Here I Go Again

From the Casefiles of Detective 'Mal' Malone

Jen Flanagan

Here I Go Again

From the Casefiles of Detective 'Mal' Malone
Copyright © 2022 by Jen Flanagan

This is a work of fiction. Names, characters, places, and incidents either are the product of the author's imagination or are used fictitiously. Any resemblance to actual persons, living or dead, events, or locales is entirely coincidental.

All mistakes are my own.

First Edition: June 2022
This edition was first published in 2022

Cover design: Haley Tenney
Editor: Moniga Bogza, Trusted Accomplice

ISBN: 978-1-7377499-3-6 (Paperback)
ISBN: 978-1-7377499-3-6 (eBook)

Printed in the United States of America
Published by: Serenity Endeavors Press
https://www.jenflanaganbooks.com/

Contents

This series pulls from a time in my life where I met and fell in love with my incredible husband, my own personal "Rhodes." His inspiration and support during the many late nights on this book is why the first draft went together in three short months. Thanks to him for the many dinners and help when I bypassed all other responsibilities during writing sprints.

Many thanks to my sister and biggest fan. She read everything first. And loved it.

Thanks to Allison for loads of inspiration. We'll always have rubber bands.

Thank you to all of my incredible writer friends. You have helped me out more than you realize. Thanks to my friends and family for your ongoing support and love.

To my readers, I'm so glad you stayed for book two! I wrote this for all of you who were rooting for Mal and Rhodes. I hope I didn't disappoint. I hope you stick around long enough to find out what happens with Dessi in book three.

On to Roscoe Village!

Chapter 1

"Confirmed," I texted into my phone, attaching the incriminating photos and hitting the send arrow.

Sad, I slid my phone into my back pocket and eased away from the car I had been kneeling behind for a good shot inside the brownstone in Roscoe Village, a charming little burg in North Center, a larger neighborhood around Chicago.

It wasn't the kind of job I liked to do, honestly. Cheating spouses were the worst, but they also paid well, and well, it was easy work. My phone pinged in response, and I knew my client would be filing her divorce papers tomorrow, secure that her husband wouldn't be able to take her money.

See, she was the breadwinner and couldn't divorce him without him taking half of what was hers. Well, not without proof of disloyalty, as per their prenuptial agreement, or so she said. I tried not to get too far into the details with work like this. It was too emotionally draining.

Still, the occasional infidelity investigation would have to do. I had recently acquired a receptionist *slash* bookkeeper *slash* busybody who had wormed herself into my life in a way I wasn't upset about, oddly enough. What it meant, though, was that I needed to keep a steady flow of income. It was good filler work.

"Hey, you there!" came a booming male voice.

Just what I needed.

I took a quick right between two buildings. Apparently, the philanderer didn't want his photo taken. Maybe I had gotten his bad side… A snort bubbled out of me. Glancing behind my shoulder, I saw a shadow bounce against the brick wall.

"Stop!" The voice was closer than I'd like.

Yeah, right. My boots caught traction on the pavement. I easily made a left and cut through an alley, then took a sharp right into another. I knew this neighborhood; these were my stomping grounds. I jogged lightly up the path, made a quick right, and burst through the back door of the aptly named Grounds, my local coffee shop. Happily shrugging off the too-warm leather jacket and hat, I threw them on a barstool and took a seat in front of Mo, the owner.

"How's it going?" I beamed at him, breath only slightly faster than normal.

Raising an eyebrow, he glanced at the back door, but no one came in.

I smiled innocently.

He just huffed and went back to drying the coffee mug in his hands, lifting it in question.

I nodded. Was that even a question? I fluffed out my auburn hair, its waves having been smooshed by the ball cap.

Turning, he set it on the counter in front of him and went to work, weighting and tamping espresso powder. The air filled with the scent of freshly ground coffee, erasing any remainders of stress.

"Keeping out of trouble, Mal?"

I shrugged. "As much as normal."

"Any luck on the jewelry case?" he asked, frothing milk for the most beautiful creation in the world.

"Not really." I sighed. I had been approached, a few weeks prior, by a seemingly sweet little old lady, claiming her son was trying to steal her fortune, starting with her jewelry. "I've been keeping an eye on vintage jewelry sales sites but haven't seen anything matching the description she gave me yet. If he's after her fortune, he'd be after the money, right?"

"Unless he's trying to make her look incompetent and gain guardianship of her assets." He tapped the frothed milk on the counter and began to pour it into the espresso, making art.

"I thought of that, but since she doesn't want him to know she's on to him, I can't easily question him."

"So, your hands are tied."

"Yep." I sighed, sipping the slice of heaven he had slid my way. "I've got to wait for his next move."

I hated that part. My jobs often had an element of stealth. It added difficulty. I just hoped the guy would get greedy and try to make a buck on the jewelry.

"How's Suzy?"

"She's taken over things." I tried to look irritated.

"Nothing new, then."

"Nope."

"No sign of Dessi?"

"He hasn't been sniffing around her, but one of Wyatt's guys is still following her everywhere."

"I bet she loves that."

"I think she's just glad to be out of the house. For some reason, she likes bookkeeping." I shuddered.

"The horror." He grinned, turning back to his cleaning.

I lingered over my celebratory coffee for a few minutes. Then, finishing up, I nodded my thanks to Mo and paid my tab.

"Should we be expecting anyone looking for you later?" he asked, eyes sliding to the back door. "And if we do, do we know you?"

"Nah, you won't get any visitors." I chuckled, heading back out to the office.

Damn, it was good to have friends.

I waved at Brian, Suzy's bodyguard and driver posted outside the brick building housing my office, as I crossed the street from Grounds. The sounds of The Police greeted me when I walked in.

Not the actual police, the English rock band.

"Did you get it?" Suzy Mennon asked, swiveling in her chair to look at me, her stick-straight, mocha-colored hair swaying against her back, giving her a polished look in her professional wear.

"Yup." I held up my phone in confirmation. "And sent."

"Nice job!" she replied, already busily typing away on her computer. "And billed. She should be receiving the final invoice notification in a few minutes, paid with the credit card on file."

"What would I do without you?" I asked. Suzy was always way better at this part of the job than I had ever been.

"You don't want to know." She shook her head grimly.

The tablet on her desk buzzed, and she pressed a green button on the overly large smile of her techie-geek husband and aspiring PI. His brown hair looked especially curly in the photo.

"Did you get it?" Sam Mennon said as his actual face, eyes wide, replaced the contact avatar.

"Yup," I repeated, rolling my eyes. "Are you *still* tracking me?"

You get kidnapped one time by the mob, and everyone worries. It had been nearly four weeks.

"You were kidnapped only four weeks ago!"

Exactly.

I shrugged, not entirely irritated by their overprotectiveness. The event had set me back a little more than I liked to admit. Hence the boots. Regardless of the heat, I wasn't getting caught without them on a case again.

"You were moving pretty fast there for a minute. Were you being chased?" His voice raised in excitement.

"A bit."

"Oh boy."

"Any calls?" I asked, heading to my office in the back.

"Nothing from Rhodes," Suzy said sadly. "Didn't you call him? You said you called him."

"I did," I mumbled. It was a lie. I was going to call him after our last coffee date a few weeks ago. But I couldn't figure out what to say. Eventually, it felt like I had waited too long. Now, I wasn't sure what to do. "I meant work calls."

"No work calls."

"Great." I sat down at my desk, the coffee turning sour in my stomach.

I didn't like lying to Suzy, but it was easier than trying to explain everything that was going on in my head.

At least I had money coming into the bank. That part felt good. Opening my computer, I rechecked a few jewelry sale sites.

An unproductive hour later, I stood up to stretch. I felt bad Ms. Lamb was paying me for the fruitless computer time even though she'd assured me it was what she wanted. From the sound of it, the lady was loaded. I tried to brush off the guilt, but I felt like I should be doing more.

I had checked the local jewelry shops too, in case they had gotten loose stones in for sale. Most of her diamonds were certified and had been etched with a serial number. They had lists and would call me if anything came in with that number, but they informed me that if someone was hocking diamonds, they only had to recut them to remove the trace. *Great.*

If her son had any idea what he was doing, he wouldn't be dumb enough to simply sell a certified diamond.

Still, maybe he wasn't the sharpest tool in the shed.

Grabbing my keys, I decided to get a bite to eat. Suzy had already left, and there wasn't much else I could do today.

After grabbing a salad from my favorite salad bar at Mariano's, I drove by a few betting parlors, windows open to let in the warm late-June air. I'd have preferred a scone at Grounds, but I needed to keep in shape.

I scanned the neighborhood. I wasn't looking for anything in particular; I was just keeping an eye out for anything unusual. The same beat-up cars sat at the same betting parlors, with a few revolving ones thrown in for good measure. Nothing new.

They were all owned by Fabian Dessi, or so Sam's slick hacking skills said. He was the sleazebag who had ordered Suzy's death a couple of months ago and my kidnapping four weeks ago. We had gotten a few of the bad guys behind bars, but Dessi was the mastermind behind them, and we had yet to get enough evidence to throw the book at him.

It didn't help that he had ties to the Marchis, a known Chicago mafia family.

I swung through a drive-thru for a black coffee and pulled into my usual spot off to the side of Dream Time Furniture in Wicker Park, another of Dessi's holdings. He had several, and I kept my eye on all of them. Apart from the betting parlors and this place, there was a strange little video-gaming winery in Oakbrook. Honestly, I couldn't see him spending time in a place like that.

Checking for my baton, I found it in my door pocket. I wasn't going to get anywhere near Dessi's goons without having it at my side from here on out. I pulled out my salad and dug in, watching the traffic.

A couple arrived, one of a long list of regulars, dressed in trendy clothes and giggling as they made their way into the furniture store.

My watch showed 5:30 p.m. Brown-haired Guy pulled up and walked in. An attractive Asian-American woman arrived at 5:45 p.m. in a hurry. The door at the back of the building, that I could see from my vantage point, opened, and Apron Guy came out with a trash bag he deposited in the bin at the end of the building. It was the usual chain of events, and I had the pattern down by now.

Munching my salad, I watched the clock, waiting for the delivery that was due to arrive. Right on time, the truck pulled up and unloaded liquor bottles through the back door. In and out, like a choreographed dance of which I had the score.

A few other regulars arrived, only it wasn't the furniture store they were frequenting; it was the business within a business, accessible only through the Dream Time Furniture Store. A speakeasy and apparent office space for Fabian Dessi.

Correction, suspected speakeasy. I hadn't been into the building yet. I was taking my time, collecting facts, being careful. I wasn't fond of the idea of getting kidnapped again. But based on the intel Sam had dug up online—liquor license, business license, and address—plus my frequent surveillance, this was Red, a hidden speakeasy in Wicker Park.

It didn't look like Dessi was here tonight, and neither were any of the Marchi-related goons. Maybe they had other business around town. I wished I had a way to know what he was up to now that he wasn't spending his time at the Arlington Racecourse. But after we'd blown the cover of a doctor who was juicing the horses so he could win, he had found another hobby.

I needed to get in and find out what he was doing in there. Maybe I could find out which guests were new business partners and get more background on them.

It was time. I just needed to set a few things in order first.

Here I go again.

Chapter 2

Steaming milk and the clattering of mugs on plates was music to my ears as I walked into HERO's coffee shop the next morning. I was in the mood for their Nicaraguan pour-over and a scone. I had gone on an especially long run this morning, and I had earned it. I had even come up with some good angles for Ms. Lamb's case I could research when I got into the office.

The sign on the wall today said, "May your coffee kick in before reality does." I smiled as I scanned the baked-goods case, letting out a huff of air as my eyes flicked over the maple-bacon long john. My thoughts drifted back to a time when I was here with Rhodes, the captain of a fire station in Bricktown, a neighboring burg. Not that he'd be caught dead eating bacon on a donut, but he'd made a crack about it and coffee-flavored coffee. He wasn't as adventurous as I was with my caffeine. As I saw it, coffee could be used as an acceptable substitute for any course of the meal, be it an appetizer, the main course, or dessert.

"Can you add a lemon-blueberry scone to that?" I asked the barista who was ringing up my coffee.

"Sure thing." He handed me the scone on a plate. "The coffee will just be a few minutes."

Taking a seat, I picked at my scone while the barista slowly poured the hot water over the beans.

I had met Rhodes at a working fire a couple of months back. And after I put one of his assistant chiefs under the microscope as the cause of a rash of fires in the area, I didn't think I'd ever get another chance with him. Especially after he had expressly asked me not to.

Not to mention I had actively looked for evidence condemning the guy. It wasn't one of my best moments, but I had been so certain, and my gut was rarely wrong. Of course, I had done the right thing by coming clean and apologizing. The thought still sat heavily on me. And he had made it clear he wasn't ready to resume our barely begun dating.

The last time we were at HERO's, we'd had a tenuous conversation, both tiptoeing around to see if we could get past the things said by the other. I had hoped we'd be able to settle as friends; it was something that was growing in importance in my life. He was a good guy, used to taking care of others.

"Nicaraguan pour-over," the barista announced, setting down the coffee. Chocolatey notes drifted to my nose in warm swirls.

I pulled out the notepad I kept in my back pocket and tried to jot down thoughts from my jog, but my mind kept straying to Rhodes.

I had avoided talking about Dessi with him. I was worried he'd try to talk me out of pursuing him, but I had to get him behind bars. Only then would Suzy truly be safe.

Frustrated by the blank page in front of me, I pushed away from the table and walked out with my coffee, leaving my scone half eaten at the table.

Back at the office, I was finally able to get my mind wrapped around the jewelry case, even though it took a walk around the block with my coffee to clear it.

Opening tabs on my laptop, I pursued several lines of thought until something stuck. I flipped back and forth between vintage-jewelry sales sites, raw-diamond resale sites, and legal sites detailing ownership. I had special access to the latter with my private investigator license.

Remembering my earlier train of thought, I opened a new tab and typed in Rosemary. Lamb's name. Then another with her son, Frederick Lamb. And yet another with Jonathan Gladstar, her financial advisor. Apparently, Ms. Lamb thought they might be plotting together. Might be true.

From her description of her assets, it sounded like she had quite an estate, and I wondered if she had someone else on hand that saw to her day-to-day life. Maybe a groundskeeper or a butler.

"What's our next move?" Sam's voice filled my office.

I sat up straight, head whipping left and right, trying to find the source of his disembodied question.

"I'm down here."

Just inside my doorway, I saw Sam's face on Suzy's tablet attached to a platform on rubber tracks. It looked like some kind of modified tracked robot.

"What in the world?"

"I built this cool bot so I could move around the office better," he said, eyes sparkling with excitement. "I can be of more help to you and still do my work here."

It was a good thing he owned his own IT development company, PhishNett. No one else would let him moonlight on another job while he was on the clock. As it was, he made enough money on apps and security software. He didn't need a second job. It was more of a hobby for him, to see what he could do.

"So, what's our next move?" he repeated.

My first instinct was to blow him off. I still wasn't used to asking for help. But he'd proved resourceful in the past.

Besides, he had his Jedi cloak on again. If I didn't keep him talking about work, he'd probably explain the story behind it. *Nope.* I had already sat through one hour-long recitation on the Star Wars story arc this month. It was enough to last me a while.

"I'm trying to dig into the son and the financial advisor's background. Maybe I can get a feel of their character."

"Found anything yet?" he said, fingers tapping on his keyboard.

"It looks like Jonathan's self-employed as a financial advisor. He's got all the paperwork in place and has been in the business for a while."

I had Sam on the books as a consultant. Thank goodness he wouldn't take payment; I couldn't afford him. And this way, we could discuss the details of the case. My job was my livelihood, and I wasn't about to cut any corners. If I was going to make it as a detective, I was going to do it the right way.

Mo was a great listener, kind of like a coffee-scented bartender, but we never talked names or other particulars.

"He doesn't have a lot of clients, though," Sam piped up. "And all of them are older."

"How do you—never mind." It was better not to ask. Okay, so I *mostly* didn't cut any corners. I couldn't control how my consultant got his intel. "That may not be unusual. I would think there are fewer younger people with enough money for a financial advisor."

"True."

"I haven't found anything particular on Frederick yet, except lots of articles where he's appeared at some social function downtown." I shrugged at the Sam-bot on my hardwood floor. My life was weird.

"Me either." He frowned, typing away. "I'll do a deeper dive later."

"I was thinking about a trip out to her house. Do you think you could come up with a small, easy-to-hide video surveillance system?"

"Oh boy."

"Something simple," I warned. We didn't need to know the ins and out of every dust particle in the house. "I just want to be able to catch the thief in the act. If she'll let me visit, anyway. I know she's trying to keep a low profile about me and not tip anyone off, but I need more information if I'm going to help her. I'm tired of just searching online for the chance a piece of her missing jewelry comes up for sale."

"You're *manually* searching online for jewelry sales?" Sam's head drew back in amazement. Like I had grown an extra eye. He wished.

"Yes?" My voice pitched up with the question. What else was I supposed to do? "Vintage-jewelry sales, estate sales, wherever I could think of. And just because they're not listed today doesn't mean they might not be listed tomorrow. I check them every few days or so."

"Mal." He tilted his head, eyebrows drawn. "That's cute."

"Oh, for goodness' sake." I threw my hands up.

"Send me the list and the jewelry description, any detail you may have, even pictures." He hurried to soothe my frayed nerves. "I'll write a simple program to check the sites and schedule it to run daily."

"Oh. That would be helpful." I didn't know he could do that.

"That's why I'm here," he cheerfully tittered, the bot backing out the door. He stopped momentarily to add, "And I'll have what you need for the cam."

I nodded.

"Did you help her?" I heard Suzy ask him from the other room.

"Yep! I'm going to automate what she's been doing every day."

"Not all of it!" I shouted. I wasn't that easily replaced by a computer search. Still…it would save a lot of time.

"Thanks, Sam. She's been spinning her wheels for weeks," Suzy said quietly.

"I heard that."

"Oops."

Ignoring it, I picked up the phone.

"Hello?" Ms. Lamb's soft voice answered. I had called her personal cell phone instead of the house phone.

"Hi, Ms. Lamb. This is Detective Malone."

"Oh, hello, dear. How are you?"

"I'm doing well, thanks. I'm sorry, I still haven't seen your jewelry come up for sale anywhere."

"That's okay, dear. Thank you for looking."

"I was hoping you could give me a little more information about who has regular access to your home."

"Oh, they wouldn't steal from me," she hurried to reassure me.

"Just the same, it's good for me to understand who's around you all the time and what they might know."

"Well, I have Nathan. He helps out around the house. And Hillary. She takes care of my plants. Rachel and Tommy also help out with odds and ends."

It was more than I had anticipated. "Are they there every day?"

"Mostly. It just depends on what I need. Nathan handles scheduling that for me, though."

"I know you're not ready to file a claim on the missing jewelry, but how would you feel if I came by your place?" I suggested. "I'd like to look around and talk to whoever works for you."

"I don't know if that's a good idea," she muttered. "If Frederick thinks we're on to him, it's going to be harder to find out what he's got planned."

"Don't worry, Ms. Lamb. I've got an idea."

"So we're okay for another month?" I asked, watching Suzy's reaction for any sign of concern.

I hated these conversations. They always made my stomach tie up in knots. Probably because before Suzy came into my life, I was living from job to job, rarely ever balancing anything and never really knowing how much money I had. I always focused my energy on getting the next case.

"Yes," Suzy replied, smiling fondly at me. "We're okay, and we will continue to be okay. You have money coming in from Ms. Lamb."

"Money to pay for research Sam figured out how to automate." It didn't feel right to charge people for work I didn't do.

"That will leave you more time to find another lead," she said confidently.

"True." I already knew what I wanted to investigate next. Maybe she was right.

"Besides, we have the money from that surveillance yesterday. It cleared today."

I took a deep breath. Okay, I was actually making ends meet. And I had been for years now, to some extent, but I had also lived in a state of constant panic about my finances.

Thank you, infidelity case.

"And I updated the bill with one final item. I charged extra for the hazard pay." She smirked.

"Hazard pay?"

"You were chased, correct?"

"Oh, yeah. But it was minor as far as chases go."

"Only because you're in shape and you know this town." Suzy put a hand on my shoulder. "It's because you're good at what you do."

The whirring sound of an electric motor announced the Sam-bot rolling back in.

"Mal," he said, eyes focused elsewhere, like on another computer screen.

"Yes, Sam." I rolled my eyes. It was hard to take him seriously in that Jedi robe.

"The search is ready to go. I beefed it up with more sites, similar to the ones you found. There are a few on the dark web that are harder to find. Also, I added the local jewelry store's inventory descriptions. There's a meta-data tag on them online that I used."

"Meta-data?" I looked curiously at Suzy, who just shrugged.

"Yeah, it's how the information is cataloged online. It has all their details. I linked it to the store's customer-supplied information."

"Is that legal?"

"Meh." He scrunched his face. "If they didn't want people to know, they wouldn't put it online."

It was hard to argue with that.

Chapter 3

Bracing myself, I pushed the aptly colored red door open, anxious and a little trepidatious to enter Dessi's lair. I hoped he wouldn't show up tonight. It was already past his typical arrival time.

The beige colors of the furniture store around me were immediately replaced by a dimly lit hallway accented by jazzy piano music. The metal-banded door at the end of the hall had no knob but had a square window at eye level.

I knocked on the door, and the window opened to show a man's face.

"Capone," I said, giving him the password. Thank God for Sam and his research.

He opened the door to reveal a larger room. Deep-scarlet fabric covered the walls, with black leather-covered booths placed intimately around the perimeter of the room. To the immediate left was a long bar made from dark mahogany wood. Edison light bulbs hung over it, and crystal chandeliers decorated the rest of the room. The bartender and other employees wore slightly 20's-themed clothing.

This early in the evening, the place wasn't crowded. I nodded at Apron Guy, who was behind the bar, filling drinks. Standing this close, I could see his leather apron had metal fittings and he wore black garters around his white sleeves. A few of the regulars I recognized sat at the bar.

Looked like a speakeasy to me.

Casually, I made my way to a barstool, nodding politely to the couple next to me.

"What'll it be?" asked Apron Guy.

"Gin and tonic," I replied. Why not?

Nodding, he went to work on it, expertly flipping bottles.

Meanwhile, in a cozy but sturdy fortress,

"She's inside," Sam said, bent over his phone, watching the little dot move around.

"Are you following Mal again?" Suzy scolded, walking into the living room with popcorn. "You know she hates that."

"Well, yes." He coughed. "But she's been going to that place every night, watching things. I'm worried Dessi's going to get wind of it."

"Personally, I don't think it's healthy how much time she sits in her car." She peered over his shoulder, sitting down.

"That's not the point, Suze." He pointed to the screen. "She's inside."

They both stared at the blinking red dot, waiting for it to move again.

I turned in my seat, taking in the surroundings. There was a smaller room off to one side, but it looked like it was for private parties. I wondered if Dessi kept it for Marchi's business meetings. A place like that would be perfect, hidden away from the prying eyes. There was a hallway to the left of it, leading to a larger dining room with additional seating. It looked like restrooms just before it.

"Let me know what you think," the bartender said, sliding the drink in front of me. "Just made a fresh batch of tonic syrup."

"You make it in house?"

"We make everything in house. From the gin to the bitters. Not the vodka. It comes from a local distillery, though."

"Impressive," I said, taking a small sip. The bright herb flavors and slight sweetness complimented the gin. "Delicious."

Satisfied, he smiled, moving on to another couple at the end of the bar.

I checked the ceiling for cameras but didn't see anything. Sam had run a sweep over the place a week or so ago and said the drone didn't pick up any video or sound data. The bar was clear, unless it was hardwired, which was possible but less likely with today's equipment. And given the owner probably didn't want anyone recording his illicit activities, I wasn't that worried about cameras inside. The front door might have been set up with surveillance, though, especially if it was part of the original construction. I had been pretty careful at lying low, parking way off in the side lot, and I doubted Dessi would be keeping an eye on every person who entered the front door.

Oddly enough, nothing around me seemed out of place. It just looked like a hip bar. Then again, that wasn't that odd. He always kept his nose clean in public, appearing as a young three-piece-suit-wearing businessman with attractive features. This place was only barely beyond the norm, as far as typical public venues went, but it was still a legal establishment, even with the hidden doorway. It didn't look like it suffered any from the lack of marketing. The thrill of being a part of a secret community had its appeal. Sounded like Dessi.

The Asian-American woman walked in from the back, wearing a feathered band around her head. She sashayed around the room, checked in on the few tables and booths scattered around the bar, and headed back.

If Sam had it right, her name was Cynthia and Apron Guy was James. Apparently, he had found their employment records and compared the drone shots to their DMV photos. It was scary what he could dig up.

I looked around the room for Brown-haired Guy, who Sam said should be Chris, but didn't see him.

"First time?" the bartender asked, wiping down the counter.

"Excuse me?" I asked, focusing back on Apron Guy—er, James—and what he was saying. "Is it that obvious?"

"You just had that kid-in-a-candy-store look," he said with a friendly smile. "Also, our clientele is mainly regulars with few newbies, who come by just to see if they can find the place."

"I had a friend tell me about this place, but she couldn't make it tonight."

"Good."

"Good?"

"Then you'll have to come back when she can join you," he winked.

"Oh, you're good at your job."

He just laughed at that. "Maybe I just like a pretty face."

Yup. Dessi had done well, hiring him, an improvement over the schmucks he employed at the betting parlors.

"So, who's your friend?" he continued.

"Jessie," I replied without missing a beat. I had thought about asking Jen to join me even though Sam thought *he* would be the best for the job. I'd known her for quite a few years, an old friend from the police academy.

She had graduated; I hadn't.

"Don't think I know her."

"I think she's only been in once before too."

"Then you can break the record. Turn the page from newbies to regulars."

"Maybe." I smiled into my drink even though I knew he was paid to be friendly. I made a mental note to ask Jen if she wanted to join me this coming weekend. "This is such a cool place. Has it been here long?"

"Yeah, a couple of years," he said, looking over the ambiance appreciatively.

"The owner must be pretty creative to come up with a place like this."

"He's got taste, for sure. He hired me, didn't he?"

I giggled, playing it up a bit to keep him talking. "Who's this brilliant owner?"

"You wouldn't know him. He's not a local guy. He keeps an office in the back."

"Really?" *Bingo.* I leaned forward.

"But he doesn't manage the place. Cynthia does." He inclined his head to the pretty Asian-American lady who had made her way back into the room and was eyeballing me pretty hard.

Shit. I hoped she didn't know who I was.

I gave her a little wave, fighting to keep my smile in place. She just rolled her eyes and strutted out. Maybe I was okay.

James wandered over to another couple, so I took a moment to slide out my phone and text Jen.

> *Mal: Wanna meet up for drinks this weekend? I found a new place.*

It didn't take her long to respond.

> *Jen: Is this related to the one you've been stalking? That Dessi owns?*

> *Mal: Maybe? I think the coast is clear. I came in tonight.*

> *Jen: Are you still there?*

> *Mal: Yep.*

I looked around. It seemed pretty safe.

*Mal: No sign of Dessi. I don't think
he knows I've been keeping tabs on it.
Mal: I think it's safe enough.*

*Jen: Okay, but it has to be Saturday.
Jen: Tomorrow night's a soccer game.*

No way would she miss that. Her nephew,
Charlie, had her wrapped around his adorable little
finger.

*Mal: Saturday works. Tell Charlie
good luck.*

*Jen: Will do.
Jen: Mal? Text me when you leave.
…
Jen: I want to make sure you get out safe.*

You get kidnapped once, and they never let you
forget it. I sent a thumbs-up.

Feeling someone behind me, I put my phone
away before anyone read the crime lord's name over my
shoulder. I turned and saw it was just another couple,
another set of regulars I'd seen from the parking lot.

"Hi," I said politely, turning back to my drink.

They both nodded in response, taking seats
next to me.

Brown-haired Guy, Chris, came out of the back
kitchen with a large wooden slab ladened with meat,
cheeses, and other little colorful items. He headed
straight for the tables in the dining area.

"They have the best charcuterie trays," the lady next to me said, seeing me watch the waiter.

"It looks great."

"It is." She leaned in. "You can mix and match what you want from a list. But not from here. This is the cocktail room."

"It's my first time here." I smiled. "So, that's the dining room, back there?"

I pointed to the hallway where Chris had headed.

"Yep. They only have small plates and the charcuterie trays, but they're delicious."

"And what's that used for?" I indicated the small room off to the side.

"I'm not sure. I've seen people in it once or twice. Looked like a business meeting. I think they rent it out or something."

"A business meeting?" I prodded, hoping for more detail.

She squinted her eyes, trying to remember. "Yes, lots of guys. It got kind of loud. I think I heard one of them was the owner, a slick-looking guy, very Italian."

"Interesting."

"What can I get you?" James asked the couple.

I retreated from the conversation. It sounded like that was all she knew anyway.

Signaling James for my tab, I pulled cash out for the bill.

"So, you're breaking the mold, right?" he asked. "From first-timer to regular?"

"Yes." I smiled. "Jessie's going to meet me here this weekend."

"I'm James," he said, sticking out a hand for a formal introduction.

"I'm Marina," I replied, using one of my usual covers. I didn't want Dessi to get wind of either of our real names.

"Looking forward to it." He gave me a grin.

Back in my green Jeep, I quickly texted Jen, letting her know I made it out alright. Then, scrolling down through my contact list for Sam's number, I paused, my thumb hovering over Rhodes' name.

I was going to have to come clean with Suzy. I shouldn't have lied to her, and it didn't sit well with me. I was okay that things hadn't worked out with Rhodes. Honest. I had been hesitant to even try a relationship. Most of my time was spent with work. Only recently had I been making an effort at any friend outside of Jen. I hadn't thought I would have the time for a romantic relationship, but he had pushed past my objections and made it all seem easy with his laid-back charm and non-cocky confidence. It was very appealing.

He was very appealing. His muscled physique only added to that attraction, the only kind of guy who really looked good with a bald head.

The regret I felt over it was because I didn't like the way things had fallen apart.

Scrolling past it, I found Sam's number.

"Hey, Mal."

"Hi, Sam. So it *is* a speakeasy." I had waited to tell him until after I left. He would have wanted to join me, and he wasn't good at undercover work.

"You went into Red?" His voice pitched up in excitement.

"Yep."

"How'd it go? What was in there? Did you see Dessi?"

"Everything went fine; no sign of Dessi," I reassured him.

"Did it look like the kind of place where mobsters would hang out?"

"Sort of." I grinned. "It's all red and black inside with a 20's theme."

"Prohibition," he whispered. "Awesome! I want to go!"

"Not yet, Sam." I tamped down his excitement. "I don't know if it's safe. I'm bringing Jen this weekend to see if we can find out more. Besides, Suzy needs you."

"That's why I want to help. I want to keep her safe."

"I know, but what would she do if something happened to you? Jen's trained for things like this. Besides, you're already helping so much with information."

"Okay," he said, voice dipping.

"But this is definitely Dessi's place, just like you said," I tried to mollify him. "According to James, who's the bartender, he keeps an office in the back. And there's a private room off the cocktail area that I think is used for business meetings."

"Mobster meetings?"

"Yes, Sam. Mobster meetings."

"So cool."

Not so cool when you get kidnapped by them. I promised to keep him informed and hung up.

Chapter 4

"How'd it go?" Suzy asked.

"Pretty good," I said, handing her one of the two take-out containers of coffee I had brought with me.

It was nearly 9:30 a.m. I had spent my Friday morning at the Adult Learning Center (ALC) in Uptown for their grand reopening. It had been one of the community centers targeted in the arson attacks a couple of months ago, and I had helped out a few times to clean up the building. After tons of bleach and scrubbing, the place was back in business.

"Was he there?" she said, meaning Rhodes.

"Sully was," I replied, referring to Assistant Chief Sullivan, who I had thought was behind the fires. "We didn't talk much, though. He was busy with the news crew."

"Sorry." She winced.

"It's really okay, Suze." I shrugged it off and headed back to my office, but stopped short. "Suze? I have to tell you something."

"What's that?"

"I lied."

"About?" she said, turning in her chair to look at me.

"I didn't call Rhodes," I admitted. If it felt bad doing it, it felt even worse coming clean. "I know. I shouldn't have lied about it. It was a silly thing."

"But why did you?" Her eyebrows were drawn in concern.

"I-I think I just wasn't sure if I was ready." I looked at the floor. "I was wrong, but he said some pretty hurtful things too. And originally, I wasn't even sure I had room in my life to date him. Has that really changed for me? But you were just so sure I should call him. So, it was just easier to say I had than figure out what I was feeling."

Crap. That made it sound like it was her fault.

"What I mean is I know you're trying to help me, but I just needed some time to think it out and decide for myself."

"I'm so sorry, Mal," she said, standing up. "I didn't realize."

"It's okay, Suzy. I should have been open with you about it. I'm not good at this dating thing. The last guy I seriously dated was Rodriguez. And you know how that ended."

He was an old flame from the police academy who had cheated on me, and unfortunately, he was also the detective on Suzy's case.

"But I thought you wanted to be friends with him."

"I do. I would." I shifted on my feet. "I kinda wish I had called him now. But I'm afraid too much time has passed. And that's okay. That was my decision. But I'm sorry I didn't just talk to you about it."

"It's okay." She moved to hug me. "I forgive you."

"Really?" I asked from within her embrace.

"Of course. That's what friends are for."

Later that morning, as I was doing a little more research on Frederick Lamb's social activities, a dark shadow filled my doorway. Weird, because Suzy hadn't announced anyone.

The last time this had happened was a few weeks ago when Rhodes came to visit and take me to coffee as an olive branch to my apology.

My heart skipped a beat as I looked up, eyes wide, to find Marty, a newsstand owner from down the block.

"Marty?"

"Hey, Mal," he said, worrying the ball cap between his hands. "I think I need your help."

"Is there something wrong?" I stood up, gesturing him in.

He sat down in front of my desk, his hands still clutching his cap in his lap.

"Well," he began. "There's these kids. They're causing some trouble, breaking things and the like."

"Someone's vandalizing your stand?"

He nodded. "They've come by a few times now. They park curbside, threaten me, and steal things."

"Have you called the cops?"

"Yes. They came by and took pictures, but they haven't been able to find them."

"Did you get a license plate number?"

"No, they park across the street. I've never been able to catch it."

I tried to think about what I could do to help. It wasn't much. He couldn't afford for me to sit and watch the place.

"What does the car look like?"

"It's a yellow convertible," he said, his lanky figure slumping in the chair. "I'm sorry to bother you with this, Mal. I know you're busy. It's just that you're on the streets a lot."

"It's okay, Marty." I tipped my head. "I'm happy to keep an eye out for them, and I'll make some extra trips by your stand during the day. Yellow is pretty hard to miss."

It was surprising that the local cops didn't know who they were. Must not be locals.

Suzy leaned back in her chair until I could see her from my desk and gave me a thumbs-up. Of course. That was why she hadn't warned me about this job. She knew I wasn't going to charge him.

"I bet Sam could set you up with a camera," she said helpfully.

"There you go. Between the two of us, we can figure this thing out. So, how many kids are there, and how old do they look? They're at least sixteen to be driving."

"Yes, I'd say about seventeen or eighteen." He shrugged. "There are three of them."

I sent him out to Suzy, who sat him down with a cup of coffee while they called Sam. He was unsurprisingly willing to help. He'd do anything for her. It warmed my heart to see how close the two of them were. My own parents hadn't been nearly as supportive. It was more like my mom did everything my dad asked.

He wasn't warm or open, and he certainly wasn't around enough to give back. At least he hadn't been when I was growing up.

A half an hour later, I had finally gotten back to the article I was reading on Mr. Lamb when I noticed someone in my doorway again.

Already?

"Are they back?" I said, quickly standing up and already heading around my desk.

But where Marty's slight frame had only taken up a portion of the doorway, this one's wide shoulders nearly blocked it out.

It was Rhodes.

I froze.

"Back?" he said, instantly going on alert. "Is there a problem?"

"No." I slowly edged back a few feet, giving us space and time for my thoughts to calm. "A business owner from down the street is having some problems with vandals. I thought he was coming for help."

Glancing at Suzy through my doorway, I saw her pointedly ignoring me, but still very obviously listening.

"From you?" he asked, eyebrows drawn. "Why wouldn't he call the cops?"

"Yes, from me." I bristled. It was an old argument, me getting involved in things that weren't my business. Sometimes, it was like he forgot I was nearly a cop myself. "He *has* called the cops. They haven't caught them yet. Also, I can get there a lot faster than the cops can."

I could see an internal battle waging in him.

Running a hand over his shaved head, he let out a sigh, his body language changing. His shoulders slumped, and he looked at me directly, lips set in a firm line.

"I'm sorry to bother, but I need your help."

Meanwhile, in a glitzy black-and-red office,

"Are you sure it was her?"

"Yes, but she said her name was Marina," Cynthia told her boss, nodding at the picture on the wall.

A slow grin spread across Fabian Dessi's face. He had known she would make it past the front door at some point.

"What do you want me to tell the team?"

"Business as usual. Let her get a look around." He sat back in his patent-leather upholstered chair and brushed the lint off his suit. "Just make sure to fill me in on what questions she's asking. Tell James well done."

"Will do, sir."

"And be ready for Saturday."

"Always."

The cat-and-mouse game had resumed.

Fifteen minutes later, we had relocated to a corner table at Grounds. I didn't feel like having Sam burst into this conversation. I wasn't sure where it was going.

Maurice—or Mo, as I called him—brought us our coffees, giving Rhodes a side-eye. He looked at me, his eyebrow raised. I nodded, letting him know he had correctly identified my guest. Between Suzy and me, he had heard the whole story.

"Thank you," Rhodes said, taking his coffee while curiously watching Mo's perusal.

"Thanks, Mo." I angled my head towards him, giving him a non-verbal shove off. If I had wanted an audience, I'd have stayed at the office. Turning back to the man in front of me, I gave him my full attention. "What can I help you with?"

Taking a deep breath, he said, "I need you to find my dad."

"Your dad?" I frowned. "Is he missing?"

"Not exactly." His full lips pursed. "We just don't know where he is. Last we heard, he was in Arizona."

"When was the last time you heard from him?"

"I don't know, maybe twenty-five years ago?"

My eyes widened, but I didn't say anything. I hadn't had the best relationship with my father either, but that was more than his adult life.

"Okay. Could anyone else have heard from him during that time? Maybe your mom or your uncle?" I knew his uncle was the one who had gotten him into the fire service, but I wasn't sure what side of the family he was related to.

"I don't think Sean knows anything more than that. And my mom died from complications from my birth."

I hadn't known that.

I had so many questions, but I had to focus on the job. It was why he had come to see me.

"Can I ask why you need to find him? Is it time sensitive?" I hated to consider it, but sometimes, when someone needed to be found, it was because of a health or money issue. Or most often, a will issue, which was kinda a mix of the two.

He looked down at his untouched coffee, cooling between his hands. "My grandma needs to go to a nursing home. I'm not happy about it, but with our schedules, it's just too difficult for Sean and I to keep an eye on her."

"I'm so sorry, Rhodes." I put a hand on his forearm.

"It's okay. She's not upset about it. She says she's excited about the facility. She knows some of the other residents already, and they have ice cream every day." His mouth edged briefly on one side. "She has dementia. And she keeps asking for Aaron, my dad. I'd like her to be able to see him one more time before she forgets who he is."

It was a sad story, and I hated that this was why he had come to visit me. Again, I wished I had just called him back to see if he'd be open to being friends.

But he had come to me with work. I knew I shouldn't try to turn it into something personal.

"I'll see what I can do," I told him, pulling back and picking up my coffee for a sip. "Do you know where in Arizona he was last?"

"Some commune outside of Flagstaff."

"Excuse me?"

"A commune. He's a hippie." He sighed. "He was always a free spirit, or so I've been told. But after Mom died, he struggled to stay in one place. He took off when I was five."

"That must have been hard."

"I had Sean and Gran. I had a better youth than most. Besides, I think I turned out alright."

"I'd agree with that." I smiled casually. "I'd like to meet her, if you don't mind."

"Gran?" he asked, tilting his head.

"Yes, she might remember something important."

"Maybe." He nodded. "Sure."

"Would Sunday be okay?" I asked, finishing my coffee.

"Sunday works," he said, standing and getting ready to leave. "She'll be all unpacked by then."

"Rhodes." I put a hand on his arm to stop him. "I'm sorry I didn't call back."

"It's fine." He dipped his head, shifting away from me. "It's your decision, and I respect it. I'm sorry I showed up today like I did. I wouldn't have if I didn't really need your help."

I winced; I hadn't meant for it to be like that. "I wanted to call you back, but I wasn't sure what to say. And then it seemed too late."

He looked at the ground, pausing, then finally sat back down. It seemed like neither of us knew how to approach each other.

"If it makes it any better, I really wish I had called you," I said, my teeth worrying my lip in discomfort. I didn't like the feeling. "And I'll have you know I don't bring just anyone to my favorite coffee shop. Grounds is like a second home to me. Or, really, like a first home. So, basically, I invited you to my house."

He leaned back in his chair and laughed; the tension eased. He had a good laugh.

"I'm glad you came to see me," I went on.

"I am too," he said, looking straight at me.

"I wish it was under better circumstances."

"Me too." His mouth twisted up.

"Let's go back to my office and talk about money." I grinned.

It looked like I wasn't going to get that research in today, but somehow, I had gotten two new jobs.

Chapter 5

There he was. I noticed the aristocratic appearance from his social pages. Frederick Lamb brushed back his lightly feathered, beginning-to-thin, sandy-brown hair as he readied his stance to swing at a golf ball. I had given up on online searches, trading them for the real thing: in-person research. Which was much preferred, in my opinion. Sam was better at the online stuff anyway.

I had driven by Jonathan Gladstar's office first, but there wasn't anything to see there, just a boring white building with a boring black-and-white sign.

The ball flew through the air, landing close to the hole on the first swing. Mr. Lamb handed the club to the caddy while talking jovially with the man to his right. There was a distinct swagger to his step as he moved aside for his associate to take his turn. The man's ball didn't land anywhere near his, and from the look on Mr. Lamb's face, he was incredibly pleased. I could see his chest shake in a chuckle as he patted the other man on the back.

Jerk.

After another half hour, they were out of my range of sight from my spot in the parking lot, but that was fine. I had another place to be.

Mantovani's Pizza smelled as good as I remembered it. Basil and oregano mingled with the scent of baked yeast dough. It smelled like heaven. Well, maybe purgatory. Coffee still held that supreme title.

I sat at the bar, nodding to Sally, the bartender. I hadn't been here since I was working undercover for the owner a couple of months back.

"Hey, Mal. How's it going?" she said, walking over to say hi.

"Pretty good. You?"

"Can't complain."

"I'm just here to pick up a to-go order."

"Great, I'll run back and let Lou know you're here."

Nodding to Phil as he walked by, I waited at the bar.

A few minutes later, Marco came out of the back to say hi. "Your pizzas are almost done."

"No problem."

"Good to see you, Mal."

"You too." I smiled. "How's school going?"

"Good." His eyes lit up. "I'm almost done with my business degree. It's so close I can almost taste it."

"That's great news."

"Things have changed since you left," said the son of one of the most notorious crime bosses in Chicago.

Domenico Poggiali had helped me escape from Dessi's kidnapping attempt. He was a competing family and happy to throw a wrench in anything to do with the Marchi family.

"Have they?" I pretended not to know.

"Aunt Shelly's no longer working here."

Not surprising since she was pilfering from the cash deposits.

"Sorry to hear that."

"But you knew that." He grinned knowingly.

I tilted my head. Him knowing that shouldn't have surprised me, considering who his dad was.

"You're observant."

"I was taught well," he said, pleased.

"Sometimes, it's good to keep what you know close to the vest." I gave him a piece of advice. "Don't show your hand too soon."

He nodded, considering my words. "Good point."

I grinned. "I'm in the information business myself."

"Yes." He dipped his head. "But I'm not going to be. I'm going to be a businessman. Legal."

"Glad to hear it." I put a hand on his shoulder. I hoped he was able to keep it that way.

"Hot and ready," Sally exclaimed, carrying three large pizza boxes over her head.

I paid my tab and headed out, promising I'd be back soon. Well, I would if the pizza was as good as it smelled. In the time I'd helped Peter Mantovani, I'd never had a chance to try it.

My Jeep and I made a short trip through town, pulling up to a towering stone-and-stucco house. If it looked like a fortress, that's because it was. Sam had outfitted the place with steel walls and artful wrought-iron windows. It could withstand World War III.

Walking up the driveway, I made my way to the Sentinel Security van parked outside. Jim, another of Wyatt's guys, was on duty tonight.

"How's it going, Mal?" he said, rolling down the window.

"Great," I said, holding out the top pizza box for him.

"Hey, thanks!" His eyes lit up and crinkled at the corners.

Suzy often made enough dinner to feed them, even though it wasn't expected. I figured since I was bringing dinner tonight, I'd keep up the goodwill.

Sam answered at my knock, having seen me on the security cameras.

"That was nice of you," Suzy said from the kitchen.

I shrugged my shoulders and set the other two boxes on the dining room table.

"Suzy made margaritas," Sam said, passing out plates and napkins.

"Would you like one?" she asked, carrying a tray with a pitcher and glasses.

"Definitely."

Sam walked over to the sideboard to get a small box.

"These are the cameras for Ms. Lamb," he said, handing them to me.

"Thanks." I opened it up to find three small USB chargers, made to plug into an outlet, and a small slip of paper with an internet address on it.

"They plug into the wall, so they don't have to be charged," he explained, sitting down and opening the pizza boxes. "Just put them in view of whatever you want to watch, and it'll send the feed to that website. You can enter it into your phone to check the viewing area when you set them up."

"This is perfect, Sam," I said, impressed. Why hadn't I brought him in sooner? Oh yeah, because I had to do things by myself.

And how was that going for you?

Suzy poured margaritas, smiling fondly at our conversation. She and Sam dug in.

Sitting down, I grabbed my own slice of Mantovani's pizza. After serving it for a week, I was pretty anxious to finally try it. I let out a moan as my teeth sunk through the melty cheese and into the spiced tomato sauce.

"This is good," Sam said, his mouth full of pizza crust.

"Mm-hmm," Suzy added in agreement, eyes closed to savor the taste.

For the next few minutes, no one paid attention to anything but the pizza in front of them.

"I saw Frederick Lamb this evening," I said, sipping my margarita. "At the golf course. He seems like a spoiled socialite."

"He's got to be in his fifties," Suzy said.

I nodded. "It's not cute at any age."

"That fits what I read about him," Sam said, grabbing another slice. "He got into a little trouble a while back, wrecked a sports car into a party tent. Got a DUI, but the venue didn't sue."

"Why didn't I find anything online about that?"

"I think Ms. Lamb paid it off. I had to dig pretty hard to find it. He has a trust fund, but there's a monthly stipend to it."

It sounded like Ms. Lamb was supporting him, or he had another source of income.

"Did you find anything on the financial advisor?"

"Nothing illegal. His business is a little odd, though."

"How so?"

"We knew he didn't have a ton of clients, but it doesn't look like he's ever had many." He took a gulp of margarita. "It's not like he's been in business for years and narrowed it down to these large accounts. It's more like he got into business only for the handful of clients he has."

"I'm not a finance expert, but that does seem odd."

"It is odd," Suzy said, listening to us. "That's not normal. I've never been in finance, but from what I saw when I worked at the bank, it's unusual. Makes me wonder if he has some connection to the families."

"I'll look into it," Sam said.

"Thanks." I nodded.

It sounded like we finally had a few leads to try. I just hoped tomorrow's visit to the estate went smoothly and Ms. Lamb wouldn't mind me setting up cameras.

Making my way up the long tree-lined driveway to Ms. Lamb's estate, I craned my neck to look at the three-story house, complete with balconies on the second and third floors. The upkeep of the gardens alone must be a full-time job.

I unclipped the expandable baton I kept attached to my belt loop, parked in the circular drive, and walked up stone steps to a large carved-wood door. The place was bigger than I had anticipated. I made a mental note to find out how Ms. Lamb had gotten my name.

A stately middle-aged man answered the door.

"Can I help you?" he said.

"I'm Mal. I'm here to see Ms. Lamb."

"Please come in while I get her," he said, stepping aside for me to enter.

The entryway was as opulent as the outside, maybe even more so. My eyes scanned the stone tile, carved wooden furniture, and paintings adorning the walls. There was a whole lot of money tied up in this estate.

Ms. Lamb came in, looking a little nervous.

"Thank you, Nathan," she said, dismissing him.

He hesitated, eyes flicking between us. She turned and gave him a direct look, and he left us.

"It's good to see you, Ms. Lamb."

"Oh, please, dear. Call me Rosemary."

"Rosemary." I smiled. The casual name sounded odd for such a fine lady.

"Let's go upstairs," she said, leaning in. "Fewer ears."

I followed her up to her master suite, and she indicated a sitting room outside her bedroom.

"We can talk here," she said, sitting.

"Nathan's your housekeeper?" I asked.

"Yes, housekeeper, groundskeeper, whatever you want to call him. He takes care of things." She waved into the air. "He hired the rest of them. They do what he asks."

"Do they all have free rein of the house? I mean, do they have a way in if you're not here?"

"Only Nathan does. If one of them needs to get in and I'm not here, he meets them."

"What about Mr. Gladstar and your son?"

"Freddy has the front door code." Her lips pressed together. "He insisted on it when we put in the alarm system last year."

"You can change it," I suggested. "It's your house."

"I'm afraid he'll try to take me to court and have my sanity checked." She bowed her head. "I want to prove he's stealing from me and that I'm perfectly sane."

"We can help you find out what's going on," I told her, hesitant to promise to prove her son's culpability. Sometimes, it wasn't who you thought it was.

"These are cameras," I said, getting the USB chargers out of my bag. "Like nanny cams. We can put them where you keep your valuables. Get some proof. Because unless your jewelry comes up for sale somewhere, we can't prove anything."

Rosemary held up a charger, inspecting the tiny dot of the camera lens. "I had no idea you could buy one so small."

"Can you show me where you keep your jewelry?" I stood. I wasn't sure how comfortable she'd be, having her privacy recorded.

Nodding, she rose and took me into her bedroom. One wall of the dove-gray room had a small cabinet. "It's in there."

"Okay." I scanned the walls for plugs and found one across the room, far enough away from her bed to keep it out of the recording. Clicking through my phone, I checked the angle. Perfect.

I took her back out into her sitting area and placed one in the view of the bedroom door and the other towards the entryway.

"As long as you walk here"—I indicated with my arms—"you'll stay out of the video. These don't record sound, only images, so you can still have private conversations in this room. Only the lower half of your bedroom is in the camera's view. I know it's not ideal, since it's in your bedroom, but at least your bed will remain private."

Rosemary looked at the feed on my phone. "Who has access to this?"

"It's a recorded video on a secure line. Only my associate, Sam, and I have it. The feed is being recorded, but we're not going to access it unless there's a reason to check it and we have your permission."

Dipping her head, she said, "Okay."

"Do you think Nathan or the others would talk to me?"

"I don't know. If they think Freddy will be in charge one day, they may be afraid to lose their jobs." She worried her bottom lip between her teeth.

It had looked to me that Nathan was protective over her, but he could be expecting to be in her will. It was hard to tell.

Footsteps pounded up the stairs.

Surprised, we both turned to the doorway to see Freddy burst into the sitting room.

Chapter 6

"Freddy!" Rosemary's hands floated to her throat. "I wasn't expecting to see you today."

"Who's this?" he said, chin jutted forward, fists clenched.

"Hi. I'm Mal," I said with a friendly smile, curious to learn how he knew I was here. I led with my hand out, keeping my body relaxed and open. "I'm with Insideonline's society page, and I'm writing an article on Ms. Lamb here. I'd like to highlight some of her generous giving over the years."

He ground to a halt, eyes narrowing and shifting between the two of us.

Rosemary still looked a bit tense, so I put a hand on her shoulder. "It's been quite a pleasure talking to your mother about her efforts."

Leaning towards me, he turned to his mom, trying to get between us.

"I'd like to talk to my mother for a moment. You understand, of course."

"Of course." I kept my face neutral. "And I've heard you've been a supporting presence at quite a few fundraising events as well. I'd love to add a chapter on you too, if you'd be so kind."

"We'll see," he hesitated, pulling his mom to the side a little more aggressively than I'd have liked to see.

I politely moved away to give them some privacy, but it wasn't hard to overhear their conversation.

"Why didn't you call me?" he asked in a loud whisper. "I'm not sure I should allow—"

"Allow?" Her voice pitched up an octave.

"A misuse of words," he said quickly. "I meant that *we* should discuss."

"Do you want me to call you over every little thing I do all day?"

"She's with the *press*." He over enunciated the word. "You don't want to sound foolish."

"Foolish?" Her chest puffed up. "Do you think I got here because of my looks? I'm perfectly capable of handling an article with a small newspaper. What I'd like to know is why you barged in without—"

"Mother." His tone softened. "I'm simply concerned with your welfare."

"Well."

"As your loving son"—he put a hand over his hollow heart—"allow me to talk to the press myself for a moment. I merely want to ensure you're being properly portrayed in accordance with your generosity."

Wow. I hadn't seen that much manure since I was last at the Arlington Racecourse.

Sliding her eyes toward me, she shifted. "I suppose you can. But I want you to know that Mal and I have reviewed the content in which she will write. I've taken the appropriate precautions."

He looked over at me. "I'm sure you wouldn't mind giving me the name of your supervisor."

"Of course not." I smiled sweetly. "That would be Paul Whitfield. I'll jot down his number for you."

"I'd be happy to escort you around the house." He gestured out of Rosemary's sitting room.

I glanced at her but didn't want to make her situation any worse. The cameras were already set; I had done what I came to do. I just needed to sell my story to Freddy before I left. Easy enough.

"That would be lovely." Nodding to Ms. Lamb, I walked out, pausing for him at the landing to the stairs. "Please tell me about the autism awareness event you went to last month. I heard you put quite a bit of money in the raffle."

"Oh, well." He ran a hand over his fine hair where it had lifted in his haste. "It was for a good cause."

My ass. It was for a private tee time with a PGA tour champion.

"Do you have a personal interest in autism?" I asked, knowing he didn't.

"Uh," he faltered. "I'm keenly in touch with all disabilities, having struggled with a touch of dyslexia when I was young."

He placed a hand on his chest, and I gave the obligatory head shake. "That's so unfortunate."

"Yes," he agreed.

"How kind of you to support those still struggling." I was starting to feel like I would have to wash my mouth out after this meeting. Probably with some coffee.

"Oh! I know just the place to talk." He led me to the front door. "You haven't properly seen the gardens."

I let him lead me out the front door and away from his mother.

Unsurprisingly, when we were safely settled on a live-edge bench under a willow tree, he conveniently remembered he forgot to tell his mother something important and hurried off.

No matter, I leaned back and enjoyed the momentary reprieve from his company.

"Can I help you?" a soft voice came from behind me.

Turning, I saw a young woman wearing overalls. She had gardening gloves on and pruning shears in one hand.

"I'm just waiting on Freddy—er, Frederick." I stood up. "You must be Hillary."

She tilted her head and raised her eyebrows.

"Ms. Lamb mentioned you"—I smiled—"When I asked who kept up these beautiful gardens."

"Oh." She bent down to pick a dead leaf off the immaculate grass and tuck it into her pocket. "Thanks."

"I'm working on an article for Insideonline. About Ms. Lamb's generosity."

"She really is." Her eyes lit up. "Generous, that is. She's such a sweet woman."

"From what I've seen, I would agree," I said. "Her son wasn't so happy to find me here, though."

The light dimmed from her eyes. "Hmm. He does try to keep an eye on her. To help out, of course."

"Of course," I repeated. "I hope I didn't cause any trouble for her."

"No." She shifted on her feet. "I'm sure he was just trying to protect her."

Hmm, indeed.

"I, uh, should go," she said, seeing Freddy assertively making his way back across the lawn.

"Nice meeting you," I said to her swiftly retreating back.

"Now, where were we?" Freddy said, approaching me.

"Should we have Ms. Lamb here?" I glanced toward the house.

"Not at all. I can fill you in on her donations...and mine."

This should be fun.

It took an hour of nods and appreciative noises before I could escape from the conversation and Freddy's attention.

Getting into my Jeep, I let out a sigh, finally able to drop the impressed-reporter act.

But before I forgot, I dialed Paul's number on my Bluetooth as I pulled out. I had fed him an arson case and hoped he'd help me out.

"Hello?"

"Paul, it's Mal. I need a favor."

"For you?" I could hear papers shuffling. "Anytime."

Making my way back into Roscoe Village, I came in from the north so I could run by Marty's newsstand and check on him. I pulled over to park on the side of the road and watched him from across the street.

It was late morning on a Saturday, and his stand was busier than ever. Half a dozen people were perusing magazines, while two more were in line to pay. His entire stand had a canopy over it with metal overhead doors, able to be rolled down at night for security.

Sitting there, I thought about Rhodes.

Was it a mistake to get involved with his personal life? It had been good to see him, but things still didn't feel right between us. Why was I so hesitant to see where things could go with him?

Maybe because he had asked me to leave the arson investigation to the professionals. If I was being honest with myself, it still stung. I had asked him to forgive me for what I said, but I was having trouble doing the same. *Except, he hadn't quite apologized for his words said in the heat of the moment.* And he had sounded surprised Marty came to me for help. I didn't need another male in my life, questioning my profession of choice.

I rolled my window down, letting in some air.

Marty glanced up, saw the Jeep, and waved enthusiastically.

Grinning, I raised a hand in return and hung around for another ten to fifteen minutes. Trouble was less likely to come knocking with such a large audience. I got out of the Jeep and locked up. The office was only another block away. I'd just walk back at the end of the day.

I waited for the light, crossed, and nodded at him while he was busy with a customer. Hopefully, knowing I was close by gave him some comfort.

Being Saturday, I only planned on staying in the office until noon. Since it was nearly lunch after my regrettably long morning at the Lamb Estate, I tried to focus on what I knew about Rhodes' case. I was glad I had some time to get my thoughts together before I met them the next day.

I ran some searches on communes around Flagstaff, Arizona, and found there was quite a large hippie population there, but nothing about communes. There was an up-and-coming community called Arcosanti, an experimental town focused on environmentally conscious and sustainable living. Basically, several areas around Sedona, Flagstaff, and Cochise County had groups of people or small communities where people lived off the grid. It was hard to find anything more about it than that, no details on the residents themselves or anything connecting Aaron Rhodes to it.

I started perusing some message boards and got frustrated. It would be so much easier to just go to Arizona; I much preferred gathering information in person. I opened another tab on my internet browser. Great, Flagstaff was only 1,617 miles away. So, either a twenty-four-hour one-way drive or an almost four-hour flight. Once I added the time at the airport and getting a rental car, it was looking at six to eight hours of travel time.

Propping my chin on my hand, I weighed my options.

Noticing the Sam-bot on the floor by Suzy's desk, I walked over to it. I wasn't sure how to turn it on, so I picked up the tablet to look at it and felt a paper stuck to the back. Turning it over, I found a Post-it note with instructions on how to make a call.

I walked through the instructions, clicking the icon and Sam's contact he had set up.

His face filled the screen.

"Mal!" He waved. "You figured out how to use Facetime!"

"I followed the instructions on the Post-it." I frowned, looking back at the Sam-bot.

Not wanting to crouch on the floor to talk, I carried it instead to my desk and propped it up next to my monitor.

"What can I do for you?" he asked, eyes sparkling.

"I'm working on that new case for Rhodes," I said. I had filled him and Suzy in on the details over pizza the night before. "You wouldn't have a way to look into these message boards to find hippie communes in Arizona, would you?"

I could see his eyes focusing elsewhere as he typed on his own home computer. "I can run a search through the text for certain keywords."

"I'll email you the websites I found."

"No need," he said, still absorbed in his screen. "I took a screen capture of your monitor."

"You hacked into my computer?"

"No, I installed remote-access software on your computer."

"You hacked my computer."

"It's not quite the same thing."

I stared at him, lifting an eyebrow.

"Fine." He shrugged. "I hacked your computer. But it makes it easier, doesn't it?"

"I guess," I mumbled.

"It looks like most of these places are completely off the grid."

"That's what I was seeing, too."

"We won't be able to get very far." He pursed his lips. "I can find out where they're located and see if anyone's mentioned his dad's name. What was it again?"

"Aaron Rhodes."

"Got it. I'll see what online references I can find on that name."

"Thanks," I said, relieved. "I hope I'm not intruding into your weekend."

"Not at all," he said, already consumed in the task. "I can get these set up to run and just multitask while I watch anime."

"Suzy's watching anime?"

"Uh, no. She's taking a spa afternoon. I get anime, and she gets a bubble bath with wine and a book," he said, glancing back at me. "But I have to warn you to keep your expectations low. If Aaron's off the grid, the best I can do is find out where to look for him. People like that don't typically have a large social presence."

I had been worried about that. "I know, but let's see what we can find."

"Will do."

It was the best I could do for now.

Chapter 7

After flicking through a few more websites and jotting down notes, I headed back out. It felt strange not having more to do, even on a weekend. Suddenly, I was keenly aware of what a difference it made to have a little help at work.

Walking back down the street, I wandered into Marty's newsstand. I wasn't much of a magazine reader, but I perused the shelves and the small rack of snacks at the corner of his booth.

"How's it going today?" I asked Marty, who was handing change to a customer. He had a few people shuffling around, but the activity had died down somewhat.

"Pretty good." He straightened items on a nearby rack. "No unwelcome visitors, so that's a plus."

I nodded, looking around. "Good to hear."

He had a small shelf of succulents stuck between a stand of books and comics. Picking one up, I looked at it closer. I wasn't particularly good with plants, having been attempting to resuscitate a dead ivy for way too long, but these were practically impossible to kill. At least from what I'd heard. Maybe it was time to let things go and move on.

I got in line to pay for it, but Marty shooed me away.

"It's the least I can do," he said.

"Thanks," I said, tucking the new plant into my elbow. I glanced over to my Jeep and decided to leave it and walk the few blocks home.

Inside my small but comfortable apartment, I set my keys down on the side table next to the dead ivy and leaned in close to give it one final inspection. No, it was good and dead. I replaced it with the new one and walked it down the stairs and outside to toss in the apartment's dumpster.

My neighbor Noelle was on her way up the stairs when I was heading down.

"Hi." I nodded, glancing at the dead plant in my hand.

"Hello." She frowned, giving me space in the stairway.

"Guess I'm not good with plants." I attempted a grin, lifting the plastic pot.

She just nodded, her blonde pigtail bobbing.

Somehow, I never ran into her doing normal things. Sighing, I banged down the rest of the stairs and out the building door, heading for the trash. Still, I hesitated before tossing my failed attempt at nurture and domestication away. The next one would be different, I promised myself. I'd pay more attention to watering it, especially now that I had more time.

Or maybe I'd get more work. If I did, I'd just have to be more diligent, I thought, heading back into the building. Besides, it was a succulent; it didn't need much watering. My feet pounded up the stairs, passing a guy, who pushed past me. I turned to watch him: ball cap and hoodie. Strange. We only had four units in this building. Maybe he was a new guy.

I hit the button on the coffee bean grinder to feed my coffee pot, Mr. Bunn, and heard my stomach growl. *Oh yeah, food.* I finished setting the pot to brew and got out some leftovers for a late lunch.

Several hours and a pot of coffee later, my apartment had been cleaned within an inch of its life and I was nearly going crazy with the lack of work to do. I had spent a good hour, searching the web for anything on Fabian Dessi, even though I knew Sam always kept an eye on that. And another half hour, researching the proper care and feeding of succulents.

Glancing at the time, I got up to change my top and swipe on some mascara.

By the time I heard Jen's knock at the door, I was ready to go and waiting impatiently on the couch.

"Hey, Mal," she said, coming in.

"Hey, yourself. Boy, am I glad to see you."

"Miss me?" She laughed.

"You have no idea." I rolled my eyes. "It's been a long day. Just looking forward to a night out."

"Even though it's kind of a work thing?"

"We still get to talk." I shrugged, grabbing my keys and walking out. "I have some things to catch you up on."

"Me too," she said, her mouth in a thin line.

"That sounds serious," I told her as we exited the building. She had parked right in front. "Do you want to drive or me? I'm parked a few blocks up the road."

"I'll drive," she said, unlocking her sedan. It looked like a cop car, but at least she had changed out of her uniform. That would have been a little conspicuous.

"Okay," I said, getting in. "You first."

"Well, Marchi's been making waves, and not in a good way." She glanced over as she pulled out.

"Is there a good way for him?" I chuckled.

She shot me a look. "A call came in at a warehouse in Oakbrook. Ten pronounced at the scene."

"Dead?" My eyes grew round.

Jen just gave me a look. *Duh.*

"At least two of them were just at the wrong place at the wrong time. Innocent civilians walking by."

"God."

"Yeah."

"How do you know it's tied to Marchi?"

"Well." She tucked a chunk of her short blonde bob behind an ear. "Because cameras in the area caught a couple of the guys."

"Marchi himself?"

"No," she said, looking at me. "Two top guys in his organization."

"Dessi," I guessed.

"Yep."

Silence filled the car. We both knew this was a dangerous case. But we'd had training for this sort of thing. We'd been through most of it together. And we both had backup. Hell, she had the whole police force. I didn't, but I had Sam and Wyatt's guys. And it was also personal for me. I wasn't leaving this one alone.

"We're still trying to figure out all who were involved and why they were there."

"Can you send me the location of the warehouse?"

"Mal. I don't know..." she started.

"I have to look into it, Jen," I cut her off. "You know I do. Suzy isn't safe until he's in jail."

"She could go into protective services. Witsec."

"And she and Sam would lose everything. His whole business, their home, everything."

"They could start over."

"He has a narrow set of skills. He'd be easy to track down. Eventually."

Jen shrugged. "That's their choice."

"It is, and this is mine," I said, looking straight ahead. "And it's yours if you deem it too dangerous to help me out on this. But I'm going to see him behind bars."

"You know I just worry about you." She let out a long sigh. "And I'll do whatever I can to help. That's why I'm here tonight, right?"

I gave her a side grin. "Thanks."

"Now, what was this other news?" she said, switching subjects.

"Rhodes came to see me."

"Did you call him?"

"No. He has a job for me."

"A job?" Her eyes cut to me. "You didn't call him all that time, and now he's got a job for you? Isn't that a little weird?"

"No, I don't think so."

"What? He's going to pay you to hang out with him?"

"That's not fair." I frowned. "It's a real job."

"He's paying you to find something?" she said, her lips thin.

"Kind of. Some*one*."

"Another missing-persons case?" she questioned, her gaze breaking from the road to glance at me.

"It's not like that. Geez, Jen. He just wants help reconnecting with someone from his past. You know I can't give you more details than that."

She hmphed.

"What's going on with you?" I asked, turning toward her.

"I just don't trust him." She shrugged. "He didn't help when Suzy and Sam went to him. When you were missing."

"He was at work."

"I would have left."

"I know, Jen. We weren't in a good place. Hell, we barely knew each other. Also, he couldn't have done anything anyway. He told Suzy he'd leave if they needed him to and made them promise to call him with updates. As soon as he got off shift, he was there."

"He wasn't very supportive of you."

"True." I nodded. "We both made mistakes. What is this, Jen?"

Turning further in my seat, I watched her, her eyes illuminated by lights from her rearview mirror.

"You forgave him, but you didn't forgive Alex."

My mouth hung open. "That is *not* the same thing."

"He really misses you, Mal. He's really sorry for what happened between you two. I think you were the one who got away for him."

"Seriously, Jen! The man cheated on me while we were in the academy together. It's not like it was brand-new between us; we had been together for months." My fists clenched on my lap. "Why are you going there? You know I'd never forgive him. I can't. I won't do that."

"I just think he's changed." She raised a shoulder. "People do."

"Some people do, and for his sake, I hope he has. But not for me. I won't have anything to do with that. And as my friend, you should know that."

Jen breathed out a sigh. "I'm sorry, Mal."

"What's going on?"

"It's just that I've been working with Alex a lot lately, and I feel bad for him. I miss us all hanging out together."

"I know." I had been stopping by Hungry Brain, the local cop bar, lately. It was nice, seeing the guys again after avoiding it like the plague for so long. But I had avoided any friendship with my ex, Rodriguez. "Look, I'll try not to be so mean to him."

"You weren't perfect back then either. You went toe-to-toe with him all the time."

"You're right," I admitted. "I've grown up a lot since then. I wasn't willing to make any concessions for anybody. I'll try to be nicer, but, Jen, I can't forget what happened. We're not going to get back together."

"Fair enough." She blew out a breath. "I just want you both to be happy."

"I know," I said quietly. "I'm trying to get there."

"I'm glad."

"And I hope he finds the right person for him and that he's ready for her."

"Me too." Her mouth twisted. "Sorry."

"It's okay." I lightly punched her in the arm. "Now tell me how the game went last night."

Her face split into a wide grin. "Oh, you should see Charlie on that soccer field. He did so well! I've never seen him run like that."

"He's growing up."

"Is he ever! I think soccer is really going to be his thing. He's already so much better than the other boys. I'll bet he could get a scholarship if he keeps it up."

"For college?" I chortled.

"Well, yes. I know it's far away, but he's got time to practice."

I shook my head. Some things never changed. My love life was in ruins, and the only man in Jen's life was her nephew.

Meanwhile, in a lavish personal office,

"I still can't hear anything," Dessi said, his fingers drumming expectantly against his desk.

"Hang on, it should be coming through," the other man said, bending to adjust the signal. White noise burst through the speakers, making them both jerk back. Hurriedly, he turned the volume down. "It's on now."

"There's still no sound." His boss leaned forward, listening.

"Maybe she's left the house? It was working just a little while ago." The man frowned. "I didn't hear much, but I did hear her moving around."

"She's here," Cynthia said, strolling into the office. "At the bar. And she's brought a friend."

"Fantastic."

"This place is kinda cool," Jen said, appreciating the interior. She had gotten quite a kick out of the password door.

"Yeah, if it wasn't owned by a megalomaniac, I'd probably like it."

Taking seats at the bar, I was glad we had come early. I didn't want to risk running into Dessi, and it would be easier to get people to talk if the place wasn't full.

"Marina! You're back," James said, walking up with a smile.

"I told you I would be." I smiled in return.

"And who's your lovely friend?" He raised an eyebrow.

"This is Jessie," I introduced her. "The one I told you about."

"Right." He held out his hand to shake hers. "This is your second time here, right?"

"Yes." Jen smiled, slipping into the role. "I'm glad I made it back."

"What can I get you?"

We both ordered gin and tonics and settled into light conversation, keeping an eye on the room. I had filled her in on what I knew.

My phone pinged. It was Paul, texting me.

Paul: FYI, that guy called to verify your reporter cover.

I hmphed. Of course, he did.

Mal: Thanks, any problems?

Paul: Nah.
Paul: I told him the article would write about Ms. Lamb in only the best light and highlight her philanthropy.

Mal: Perfect.

Paul: He seemed more worried about Mr. Lamb than Ms. Lamb, though.

Mal: Mr. Lamb? Isn't that who you were talking to?

Paul: No. It was Jonathan Gladstar who called.
Paul: Is that okay?

Mal: Yes.
Mal: Interesting.
Mal: Thank you.

Paul: NP. Just remember me if you get another good story.
Paul: Maybe this one.

Mal: If I can.

> *Mal: Don't worry, I'll keep you in*
> *mind.*

A group of men walked in, heading for the private room. I kept my eyes peeled on them. They didn't look familiar, but they didn't look like they were here just to hang out on a Saturday night.

"Is there a party tonight?" I asked blandly when James walked by.

He glanced to the back, raised his eyebrows, and looked down. "Looks like it."

"It looks more like a business meeting," Jen said, absently stirring her drink.

"Might be." He lifted his shoulders. "People sometimes book the room."

"Any idea who they are?" she asked.

"Ooh, I love this game," I broke in, worried the question was too direct. Maybe it had been a while since Jen had gone undercover; the cop in her was showing. "I'm guessing it's a finance mogul from one of those buildings on Michigan Avenue."

"Nah, they're not slim enough for that." She giggled. "Maybe they own the Cubs."

"I like that." I laughed, stirring my drink, then casting a coy look at the bartender. "Are we close?"

I paused, waiting to see if he was going to spill.

"I don't think they're either of those things." His mouth tipped to one side as he twirled bottles with moves that rivaled *Cocktail's* Brian Flanagan. "They're all businessmen and own buildings in town, but I'm not really sure what they own."

Interesting. I mentally noted all the people who had come in, trying to catalog their descriptions to jot down later. Between Jen and I, we should be able to remember all the details.

"Oh, I do know one thing," he said excitedly, drawing my attention from the group. He put an elbow on the bar top.

"What's that?" I leaned in, thinking his inside information was more important than getting notes on everyone.

"One of them just got in trouble for fixing horse races. I've heard he's been banned."

"One of them here?" I started to turn.

"No," he cut me off. "Not here today, but he meets with these guys. It's an interesting group. They come in regularly."

Now we're getting somewhere.

Jen and I caught each other's gazes. This was it; these were the guys.

Chapter 8

"Thanks," I said to the attendant at Hillview Homes who had led me to room 114, where Eleanor Rhodes was staying. It was early, and I wished I had stopped for a cup of coffee before leaving the house. Jen and I had waited way too long at Red, hoping to see or hear something from the group tucked in the private meeting room.

"No problem," she said, indicating the door. "Miss Ellie's in there with her son. They're expecting you. If you're lucky, you'll see both of those hunky men she's got. Woo-ee, girl. I would have transferred to this wing just to work with her and get an eyeful of those guys. Do you know them well?"

The corner of my mouth twitched up. "I know the younger one."

"Mercy." She put a hand over her heart. "You're one lucky thing, you are."

Shaking my head, I turned to knock on the door.

I had to take a small step back at the sight of the man who opened it. He looked so much like Rhodes, but about fifteen to twenty years older. Only, he had dark-brown hair speckled in gray, with a heavily receding hairline. I guessed that was why Rhodes preferred to shave it; early onset of hair loss must run in his family.

"Detective Malone," I said, sticking to business, unsure of his opinion of my investigation.

"Sean," he said, thrusting out a hand in greeting. His eyes flicked over me, taking note of details. Opening the door further, he stepped back to let me in.

It wasn't a large room, but it didn't look crowded. An heirloom buffet sat under the window, near a small half kitchenette with a mini fridge and microwave. Matching wooden furniture was scattered throughout the room, revealing that they had tried to make it feel like home.

I found Eleanor sitting in a small, padded rocking chair. It was obvious why the attendant called her Miss Ellie; the sweet countenance on her round face framed by soft white curls didn't fit the stately name Eleanor.

"Mom, this is Ms. Malone." Sean gave me a direct look. Apparently, they didn't want her to know I was a PI. Either that, or he disapproved of Rhodes hiring me. "She's a friend of Marlon's."

I had to pause at hearing him refer to Rhodes by his first name, but of course he wasn't going to call his nephew by his surname.

"Please call me Mal." I took her soft hand.

"Hello, dear." She smiled up at me.

"You're welcome to ask her about Aaron." Her son said to me. "But she hasn't seen him in a very long time."

"I don't want to upset her," I said, suddenly hesitant now that I had met her.

"You won't." He gave a slight shake of his head.

"Miss Ellie." I sat down in one of two chairs at a bistro table set. "What can you tell me about your son Aaron?"

"Aaron?" she said, her brows pulling in slightly. "Is he here?"

"No, I'm sorry. He's not." My heart clenched. "I wanted to give him a call to let him know you're here. Do you know where he is?"

"No," she said, tilting her head. "He had to go off to heal. He's sad."

"Sad?"

"Always searching for something. He'll come back, though."

I looked at Sean, whose thin lips said he'd heard it all before. I tried again. "Do you know where he went to look for it?"

"Here and there." She lightly lifted her shoulders, then smiled. "He's been everywhere. He'll come back."

I frowned. "Have you seen him?"

"Sometimes, he comes to see me."

My heart stopped. Was he visiting her secretly? I shot Sean a look, but the sadness in his eyes stopped me.

"Sometimes, she gets Marlon confused with Aaron," he said, his mouth tucking in. "They look a lot alike."

"Well, I'll do what I can to find him," I told her resolutely. It didn't make sense that he'd stayed away for so long. I wondered what shape he was in or if he was even still alive. For the family's sake, I hoped he was.

"If you can." He bobbed his head slowly. "It'd be a good thing. It's well past time for him to grow up."

"Grow up?" I tilted my head toward him.

Letting out a deep sigh, Sean said, "Apparently, Marlon didn't tell you everything." Then, looking over at his mom, asked, "Mom, would you like some iced tea?"

"That would be lovely, dear." She smiled, resting her head back in her chair.

Getting up, he got out tea bags and a pitcher from the small cabinet. I rose to follow him.

"Aaron was always a free spirit." Sean put tea bags in a microwave-safe Pyrex bowl and turned on the tap to add water. "Lily, Marlon's mom, was instantly attracted to his charisma and energy. They were both young and traveled a lot, even though they never had any money. One time, they came back into town following some band or camping group—I never knew which—married and pregnant."

I leaned against the counter, listening quietly. He set the microwave to heat the water and tea bags.

"Aaron took to calling himself something crazy like Leaf or something. Anyway, Lily died at the hospital. They hadn't taken her to any doctor, no prenatal care, nothing. The baby came a bit early, and because of the way they were living, she'd had no medical care and was eating what she could, when she could. Well, we were lucky Marlon made it."

"That's terrible," I said, my heart constricting at the thought that he might not have made it into the world. And at what the family had to have gone through during that time. "Were her parents around to help at all?"

"Never saw them." He shook his head, measuring sugar into the pitcher. "I don't even know where he met her. Somewhere around Chicago, I'd guess, but I don't even know her last name. Aaron named the boy after Marlon Brando—crazy thing. Thought he was the toughest guy alive. The man's just an actor."

"Still, it suits him."

Sean huffed. "Yeah, I suppose it does. Anyway, being a dad didn't mean much to Aaron. He still traveled like he did before. Said he was looking for meaning in his life, or some crap like that."

"With Rho—er, Marlon?"

"No, he left him here, with Mom." He gestured as the microwave beeped, but he left the bowl where it was, to finish steeping. "He had meaning right here. His son should have been his meaning. He was a part of him and Lily."

"How old were you?"

"When he was born?" He looked up. "I guess I was eighteen. I had just taken the exam for the fire department. I took classes after."

"Marlon said you helped raise him, too." It sounded like he had taken over his absent dad's duties.

He just lifted his shoulders. "I tried to help when I could. I had a good-paying job, a house. It was the least I could do. But I worked every third day, so little Marlon went back and forth between Mom and my house. I lived close to make it easy with school and all. God, he was such a little runt back then."

I smiled at that. "It sounds like a great childhood. He had all the support he needed."

"We tried." He grunted.

"Did he see his dad at all?"

"Here and there. He'd come back, then leave again. Once, he went to Tibet for a full year; Marlon was three. He had made some money on the traveling circuit, Lord knows how. Anyway, when he came back from that, he said he had found a home, people like him, and was moving into a commune in Arizona, outside of Flagstaff. A while back, I tried sending mail to the address I had, but just got a return to sender. Apparently, it's an old one. Maybe they moved to another location. I've heard these communities are popular there. It's not something I know much about."

"Yeah, I've looked. There are definitely groups of people living off the grid in that area. There's not much listed online, but I've got a friend digging in deeper."

"He wanted to take Marlon." He looked up at me, jaw working. "But he had just started school. The boy didn't want to leave, and I wouldn't let him."

"Sounds like his life was here," I said, trying to stay open to the conversation. It was obvious Aaron wasn't ready to be a dad and was grieving over the loss of Lily, but it was hard not to get angry at the guy who had left Rhodes without either parent.

"I did take him to see him a few times, in those first years. But eventually, school events got in the way; besides, he didn't want to go. He was just a kid. He was used to living a different way, you know? He wasn't comfortable there with him. And at some point, I said enough was enough and refused to take him. Aaron could come here if he wanted to see him."

"That seems fair," I said. He'd already done more than most young adults. Hell, he was practically a kid himself, like a big brother stepping in when the parents died. I wondered how he'd managed it all.

"I thought so." He sighed heavily, then gave a small shake to his head and got the steeped tea out of the microwave before pouring it into the pitcher and stirring it together. "Can you get a glassful of ice?"

"Sure." I flipped through the overhead cabinets until I found the glasses. The mini fridge had a small freezer at the top with two ice-cube trays. I filled the glass and set it next to Sean.

"Thanks." He nodded, adding cold water to the concentrated tea and pouring some into the glass for his mom.

"And Aaron hasn't called since then?"

"He called a few times. But I honestly can't remember all he said. I just filled him in on Marlon, not that he cared."

"So, as far as you know, he never left Arizona."

"Right." He nodded, setting the glass next to his mom's chair, where she had fallen asleep. He stopped, eyes focused off into the distance. "Or maybe something about Tennessee. Sorry, I wish I could help more. Feels a bit like a fool's errand, but it would be good for Mom to see Aaron again. Marlon too, probably."

"Marlon, what?" came a voice from the doorway.

Turning, I saw Rhodes, casual in jeans, T-shirt, and boots. It was early, but there was a puffiness around his eyes, suggesting he hadn't gotten much sleep the night before.

"We were just talking about you," Sean said to his nephew, then turned to me. "He was so difficult to potty train. Stubborn. Wet his bed till he was nearly eight."

Rhodes just rolled his eyes, apparently used to the ribbing, and strolled into the room.

"Has she been resting long?" he asked, standing in front of his grandmother.

"No, she drifted off just a bit ago when I went to make her tea," Sean said.

Rhodes turned to me. "Sorry I didn't get here earlier." He ran a hand over his head. "Rough night."

"Work?" I asked, knowing he worked a twenty-four-hour shift.

"Yeah, we ran our asses off. Four BLS calls throughout the night." He slowly shook his head. "Did you get a chance to talk to Gran?"

"Yes."

"Probably didn't get a lot from her."

"No, but I got to talk to Sean, too. Go over the facts you gave me. See if he remembered anything more."

He nodded, glancing over at his uncle, probably knowing he had shared his background.

"I think I got everything I need for now." I made my way towards the door to give the family some privacy. "You don't have to stay on my account. Maybe you can get some rest."

"Nah." He brushed it off. "I'll be fine."

I angled my head to Sean. "Thanks for your time this morning. I appreciate it."

"No problem." He walked over to shake my hand. "It was a pleasure to meet you, Detective Malone."

"Please, call me Mal."

"I'll walk you out." Rhodes turned to follow me.

I paused in the hallway. "They wouldn't happen to have any coffee here, would they? I'd love to take some to go."

It was a good excuse to make sure he was doing alright, I told myself. Sean's story had me looking at Rhodes in a different way. Sure, he was still that confident wall-of-a-man with a kind side I had grown to respect, but I wasn't expecting the sudden protectiveness I was feeling toward him. He'd probably hate that.

"They do." He leaned in, lowering his voice. "But it's terrible."

"Eh, bad coffee is still better than no coffee."

"I'll hold you to that opinion." He led me down the hall.

"So, BLS calls?" I let my voice tip up in question at the acronym. He'd explained once before but I couldn't remember some of the finer details in his line of work.

"Basic Life Support." He reminded me. "Last night, it was mostly domestic-violence calls and bar fights."

"Fun," I said sarcastically.

"Yeah, my kind of Saturday night." He chuckled, motioning me into the main kitchen and toward the lone coffee pot sitting on a burner. To-go cups sat next to it. "Now, are you sure you want to try this? I think it might be included as one of those extreme dating activities."

Leaning back, I stuck my hands in my back pockets, considering the pot. It was still somewhat early and didn't smell too burnt yet. "Yeah. I'm up for it."

"Brave soul," he said, filling a cup for me. He hesitated a moment, holding it in front of me. "Now, for the final test."

Taking the cup from him, I gave it a whiff. Maxwell House from the can, if I had to guess. I took a sip and didn't grimace. "It'll get me to my next stop."

"And where's that?"

I wondered what he would do if I suggested going to get coffee.

"Oh, I'll probably run by that business owner I told you about," I said offhandedly. "Sundays are generally pretty busy, but he closes early. Hopefully, they're leaving him alone."

"Hopefully." He frowned.

"I've got a few jobs I can look into today. Follow up on some leads." Taking a chance, I threw out, "I'm still trying to find hard evidence against Dessi. He just keeps walking."

I knew that would likely cause problems, but we both needed to know where each other stood.

"Aren't the cops handling that?"

And there it was. Taking a deep breath, I said, "They would if there was some evidence. I'm not saying they don't keep an eye out for him, but they're not actively pursuing him just to pursue him."

"You're following him around, then."

"Not directly."

"Christ, Mal." He broke away from me to stalk in a circle. "The man had you kidnapped."

"He did. But I got out."

"This time."

"I have to end this," I ground out. "Or else, Suzy will never be safe."

The kitchen was silent for a moment.

"At what cost?" He crossed his arms.

"Whatever it takes."

It didn't seem like he could understand that, which didn't make sense at all to me. Family was important to him. He, of all people, should get that.

Oh well. It sounded like coffee was out and it was time to go.

Chapter 9

A half hour later, I found myself on a stool at Grounds. Coffee with Rhodes might have been out, but that didn't mean I couldn't take myself out for coffee.

I definitely needed a proper drink.

"Is it that firefighter?" Maurice asked, watching me hover over my mocha latte.

I swiped a smear of foam off the side of my coffee cup and licked my finger.

"I don't know. I—Every time we talk about my work, I get the impression he disapproves of what I'm doing."

"Of your profession specifically?"

"Not particularly. But he questions why I'm involved and not the cops."

"In his line of work, he interfaces with law enforcement on a regular basis."

I shot him a look. I knew what he was doing. "Suzy's case was with the cops. They would *not* have found her. 'Course, to be fair, *she* set off the alarm that notified the fire department. So, hiring a private investigator wasn't strictly the turning point in finding her."

"Stop that." He put his hands flat on the counter. "You did find her. You were moments from getting her out."

"I was. But in the end, she didn't need me."

"You don't know that." His gaze pierced mine. "The bad guys could have gotten there first, and you know that. I don't even want to think about what would have happened." Stepping away, he leaned against the back counter and looked up at the ceiling. "That sweet lady. And you'd never know she went through what she did."

I hadn't realized he had such a soft spot for Suzy, but it wasn't surprising. Anyone who met her seemed to bend to her will. She had a way with people and was one of the most honest human I'd ever met.

"I don't know, Mo. Maybe I'm doing things wrong." I paused. "Jen seems to think I should forgive Rodriguez."

"She does?"

I nodded.

"Well, there's a big difference between forgiving and forgetting."

"Exactly."

"It doesn't mean you have to put yourself into that situation again. It doesn't negate what he did or guarantee a resolution between you two."

"True."

"But you could try to let go of some of the anger you have toward him."

"Maybe," I said, rocking my leg on the rung on my chair.

"Maybe is good."

"Anyway," I blew out. "I'm at a loss on the jewelry case."

"Still not showing up anywhere?"

"No, no trace of any of the pieces. At this point, I'm not sure what I can do. I've set up surveillance, and Sam has some sort of online job running to catch a listing."

"You can get a search warrant."

"My client doesn't want the cops involved." I sipped my coffee. "What if the son doesn't steal anything else? Short of going through his things, my hands are tied."

"Don't even think about it." He raised an eyebrow. "I know Sam's online machinations aren't always in the legal realm, but he's careful and apparently only uses his powers for good." The corner of his mouth rose a notch. "You don't need those legal ramifications. No one's life is in danger here. The cost is too high."

"I know that. I wouldn't," I said. I had only barely considered it. Mostly.

"What would the son do? If you were him."

"Considering it *is* him?" I tilted my head. "I'd try to make the aging mom look incompetent. With as many people as I could. Not just stealing jewelry."

"But the jewelry is the most concrete evidence."

"Yes."

"She's going to have to decide how far she wants to take this."

He nodded.

"Thanks, Mo."

"Anytime."

Walking out into the sunshine, I texted Rosemary to ask her to call when she had a chance. I wasn't going to put her in the middle of issues with Freddy again unless I had to.

She didn't call right away, so I put my phone in my back pocket and walked down to say hi to Marty. He would still be open for a bit before he closed up shop at noon.

"Hey, Marty." I waved.

As he handed change to a customer, he waved back.

"Everything good today?"

"Yep, no sign of trouble."

"Good to hear."

"Hey, Mal," he said, moving away from a couple of customers inspecting magazines. "I really appreciate you helping me out. I'm worried I can't pay you."

"You gave me the plant."

"It's not the same as you normally get paid."

I rubbed the back of my neck. "It's nothing."

"Well, it means something to me," he said, handing me an apple from his kiosk.

"Hey, thanks!" I lifted it happily. I liked apples.

Crossing the street, I dialed Sam before I forgot.

"Hey, Mal. What's up?"

"Try Tennessee," I told him, crunching into the apple.

"Tennessee?" he asked. I could hear his fingers clicking over a keyboard. "For?"

"Aaron Rhodes."

"On it."

"And, Sam? Also look for Leaf. Leaf Rhodes."

There was a pause on the line. "Ah, I get it. Hippie. He should have gone with Rock. Rocky Rhodes."

A peel of laughter came through the line, and I couldn't help but smile.

Driving down the street, I scanned for the warehouse address Jen had texted me.

There, between the meat-packing plant and a storage facility, was the brick building she had described. The police tape over the door and broken windows in the front made it easy to spot.

I pulled over to park on the side street and pocketed my ASP baton before making my way to the building. There wasn't any pedestrian activity, so I edged around the back, finding a door. There was a piece of plywood covering its window but no police tape.

The lack of police tape eased my B&E concern, and I bumped up the doorknob, grinning when it lifted easily from the dilapidated frame. Easing inside, I stood still for a moment, letting my eyes adjust to the dark.

Slowly, the room came into focus. Bare rafters and I-beams exposed the upper stories. Partial demolition showed the wall studs behind the drywall in places. I walked through to the front of the building, where the police tape cordoned off a large section.

Standing on the outside edge of it, I could still see bullet-sized holes in the drywall here and tape on the ground, outlining fallen bodies. It was a grim scene, eight inside the building. And from what Jen had said, there were two outside. Bystanders just out, walking their dog.

I took a deep breath, letting it out in a whoosh. The weight settled on my shoulders. I had to do something about this.

This location had been found by the police, but maybe Dessi had others. I made a mental note to start cataloging the other places he had shown up and keeping an eye on all of them. I had been focusing on the speakeasy, but if that's what it would take, I would do it.

The peal of my phone ringing broke the musty silence.

"Hello?" I said, one hand covering the speaker as I backed away.

"Where are you?" came Jen's voice.

"The warehouse." I looked out the door, but as far as I could tell, it was clear. I slipped out.

"Mal, you really shouldn't tell me these things," she scolded, then sighed. "You could have at least called me for backup."

"Next time," I promised. "I was just looking around a bit. I didn't cross the tape."

"That's the least of my concerns." Her voice was tight.

"What's up?"

"Word on the street says Marchi's guys were buying guns."

"A reliable informant?"

"Yes."

"And the sale went south."

"It would seem so."

"Any idea what for?"

"No, but, Mal. He saw two full crates. That's a lot of guns."

"What would they need that many guns for?" I paused. "Shit."

"My thoughts exactly."

The next morning, I was grateful to be back in the office, at my desk. It had been a quiet night, but I had trouble enjoying it due to the newfound threat of Dessi with guns. Suzy had some mellow trumpet music playing that was oddly relaxing, and I settled into my chair, scanning through emails. I tapped my fingers absently against my desk.

The sound of metal pinging jolted me upright. *What was that?* Looking behind me, I scanned the floor. No rodents.

Ting. There it was again. Searching the room for the sound, I finally noticed something hit my door. *Ting.* Three little paper clips sat in a two-foot circle on the floor in front of my open door.

Apparently, Suzy was bored too.

I pulled open my drawer and found a handful of paper clips. I threw one through the air, and it fell flat on the hardwood floor, only halfway to its mark. Frowning, I wrenched my drawer back open to find a rubber band. Extending a thumb, I pulled back on the stretchy tan band, aiming at the door but at an angle, and let it rip. It bounced against the door and ricocheted towards Suzy's desk.

"Ha, ha!" she let out, her chair squeaking. Then moments later, a rubber band arched through the air, hitting the door more centered than mine had but still at enough of a tilt to rebound and land squarely on my desk.

How did she do that?

"No new work?" I called through the open doorway.

"No new meetings," she said, leaning back to see me, a mischievous smile painted across her face. "Are you bored? You could advertise more."

"Not quite," I said. *Yet.* "Just checking."

Rolling my shoulders, I clicked back onto my computer. I still had work to do. Running a search on past mafia and Marchi-related articles in the Chicago area, I didn't find any including the guys we had seen at Red. I also ran a quick search on Dessi, but there was nothing new.

No surprise; Sam would have told me about it by now. He said he had popped up on the city cams, though. I could get a list of those. I drummed my fingers on the desk, stopping when the Sam-bot rolled into the office.

Finally.

"Morning, Mal." The tracked robot made its way to the center of the room, easily rolling over the scattered paper clips.

"Morning."

"So, I found a lead in Tennessee."

"So quickly?" I sat up straight in surprise. "Sam, I didn't expect you to spend your Sunday night working."

I didn't even pay the guy. Guilt swirled in my stomach.

"Hey, don't worry about it. I set up a little search while we were playing D&D last night."

"D&D? With Suzy?" I looked to the doorway curiously.

"Hey, I'm a level-ten cleric," she called from her chair.

"Of course, you are," I muttered.

"Her character is pretty hot." Sam's eyes widened, and he wagged his eyebrows.

"Moving on."

"Anyway, I found a message board online mentioning Leaf. Someone named Amity. The conversation is many years old. Dried up, really. But they were talking about some of the Arizona transplants being fed up with the lack of governmental support for the community there. They were relocating to one in Tennessee. Apparently, the Amish communities there have already established workarounds for living off the grid."

"Do you have an address?"

"No, but I tracked Amity's IP address to a yoga studio south of Nashville, near the Alabama border."

"You're an internet god."

"I know." He preened, brushing invisible lint from his shoulder.

"Do you have the phone number?"

"I do, but I've already called her," he said sheepishly. "I wanted to get into the actual investigation."

"And?"

"She'll talk to you, but only in person. She doesn't like phones so much."

"That's a long drive." I pulled up an internet browser.

"Eight and a half hours," he supplied. "Or you could fly. There are flights from Chicago to Huntsville, AL. It would get you within a couple of hours of the place."

I sat back in my chair. I had never left Chicago on a job. I'd be out of my jurisdiction and my PI license. Still, I could ask questions if she was willing to talk. I'd just have to be careful.

"Did she say anything about Leaf? Is there any way to know if it's Aaron?" My fingers itched to pick up the phone and call her myself, but I didn't want to discredit Sam's efforts.

"You never know. He's like a *leaf on the wind*," he said in a starry voice.

"Huh?" I asked, feeling like I was missing something with that reference.

He cleared his throat. "Anyway, like I said, she doesn't like talking over the phone, but when I mentioned Leaf, she indicated he was still there, living with the community. Some kind of farm, I think."

It was enough for me.

"Hey, Sam?"

"Yeah?"

"I think I'm going to be taking a trip. Tomorrow. Can you do me a favor?"

"Sure, I've already sent the details. They should be in your inbox."

"I was kinda wondering if you and Suze could hold down the fort while I'm away."

Sam's eyes widened to a point I thought was possibly unhealthy.

"Heck yeah!" he exclaimed. "Totally, like, for sure we can! I can keep an eye on the cams, call and check in with Marty, and even set up a cam outside of Red's if I need to. Suzy's got the books and the phones, like normal."

"I can check in with Rosemary while you're gone," Suzy's voice came from her desk.

"You don't need to put up a cam at Red's." I held my hands up. I didn't want him to get caught rummaging around there. "I think we have a good idea of the regulars. And if we need to, I can set one up sometime."

"Sure. Whatever you want." He grinned from ear to ear.

I shook my head and opened his email before going through all the documents. He had even sent me driving directions. Looks like the Jeep was getting to stretch her legs.

An hour later, my phone rang.

"Mal?" It was Rosemary.

"Hi. Thanks for calling me back," I said. "I wanted to discuss your case. I've followed up on a few leads here, but frankly, I'm at a loss as to what to do next. If Freddy puts your missing jewelry up for sale in the area, we'll find it. If he steals again, we'll have proof. But, unless I can get your workers to talk, I've hit a dead end."

"If Freddy gets wind of you questioning them, he'll know something is going on."

"True. It's just that I appreciate your business, but I can't, in good conscience, continue to bill you for following leads where I think there are none. If you're willing to file a theft report, we can probably get a warrant to search his place."

She didn't answer, but I knew from previous conversations that she was opposed to that.

"Listen, I'm going out of town for a few days. How about I let you think on it and call you when I get back?"

"That sounds good," she said slowly. "Have a safe trip, dear."

"Thanks." Then, curiosity got the better of me. "One other thing. Do you mind if I ask how you got my name?"

"Oh, that." I heard a light chuckle over the phone. "I did a little investigative work myself. You were listed in the Insideonline as instrumental in all the scandal that went down with that Mayor Koch and the Tribune. I thought you might be a good person to reach out to for my problem."

I knew Paul had listed my name, but it hadn't been a paying case, and I hadn't realized it'd be good for business. "Well, I'm glad you got my number."

"Me too, dear. Regardless of what happens next."

"Good luck with that." I shifted away from my desk and added, "Be careful."

Chapter 10

Stepping out to stretch my legs, I swung by Marty's. But as I got closer, I saw newspapers and magazines all over the street corner.

Speeding up to a jog, I raced over to find him hiding behind his cash register, on his knees.

"Are they gone?" he asked, looking up at me with wide eyes. His take-out coffee cup lay smashed on the ground.

I scanned the area, looking for a group of kids or a yellow car.

"I think so." I helped him up. "Are you okay?"

"Y-yes," he said, taking jerky steps to his stool. He leaned over, pulling it underneath his frame and sitting gingerly back on it, his breathing still trying to calm.

"I'm sorry I didn't get here sooner." I bent to pick up some magazines and put them back on the shelves.

"You don't have to do that." He stood, unfolding his long legs from his stool.

"I can at least help you." I scowled, not stopping, frustrated that these kids were causing trouble on my street. If I had only hung up with Ms. Lamb a few minutes sooner, I would have been here to help him.

I was just glad he hadn't been hurt. This time.

"I'm sending the feed now." Sam's voice rose from the Sam-bot. I could hear him busily clicking away at an unseen keyboard.

I had brought Marty back to the office after helping him close shop early. The cameras Sam had set up weren't a live feed like the ones at Rosemary's house. These were larger cameras with their own batteries, recording on a looped feed.

Suzy and I hovered around Marty, who had settled into a chair with a fresh cup of coffee. Suzy had seen to that. My monitor, turned to face us, was buffering with whatever Sam was sending through.

A grainy video appeared, the street corner suddenly popping into focus. Sam must have helped him position the camera. It had a nice, wide view of his stands and the stool where he took payments.

The feed fast-forwarded until a convertible pulled into view, then rewound to get the scene from the beginning.

The car pulled in across the street, facing the stand. It was too far away to get a good look at it, and since Illinois law didn't require front plates, it would be impossible to tell the license number.

"Can you zoom in to get the make and model?" I asked.

"Probably," the Sam-bot answered. "I'll see."

The car door opened, and Marty made a strangled sound, looking into his coffee cup. Suzy put a comforting arm around his shoulders.

A large, booted foot slammed down onto the pavement, followed by a long bare leg and a flirty skirt.

I stilled, frowning, and looked down at Marty, who made a soft moan.

"Is that...?" I raised a finger, unsure what to say.

Another car door opened, and heeled boots followed, thigh-high ones topped with a short A-line skirt. The two girls waited while a third came out of the driver's side door, hip thrust to the side until there was a break in cars.

The three girls strutted across the street, where Marty jumped up from his chair, knocking his coffee cup to the ground.

I could see the girls circle him, posturing and yelling at him, their faces twisted in mocking insult. One of them went over to the magazines, shoving the neatly lined issues to the sidewalk where they scattered in the wind.

Marty jolted forward to stop her but was pressed back by the girls' waving hands and apparent yelling. The driver and obvious leader of the group gave him a push, sending him stumbling backward. His arms cartwheeled in an attempt to catch himself, but he thudded down on his tailbone.

My nose scrunched up in reflex. That looked like it hurt.

I watched as they bent over, laughing at him. The three knocked over stacks of newspaper, throwing things in the air. Marty crawled behind his cash register and covered his head.

Then, just as fast as they had appeared, they took off, grabbing some magazines like trophies and swaggering back across the street to their car.

The feed paused when the car drove out of the scene.

"Girls?" I said, unable to finish my statement.

Silence filled the air.

"Uhn," Marty gurgled.

I looked over at Suzy, whose lips were open and rounded.

"Well," I started. "I'll send the video to Jen and Officer Mathews and see if either of them has seen these *girls* around town. Maybe they've been creating havoc elsewhere as well."

"Thanks," Marty whispered, clutching his coffee.

"Don't worry about it." I patted him on the back.

Girls or not, they weren't going to terrorize my neighborhood.

After the excitement in the office died down and Marty went back to reopen his stand, with Jen promising to keep an eye out on things when she could, I made plans to leave in the morning, booking a small motel near Amity's yoga studio. I secured it for two nights. From the sound of it, the place wasn't terribly busy and the room would be available as long as I needed it. Hopefully, it wouldn't be longer than that.

It would take most of the next day to drive south, but if I started early enough, I would make it to her studio before she closed for the day.

Leaving early to go home and pack, I reluctantly dialed Rhodes to update him on the case.

"Hi," he answered on the first ring.

"Afternoon," I said, waving at Marty as I walked by. He seemed to be doing okay. I crossed the street to walk home. "I got a lead in Tennessee."

"For my dad?"

"Yes. Sean mentioned he had heard him say something about Tennessee once and that, at one point, he had taken up the moniker 'Leaf.' That's how we found him." I held up an aggravated hand at a car that honked at me in the crossing lane. *Eh, that was Chicago, for you.*

"Leaf," he repeated the name slowly, like he didn't understand what I was saying. "Are you sure it's him?"

"Pretty sure." It must be hard for him to think about his dad with another name. A strange one compared to our walk of life. "I'm leaving in the morning to go see her; she doesn't like telephones," I added drily. It would have made this case so much easier. "But apparently, there aren't any phones where he's at anyway. As long as it's a good lead, it's worth the trip. I'm hoping to get her to take me out there to see for myself. If it is, I can give him the message about Miss Ellie."

"I'm coming."

"Excuse me?"

"Er, I'd like to come," he corrected. "It's my dad, Mal. He may not come, and well, I'd like to see him myself, regardless."

I let it hang in the air while I considered it. A long road trip would be uncomfortable for us right now, not exactly ideal.

"I know we've been rubbing each other the wrong way," he said, his voice pitching low. "Maybe it'd be good to talk on the trip."

Exactly what I was hoping to avoid. That hadn't been ending well for us lately. Still, a part of me wanted to try. I wasn't quite sure why, but I did.

"Please, Mal?"

Images of the little boy Sean had told me about shot through my mind. The stubborn little kid, refusing to go back to Arizona, uncomfortable with staying with a man he barely knew.

"I'm leaving early," I said.

"Thanks, Mal." I could practically hear his relief over the phone. "I'll be ready anytime you want to leave. I'm scheduled tomorrow, but I can call in. Do you think we'll be gone longer than a few days?"

"I hope not," I said, knowing he worked twenty-four-hour shifts, then had forty-eight hours off.

"I can take another day if needed."

"I'll call the motel. Get a second room."

"Thanks," he said. "I can drive."

"I'm driving," I said. I wouldn't bend on that one. Driving the Jeep sometimes helped me think. Besides, if the conversation went south, I wanted something to keep me busy.

"Okay." He chuckled. "You drive. Where do you want to meet?"

"I can pick you up." He hadn't been to my apartment, my personal space. I wasn't sure yet if I wanted him to. "We leave at 6 a.m."

"I thought you said it'd be early," he joked.

I hung up. This was going to be fun...

Bags packed and plans for the next few days sorted, I got into the Jeep to pick up some dinner, but she had other things in mind. Pulling into the parking lot at the furniture store, I stared at the beige exterior. It wouldn't hurt to take another assessment of the patrons.

"Back again?" James joked, heading over to where I sat at the bar.

"I guess I'm addicted to the gin & tonics," I joked.

"Jessie not able to make it tonight?"

"Not tonight. She had to work late."

"Maybe she can swing by when she gets off."

I shrugged, eyeing the room.

"That was quite the party the other night." I nodded to the now-empty room. The group had gotten boisterous throughout the evening. "I'm hoping they made some grand business plans. That's what I choose to believe anyway."

James laughed, shaking my cocktail. The ice and liquor made a swishing, clinking sound in the shaker. "I think you're not far off."

He winked, sliding my drink in front of me. "I need to get more limes; I'll be right back."

Wiping his hands on his apron, he left for the back kitchens and offices. I angled my chair to the room to see what else I could observe while I waited.

Hopefully, I could get more out of James. He certainly seemed to be in a sharing mood.

Meanwhile, in an opulently adorned office,

"It's just that the Family is due to arrive any minute," James said, hands on the back of the chair in front of him. "I know you said to let her poke around."

"You might have to *redirect* her again," Dessi replied.

"That was a close call the other night." He shook his head. It would be so much easier if the boss would just agree to get her out of there. He could figure out a way to make her leave without showing his hand. "When Mike walked in, I thought for sure she'd recognize him. But I kept her talking until he made it into the back."

"Good work." Dessi folded his hands behind his head, swiveling in his chair. "Just do the same tonight. I trust you can manage."

"Okay, boss." He gulped. He didn't like it, but he'd do what he could. "You've got it."

"Limes," James announced, holding them up as he walked out of the back.

"Then, we're all set if we have a rush on tequila," I joked.

"Yeah," he smirked, watching the crowd.

Taking a sip from my drink, I tried to think of the best segue back to details of the meeting the other night.

"You know," he said, straightening. "We never did give the meeting room a good cleaning. Those guys sometimes leave things behind."

I perked up. This was going to be easy.

"Wanna investigate with me?" He wagged his eyebrows.

"For sure!" I hopped off my barstool, clapping my hands together. "What do you think we'll find?"

"Who knows?" He tiptoed exaggeratedly toward the room, watching the front door for new guests.

I giggled, following.

We skirted the room, turning over napkins and looking through the trash cans, but all the while, James' gaze kept flicking towards the door.

Frowning, I edged toward it, only to have him cut me off.

"I think I saw a piece of paper behind this chair." He bent over in front of me.

Looking past him through my narrowed view of the cocktail lounge, I saw a group of men in suits walk past, turning to go in the back. The back of one head bore a striking resemblance to Marchi, but I couldn't be sure.

I stumbled backward, blood draining from my face. Coughing, I leaned over, my hand covering my face and, more importantly, my faux pas.

Gullible. Ignorant. Naive! I was all those things and more.

James had been managing me, leading me to this meeting room and its clients while the real deal was going on right underneath my nose. Dessi probably even knew I was here.

It felt like I had swallowed a stone. My list was useless.

Dessi had an office in the back. Of course they would be meeting there, not out in the open. What had I been thinking?

I needed to get out of here. I needed to regroup and make a plan.

Chapter 11

True to his word, when I pulled up at Rhodes' brick house at 6 a.m., he was sitting on his front porch, a duffle bag on the concrete between his feet. But it was what he had in his lap that drew my attention, two to-go coffees nestled in a carrier. He had to have driven clear to Near West Side to find a coffee shop open before 7 a.m. Even the local chain coffee shop didn't open until 5:30 a.m., not nearly enough time to get there and back. I would know.

The tightening in my chest softened a little. I hadn't even realized I was holding onto so much tension. Between my hasty exit from Red's last night, when I thought I was sure to get backed into a bad situation, and the next few days in close proximity with someone I just couldn't seem to get on the same page with, uncertainty was weighing heavily on me. Despite our differences, I was still frustratingly attracted to him. And as well as it had worked last night, I was fairly certain an exaggerated coughing fit wasn't going to help me out with my current situation.

"Good morning," I said when he opened the passenger side door. "You can throw your bag in the back."

"Morning," he said, climbing in. He handed me a cup, then put his bag in the back, a flannel shirt tossed over it.

Taking a sip, frothy goodness met my tongue, and a moan slipped out.

"It's good." I quickly said to cover my reaction, glancing over to see if he noticed.

"I'm glad." He grinned, buckling up.

"Thanks for the coffee."

"Well, you are letting me tag along. I appreciate it."

"Are you ready?" I asked, giving him a once-over. He was dressed even more casually than usual in a T-shirt and jeans, and was freshly shaved. I could smell his woodsy aftershave.

"I'm always ready," he cast me a playful side glance, running his hand over his freshly sheared head.

The look in his eyes when they met mine told a different story, though. Worry clouded his still-tired-looking eyes. This time, I knew it wasn't from work. I could only imagine what he must be feeling. The possibility of seeing his dad for the first time in twenty-something years. I mean, I didn't see mine all that often, but our issues were nothing like his.

Nodding, I let it lie. I didn't like being called out on my insecurities, either. After tapping the address on my phone, I pulled out of his driveway and made a right.

"What kind of music do you like?" I asked, fiddling with the radio. Not really sure what to say, I hoped the background noise would help fill the void.

"I'm good with anything," he said. "Oh, except maybe death metal."

"Oh, shoot." I shook my head. "Death metal is my life."

He snorted. "Well, by all means, then. I can't have you dying on me. I mean, how would that look for my career? My entire job is about saving lives."

I had never thought about it that way. I mean, I knew he was a firefighter, but I had focused on the fact that he fought fires. That wasn't nearly all he did. He handled all the basic life support calls as well, kind of like a paramedic, only not as extreme.

"I think I can make do with some eighties music for today," I said, hitting a button on my dash. Whitesnake came on, rocking on about a lonely street of dreams. It should have been inspirational, but this morning, it just sounded sad. "I figured we could drive for an hour or so until we get hungry enough for breakfast."

"Works for me."

"What do you like? I'm not really fond of fast food unless you're talking coffee." Cause coffee is food.

"Oh, I'm not picky. I'd be happy with a truck stop or a diner, so whatever you choose is fine. Remember, I'm the one tagging along here."

"Right." It was true, but it still felt right to include him. We were still friends, right? "I like diners too."

"Some of the best meals I've had have been at diners," he said.

I glanced over at him momentarily while shifting lanes. "Have you traveled a lot?"

"Not so much lately," he said quietly, then paused. "Back when Sean used to take me to Arizona. He made it a lot of fun to find a good diner to eat at on the way."

"He's a good guy, your uncle." I didn't want to press, but this was the first he'd ever really shared about his private life.

"Yeah, he is. Lord knows what woulda happened to me without him, Gran, and the guys at the fire department."

"The fire department? Wasn't that before you joined? You were a kid, right?"

"Yes, but even then I was at the station all the time. I'd race over after school to hang out while Uncle Sean was working." I could hear him smile. "It was like the whole crew raised me. And, God, I loved every minute of it."

"I bet. What kid didn't want to grow up in a fire station?"

"Exactly. It was a kid's dream." I could hear him drift off again. "There are worse ways to grow up."

"I bet they even let you hit the siren," I piped up, trying to get the conversation onto more lighthearted territory.

He let out a short exhale. "You have no idea. One time, back when I was really little—I honestly didn't have any reason to be in the apparatus bay—I climbed into the machine, all geared up in my uncle's bunker gear. I sat there, hat pushed up on my head so I could see, and got the truck started. Lord." He laughed out loud. "The smoke poured out of the engine, soot coating the door. See, you're supposed to raise the door before you start it, to prevent just that. But of course, I didn't know that. I was just a little thing. I hit the alarm, thinking I would be like one of the guys. Wow, I got in trouble for that one."

"I'll bet." I couldn't help myself from smiling.

"I had to scrub that damned door for the next two hours. But it was worth it. That's when I knew I wanted to be a firefighter, too. I wanted to be like them and race out there to save whoever was in need. They were the bravest people I had ever seen."

"I know what you mean," I said. "I joined the police academy because of the same thing."

"Your dad was a decorated officer, wasn't he?"

"Yeah." I nodded, leaving it at that. "He did instill a strong sense of right and wrong."

"It makes a difference when you're small. In fact, I waffled between firefighting and social work."

"Really?" I said, surprised. I hadn't known that. "I just figured it was in your blood."

"Well, it was. Even my grandpa was a Chicago volunteer firefighter back in the day. But when I was a teenager, as teenagers do, I got into trouble."

"Naturally."

"When Sean had enough of my bullshit, he arranged for me to hang out with a basketball team after school."

"Were you into basketball?"

"Not really, but after that first summer, I sure got better at it. Competition does a lot for a teenage boy."

"Not just for boys. Girls too." I slid him a side-eye, then rolled it. I always had to one-up the boys. Hell, I still felt like it some days.

"Sean knew what he was doing, though. It wasn't just a neighborhood basketball team like I was led to believe. It was a community center putting it on. Set up to keep kids off the street."

"Is that where you met Sully?"

"Originally, yeah. Back then he volunteered at the center. Of course, I got to know him better on the job, in a different capacity. But back then, the center gave me what I needed, a place outside of home, outside of my family, who at the time I thought couldn't even begin to understand me. Truth was, I didn't understand myself. I was growing and changing and mad at the world."

"I think we all were at that age, trying to figure out who we are."

"Yeah." He blew out. "No way would I want to be a kid again. Life's so much better from the adult side."

"It has its moments." I agreed. "More stress, but still."

"Is it, though?"

I thought about that. "Maybe not. Just different, I guess."

He nodded.

We both let Queen encourage us that we were champions as our minds drifted off into a comfortable silence.

"I think I found one," Rhodes said suddenly, pointing out the window. "Take the next exit."

It was over a couple of hours later. My stomach was growling, and I still hadn't found a good place to pull off for food.

"Oh, finally." I sighed. "I hope they're still serving breakfast."

"Mal, it's not even nine o'clock."

"Still." I glanced at him, turning the wheel to take the exit. "You have no idea how much I need another cup of coffee. And a restroom."

"I'm sure they'll have coffee all day."

"Breakfast coffee is fresher."

He just chuckled.

The diner was tucked into the rest stop. We were going old school. I liked it.

I pulled in and found a place to park. I'd get gas to feed the Jeep after I fed my stomach.

As we walked in, Rhodes paused to open the door for me. That was new for me. Well, unless I counted Jimmy Ankenbrand from Freshman year, but he was definitely trying to get something out of the deal. I didn't get the feeling Rhodes was angling for anything from the casual nature of it. Which was good because it hadn't gotten Jimmy anywhere, either.

Settled in the booth, I tried to keep my mouth from watering as I scanned the menu. It was simple but had hearty comfort food. Country fried steak, pork steaks, and meatloaf all called to me, but I still wanted breakfast. Settling for a large breakfast skillet, I placed my order and hurried off to the restroom.

When I returned, two steaming cups of coffee sat on our table.

"Oh, bless that waitress." I pulled mine close to inhale its goodness.

"I warned her that you may need an IV drip if we didn't get caffeine into you soon," he said drily.

"Smart move." I took a sip. It was pretty good, as far as diner coffee went. Not strong, but that's because it's meant to be consumed by the pot, not the mug. Comparing it to Ground's coffee was like comparing Pop-Tarts to pie. Both were tasty, but they certainly weren't the same thing.

"So, at what time do you think we'll get to the yoga studio?" Rhodes raised his coffee.

"Probably about 4 p.m. It doesn't close until 6, though, so with any luck, we'll be able to talk to Amity before she closes for the day. But we really don't know what we'll run into," I warned him. "I'm not a cop, and I'm already out of my jurisdiction, so I really can't make her talk to us. Sam seemed to think she would, in person anyway, but it's still a shot in the dark."

"Yeah, but you can be very persuasive." He gave me a soft smile. "I have faith in you."

"Thanks," I said, my face warming at the compliment. "I'll do what I can. I just don't want you to get disappointed if things don't work out the way we think they will. You never know. She may have called in sick today, or it could be her day off. Investigations like these can spin off in all sorts of directions and take longer than you'd think."

"I'm a big boy, Mal." He reached over the table to put a hand on mine. "Don't worry about me. I'll stay out of your way if you need me to. Just let me know what you need."

I hoped that would be true. I wanted to believe he trusted me. We were both take-charge kind of people, and I had a feeling if things went south, he wouldn't hesitate to take over.

Unsure what to say, I left my hand under his. If nothing else, because I wanted to. But it was still a relief at her good timing when the waitress arrived with our food. The scent of the fried potatoes and bacon wafted up to me. Few things smelled better than that. I mean, coffee, obviously, but few other things.

We both dug in, our conversation forgotten.

Chapter 12

"So, what other cases are you working on right now?" Rhodes asked, breaking through Alannah Myles' *Black Velvet* playing softly in the background.

"Um, you know my cases are confidential," I said, hesitant to talk about work. We hadn't really dealt with the issue of him thinking I wasn't capable of handling my investigations. And being stuck in a vehicle for hours didn't quite feel like the right place to have that conversation. Nowhere to get a break from each other if needed. After we located Aaron would be a better time. The irony wasn't lost on me that he had hired me to do a job he didn't think I had any business doing. Or maybe it was just because cops wouldn't take a case that wasn't legitimately a missing person.

"True." I noticed him watching me. "But can't you talk about your cases in general?"

I smirked; it was similar to what I had asked him a few months ago when I was looking into the arson cases.

"Yeah, I could probably do that." It's how I talked to Mo about work. Basic facts still got the gist across. "I'm working on one case with an elderly lady. She thinks her son is trying to steal from her."

"Is he?"

"I'm not quite sure yet, but he sure doesn't seem like a model citizen."

"That doesn't make him a thief, though."

"True." I glanced at him, hoping he wasn't thinking about Sully and how I had pushed to find evidence against him. It still sat heavily with me. "I've been staying unbiased, trying to find evidence of *anyone* stealing from her. There's a chance it's her financial advisor or her housekeeper."

"But she had a theft?"

"Yes, but she doesn't want to call the cops," I threw in.

"In case it's her kid."

"Correct again." I watched the exits. We were getting close. "Ultimately, she thinks he's trying to make her look senile and get power of attorney over her money."

"That sucks. I hope she's wrong."

"Yeah, me too."

I put my blinker on, finally. I really needed to finish thinking through my next plan of attack for Dessi, but I wasn't ready to include Rhodes in that conversation. I wished I could, but not until I knew where he really stood.

Maybe I was worried I already knew.

By the time we located Amity's yoga studio, tucked behind a general store at the end of Main Street, I realized the town wasn't just a normal Southern town in Tennessee. We had passed several buses and vans decked out with tie-dye and peace signs. Dated buildings weren't that unusual to find in the South, especially this close to the Alabama border, but the lack of chain restaurants and gas stations cast an unusual feeling, as though we had stepped back in time. It was going to be an interesting visit.

"You're sure this is it?" Rhodes asked, looking through the windshield at the yoga studio. Sanskrit symbols on the window glinted gold in the late-afternoon sun's reflection.

"This is the address Sam gave me," I said, opening the door. "Only one way to find out."

There were few cars outside, so I hoped at least someone was free to talk. Trying the front door, it swung open, and a small bell attached to the back of the door tinkled, announcing our entrance.

The smell of patchouli and Nag Champa hit me as I stepped in, ducking under a strand of crescent moons hung across the doorway. The wooden interior of the building looked both rustic and well cared for.

"Hello?" I called out, looking through a doorway to another room since the small entry space was empty.

"We're in here," a voice called out.

I glanced back at Rhodes, then pushed through the beaded curtain to introduce ourselves.

Two women sat on yoga mats in front of a small table at the end of the room. Incense burned in front of a large bowl sitting on the table.

"No shoes, please." The woman on the left pointed to a row of cubbies stacked next to the door. She had on colorful flowing pants and a scarf tied into her curly sandy-blonde hair.

I bent to unlace my boots and saw Rhodes was already doing the same, silent as he stacked his boots next to mine in the cubby. They looked at odds with the slip-on shoes nearby, rigid city-ready, next to soft, country-relaxed.

"I hope we're not interrupting a class," I said politely. "We're looking for Amity?"

"I'm Amity," the blonde said, rising from her cross-legged position to take my hand in both of hers.

"Mal." I gave her a friendly smile, watching her go to Rhodes next.

"Marlon," he said, nodding lightly. He shifted on his feet, wiping a hand down his leg before extending it.

"I was just finishing with a meditation session." She turned to the other woman, who was rising to roll up her mat.

"Do you have a few minutes?" I asked. "My friend, Sam, called a few days ago, asking about a friend, Leaf Rhodes. He thought you might have an idea where he is."

Her eyebrows rose, then narrowed as she glanced between us. "I hope this is a friendly visit. We don't promote negativity in this space." Settling on Rhodes' face, she paused, tilting her head. "You're related."

"Yes, ma'am," he said quietly.

"We're just hoping to talk to him about a family matter," I said. "The last address we had was in Arizona, so we haven't been able to get ahold of him for quite some time."

"Ah. Well, a bunch of them came from that community in Arizona," she said, pausing to hug the other woman before she left. "And they don't have phones, out at the farm."

"The farm?" I asked.

"The community Leaf's living in."

"Do you think you can give us directions? It's pretty important that we talk to him."

"I don't know." She scratched her head. "You'd probably get lost. It's a bit out of town. Besides, you can't drive all the way out there. It's best to park and walk the rest of the way in. They don't like cars making ruts on their land. Or the fumes."

"We can walk in," Rhodes offered. "If you tell us where to start and give us a direction."

"Where are you staying?" she asked. "You're big-city folk, right? From Chicago?"

"At the motel," I said. From what I remembered, there was only one.

"Best that you don't head out there tonight," she said, shaking her head. "By the time you find the place, they'll be settling into dinner activities and meditations before bed. Unless you planned to stay there overnight."

Rhodes' eyes flicked to me, widening slightly. I put a hand on his arm.

"We'll be here for a few days," I said. I didn't want to stay overnight, either, but I didn't want to lose the opportunity. "We can head out tomorrow morning if you think that would be a better time for them."

"Meet me here tomorrow morning," she said. "A lot of these roads don't have signs on them. You can follow me out there after my morning classes. I'll be ready around nine."

"That would be great." I leaned in to shake her hand again. "I really appreciate your help."

"I'm happy to help," she said. "I'm sure Leaf will be happy to see you."

Rhodes didn't say anything, just glanced down.

"I'm sure it will be a happy reunion," I said, trying to keep the conversation light.

"Would you two like to stay? I have another yoga class starting soon," she said, walking away from us. She picked up yoga mats and rolled them out on the floor, getting set up. "Or if you'd rather, I have a yin yoga class this evening that ends in a nice, long meditation. It's perfect before bed. You'll sleep like a baby."

"That sounds great, but I think we've got a few things to do this evening already," I said, easing to the doorway to slip my boots back on.

"You're missing out," she called out. "I'm going to play the singing bowls."

I wasn't sure what singing bowls were, but I couldn't imagine how you could play bowls. Unless she was talking about glasses. I'd seen people play glasses with water in them. But that was something adults did to entertain kids, I thought.

"Maybe next time," I said, already out the door. "See you at nine!"

Back on the porch, we both took a big breath of fresh air.

"That was close," Rhodes said, staring off.

"You mean you're not a fan of yoga?" I teased, looking around the quiet streets so different from the car-clogged, honking ones back home.

"Not really," he mumbled, heading back to the Jeep.

Shrugging, I followed. I'd had to sit through worse for a good lead. At least it sounded like we had a good shot at seeing Leaf tomorrow. We had time to find some food. It had been a long drive, but so far, the awkward conversation was at a minimum and we hadn't had any arguments. I hoped we could keep the good luck up.

Meanwhile, back in a little brick investigation office,

"Ms. Lamb?"

"This is she."

"Hello, this is Suzy Mennon, ma'am. I work for Detective Malone?"

"Ah, yes, dear. How can I help you?"

"Mal said she told you she had to go out of town for a few days. I just wanted to check in with you and make sure things were going okay."

"How sweet of you. Well, everything is going just fine. Except—" She paused.

"What's wrong, Ms. Lamb?" She clutched the phone. If that man was stressing out this sweet old lady, she would head right over. Well, she'd take Wyatt's guys and head over. Not that she was scared of the spoiled brat, but the security team was her ride, and more importantly, Sam would hate it if she ran off without them. He worried about her, the sweetheart.

"Oh, it's nothing, really. I'm just not sure what to do."

"What do you mean?"

"Well, Mal thinks I should file a police report."

"What do you think you should do?"

"Do you have children, Suzy?"

"No," she said, her heart twisting. She hadn't been able to, not that Sam seemed to mind. He swore he didn't, that she was enough for him and their future, but sometimes she worried. He would have been such a great dad.

"Then you might not understand it, but I feel like I have to protect him."

"Even if he's doing something wrong?"

"Even so."

"If you don't mind me asking, why don't you talk to him, then? Stand up to him?"

"Because if I'm wrong, I'll look even worse." She humped. "Like the senile old lady I'm probably becoming."

"I doubt that."

"It's just the boy doesn't know how to manage money. But he sure knows how to manage me. He learned from his father, and it's just the way it's always been. I tried standing up to him a while back, and he acted like I had gone crazy. I've never acted like that before, and maybe I *should* go see a doctor. It'll be the perfect excuse to have my faculties assessed."

Anger boiled up in her. If there was one thing she couldn't stomach, it was manipulative men. "You know, I might have an idea."

"Amity sounded pretty sure that Leaf would be at the farm tomorrow." I sat across the table from Rhodes in a diner up the street from our motel. We had checked into our rooms, right next to each other, and walked over. The rooms weren't much, but they looked clean enough.

"Yeah." He studied the menu.

"Do you think he'll come back?" I asked, pulling my shirt away from my body to cool off. It was hot even though the sun was setting. Back home, the evenings always cooled off, unlike here.

"Who knows."

"Maybe we can get him to come back with us," I offered. "One of us could drive him back home if he doesn't have a car."

He just shrugged.

Okay. Apparently, we weren't talking about his dad tonight. He must be more worried about seeing him than I had thought. It was a side I hadn't seen in him. Gone was his calm demeanor and easygoing confidence. He wasn't the type to flake, but if he did, I could still handle the conversation with Leaf. And if I could bring him home for Miss Ellie, I would.

After an uncomfortably quiet dinner and walk back, we both went our separate ways to spend some alone time in our own motel rooms.

I was just settling down to flick through the television for a few minutes before bed when I heard a knock at the door.

"Hello?" I opened it to find Rhodes, standing there with his shoulders tight and fists stuffed into his front pockets.

"Look," he said, raising his head to meet my gaze. "I'm sorry I'm not myself."

"That's okay. Family can bring out the worst in us."

"Sometimes." He nodded. "It's just been a long time. I'm not sure what to expect."

"Makes sense. Look, do you want to watch some pointless TV?" It didn't feel right, sending him back to his room to overthink his reunion alone. What he needed was a friend. "I can make crappy coffee in the room's coffee pot."

It wasn't Mr. Bunn, but it would work.

His gaze slid into the room, then back at me.

"I think I saw X-Files reruns." I opened the door further, giving him room to enter if he decided to.

The side of his mouth ticked up. "I'll just bet you're a Scully, aren't you?"

My head shot back. "What is that supposed to mean? *Are you a Mulder?*" I shook my head, then narrowed my eyes. "Figures. You look like the type to believe in aliens."

Throwing back his head, he laughed a big belly laugh and walked in.

Chapter 13

"Sorry." I grimaced again as the Jeep's wheel landed and bounced out of another pothole. I wondered how Amity's little sedan was navigating around all of them.

"Not your fault. These roads are a mess," Rhodes said, firmly gripping the roll-bar-grab handle.

We had been following down winding side roads for fifteen minutes. We had to be getting close.

Sliding off the side of the road on a large shoulder patch of grass, the sedan rolled to a stop.

I signaled, following. Apparently, they didn't use turn signals in the South.

Glancing over at Rhodes, I could see a deep crease on his forehead. It wasn't a full-on frown, but it was obvious his stress was back. I could relate, not to the stress but to the feeling of being unprepared. I had no idea what to expect of what we were going to be walking into. I knew the place was supposed to be peace and love, but did that also mean drugs? To each their own, but I wasn't going to lose my PI license over that.

It would have helped if I could have slept last night, but between the lack of city noise and planning what to do next with the Dessi situation, I had tossed and turned all night. Hopefully, we would have good luck here and get back home to deal with it.

"Looks like this is where we walk." I turned off the ignition and opened the door to let the humid heat in. I was glad I had packed a tank top, although I only had jeans, same as Rhodes.

"Leave your cell phones in your car," Amity said, looking much more comfortable in a skirt and tie-dyed tank, which was tied up on one side.

"Our phones?" I asked. "Why?"

"They don't allow cellular frequency in their community," she said. "It's disruptive."

"Okay," I said, turning back to my car. I considered taking it anyway. How would they know? But I didn't want to leave any reason for them to toss us out. Who knew what kind of security we would have to pass through when we entered. We both left our phones in the center console and relocked the doors.

"It's only another mile up ahead." She pointed to a walking path in the woods in front of us and headed towards it. A wire was stretched across it to prevent cars from making their way through.

Rhodes nodded, trudging slowly behind.

I fell back until we were side by side. "Do you want to take the keys?" I held them out.

"What?"

"I'm sure things will go fine, but if you need some space, you can come back and wait for me. I can handle it alone."

His eyes softened. "I'll be okay. You don't have to protect me, but thanks for looking out for me."

I just shrugged, flushing, suddenly wishing I had brought shorts. It had to have been the heat.

After several minutes of walking, the pathway opened to a small clearing. Buildings dotted the grass, and a large field surrounded at least half of the area I could see. The nearest structure was marked for visitors.

"You have to check in there first," Amity said, gesturing. "That way, they know who's here, for safety reasons." She looked back at us. "Do you have it from here? I have a class in an hour."

"Yes," I said, stepping in to shake her hand, but she stood on her tiptoes to hug me instead. "Thanks for getting us this far."

"Someone inside will be able to help you find Leaf," she said, hugging Rhodes next. "Have a peaceful reunion."

"Thank you," he said.

I could only hope.

Inside the building, it was only a few degrees cooler, and it took my eyes a few seconds to adjust to the darkness. There were windows, but no light fixtures that I could see.

"Blessings," a cheerful voice said in the dim light. I was just able to make out a woman's face, wavy brown hair tied back in a bandana. She stood behind a large desk with a big spiral notebook in front of her.

The wall across from her was full of items for sale. Natural and colorful bracelets, tie-dyed clothes, and sandals hung from hooks or sat on a shelf. Most of it looked handmade, even the table with random pottery pieces. Handmade or not, they looked professionally done.

"Hi, I'm Mal." I put on a smile, walking to the counter. "And this is my friend Marlon." It sounded weird coming from my lips, but it was how he had been introducing himself outside of work. "We're here to find an old friend, Aaron Rhodes. I think he's going by the name Leaf?"

"You know Leaf?" A smile split her face, filling it with joy and warmth.

"Is he here?" I asked, feeling hopeful. It seemed like Leaf had a good reputation.

"He lives here." She nodded. "I'm sure he's around somewhere."

Rhodes walked over, eyes hooded.

"Do you think you could tell us where to find him?"

"I'll do more than that!" She smiled warmly. "I can take you to him."

A heavy breath released from Rhodes, like he had been holding it in all this time. I put a hand on his arm in support.

"But you'll need to sign in first," she said, sliding the spiral notebook in front of us.

"Of course," I said, scratching my name in and handing the pen to Rhodes.

"Leaf will be so happy to have visitors." She walked around the makeshift counter. "I'm Charity."

As she leaned in to hug me, the scent of patchouli and something I couldn't place drifted out of her hair. It wasn't unpleasant, just earthy and different, and maybe a little bit like celery.

"It's nice to meet you."

"You said your name is Mal?" she tilted her head.

"Yep, it's short for Malone. My last name." I didn't go by my first name. Ever.

"Ah," she said, turning to hug Rhodes. "How long are you planning on staying with us?"

"Oh, just for the day," he replied.

"That's a shame. It's so peaceful here. I'm sure you'll love it." She led us back out the door. "And we can always use another strong pair of hands."

Apparently, if you stayed here, even as a visitor, you earned your keep.

"That's quite a big field." I squinted in the bright sun. She was leading us towards tall ears of corn behind the buildings.

"We grow everything we eat." She beamed at me. "This time of day, Leaf's generally in the gardens. He likes to get his hands in the dirt at least once a day; it really grounds him. And the plants, they just respond to him."

"That's great," I replied, not knowing what else to say.

"But first, it'd be good to sit in a meditation class." She clasped her hands excitedly, heading towards a large pavilion. "Get rid of that city energy riding on you. You're both too tense."

I shot a glance at Rhodes, meeting his gaze. I raised my shoulders in a discreet shrug, and he responded with a roll of his eyes in a *"whatever"* response.

Large, structured pillows were scattered around the wooden floor, and a table at one end had a myriad of candles, incense sticks, plus items from nature, like rocks, sticks, flowers, and leaves. It was like they had collected little bits from their surroundings and set them out to meditate on. It reminded me of bringing in my favorite rocks from the yard when I was little, but on a much bigger scale. My mom never let me put them on our dinner table, though. I usually just stuffed them into my jeans pockets, to be found on laundry day.

Rhodes toed off his boots as he stepped up the stairs and plopped down on a square pillow, crossing his legs and settling in like he had done it a million times before. Maybe he had. I forgot he had been in contact with his dad until he was six or so. He probably knew what was going on.

I followed his lead, unlacing my boots, leaving them next to his, and selecting a poofy pillow next to his. I was out of my comfort zone but had done stranger things on a job. I mean, was it more or less strange to crouch behind a city bush to take pictures of someone's bedroom?

Charity lit another incense and settled down on her own pillow, across from ours. I watched them close their eyes and relax their shoulders, and a low hum came from Charity's direction. That seemed to be all we were doing, so I let my eyelids drop, trying to follow suit and relax.

After what felt like a few minutes, I peeked to see Charity and Rhodes both still in the same position. I closed my eyes again. Eventually, my mind began to wander, less worried about what I was supposed to say and do here. There was nothing else I had to be doing at the moment.

I thought back to Suzy. I wanted to sit down with Sam and Wyatt to talk about our next steps with Dessi. I felt certain we could come up with something together as a group. Or maybe I just needed to talk it out. It felt like we had hit such a hard roadblock, but I knew we could still find an angle. We just had to find the right place for him to trip up. And make sure we got evidence this time.

"That was just wonderful," Charity said, jolting me out of my reverie. "Thank you for joining me."

I opened my eyes, hands going to the ground to push myself up. I had forgotten where I was but felt oddly refreshed. Looking back at Rhodes, I found him standing, more relaxed than he had been a few minutes ago.

At least I thought it had only been a few minutes, but I wasn't exactly sure. The light and shadows under the pavilion looked to have shifted a little.

"It is peaceful out here," I commented, echoing her earlier sentiment. I noticed flowers scattered on the floor for the first time. It was surprising I had missed them when we walked in.

She just smiled. "I can take you to Leaf now."

We bent to put our shoes back on when another group of people entered the pavilion. Only these people had a distinct lack of clothing. My eyes shot to Rhodes', which widened in response. Definitely not something you'd see in Chicago. That wasn't exactly true. It happened, but it typically wasn't a group of people.

"Uh." I reflexively turned away, trying to keep my gaze from dropping south of their faces. What was it with naked people? It was so hard not to look down, I thought, my eyes flicking upward to the building's joists, especially when I could see things moving and swinging around.

"Oh," Charity said, her eyes twinkling. "Some of our residents prefer to go unclothed."

"Ah," I said, like it made sense. I really hoped his dad wasn't of the same persuasion. That would make meeting him a little more uncomfortable, for both Rhodes and me, if I had to guess. "Guess that makes this heat easier."

"*So* much cooler," a voice came from my right.

I dared to look, hoping I would be able to find his face quickly. It was a sweet-faced elderly man, grinning broadly at my discomfort.

"But just wait until the mosquitoes come out at dusk." He shuddered.

My face blanched, which only caused him to bellow in laughter.

We hurriedly followed in Charity's footsteps, eager to move on.

"So, it's meditation hour?" I searched to find something to say.

"No," she smiled, pressing her lips together. "It's their yoga hour."

Rhodes and I looked at each other, unsure if she was serious or not.

Winding our way into the field, we could see it wasn't just planted with corn. Other garden patches spread out in large squares with different plants in each of them, separated by walking paths. Several people were bent, weeding or picking vegetables, and aprons with large pockets covered their clothing. I let out a breath, glad they had clothes under the aprons.

Rhodes' eyes were fixed on the gardeners, taking in one after another.

"There he is," Charity said, pointing towards a bald man whose back faced us. He was hunched over a patch of dirt, hands dug in deep, pulling out what looked like potatoes.

I could see Rhodes take a short step back, sweat beading on his forehead.

"Are you ready?" I asked under my breath.

He just nodded, eyes focused on the man working in the dirt. Stepping forward to take the lead, I hoped it would take the attention off him for the moment and give him a chance to compose himself.

"Mr. Rhodes?" I asked when I reached the man.

He stilled, turning slowly to see me, squinting through the sunlight.

"Well, now. No one's called me that in years." He turned his head to look at me.

"I'm Mal," I said, extending an arm, having forgotten for a moment that he had been gardening.

Dropping the potato he was holding, Aaron stood and took my hand, not even concerned that his hands were covered in rich, black dirt. He had a light smile on his face, looking over at Charity before his eyes found Rhodes. Quietness filled the man. He stopped breathing for a long moment, maybe two, his eyes filling with emotion. Slowly, he dropped my hand, taking a large, shattered breath in.

"Marlon."

"Hi, Dad."

Meanwhile, in a trendy but high-tension office,

"What do you mean she hasn't been home? Where is she?" A fist slammed hard on the desktop, causing things to rattle. Dessi placed both hands flat in front of him, leaning menacingly forward.

"I-uh, I don't know where she is," the man replied. Sweat formed on his brow.

"She's not the type to go on vacation. Didn't you hear her tell a friend or a neighbor where she was going?"

"Um, no. She was on the phone, but I didn't hear her talking about leaving town or anything."

"Does she have a boyfriend?'

"I don't think so."

"When was the last time you heard anything?"

"Not since the night she was here."

"Two nights ago?"

"Yes, sir."

"Well, goddammit, Eddie. I'm paying you to keep tabs on her. Find her! I need to know what she's up to," he said through gritted teeth, his eyes narrowed. "I helped you out last year when you couldn't pay your rent. Don't you forget that."

"Yes, sir," he said, swallowing the lump forming in his throat. He was good at getting in and out of places quietly, but he wasn't good with intel or with people. He needed to get help.

Chapter 14

Meanwhile, in a small but surprisingly technologically advanced brick office,

"She's not answering her phone," Sam said, his eyes looking pinched on the screen of the iPad on Suzy's desk.

"She's probably just busy," Suzy replied, trying to calm his nerves.

"She didn't say anything to you?"

"No." She chewed her bottom lip. It was unusual. Mal typically texted if she was going to be unavailable, but that was mostly for billing clients or to get a timeline established if she was going somewhere dangerous. Suzy always kept the police's number ready to dial if she didn't call back within the allotted time. But Mal hadn't called.

"That was the third call that went to voicemail." His hands waved up into the air. "She never ignores that many calls."

"True. But, Sam, she's in Tennessee. With Rhodes. Surely, they're not in any danger in Tennessee."

"It might not be Chicago, but the South has its own hazards. I'll track her."

His gaze flicked off, following some unseen data on another monitor.

"Where is she?" Suzy watched him helplessly. She punched out a quick text to Mal, just in case. It couldn't hurt.

"Sitting on the side of the road, in south Tennessee. It looks like a remote spot."

"I wonder if they had car trouble or ran out of gas. Maybe they had to walk to get help?"

"Without her phone?"

"Maybe it died."

"It's an Android phone. Ha! Probably. Let me check. No, it has forty-eight percent." Sam stilled, turning to look at her. "Do you think they're, you know, foolin' around?"

"I highly doubt that," she started, then looked off to the side as she considered. "Well, I don't know. There is some mighty strong chemistry between those two. But they've also got some things to work out. Mal's not going to jump into anything rashly."

"You never know." He shrugged. "She can get pretty focused on things."

"Can you tell if her phone's on silent?"

"It's not."

"Well, then that's a no." She rolled her eyes. "No way would she be ignoring that many calls, no matter what's going on in that car."

"That means she left her phone."

"Ugh, that's worse." Suzy put her head in her hands. "This feels like last time. My stomach is in a knot!"

"You're telling me," Sam replied, eyebrow raised. He slowly shook his head, jaw set. "I'm not losing either one of you again."

"Dad?" Charity said, perking up, which was a feat for someone as preternaturally perky as she was.

Rhodes looked around with a frown. People were starting to stare.

"Hey, Charity," I said. "Is there a good place where we can all sit down to talk? It's getting mighty hot here in the sun, and I could use some water."

He shot me a look of thanks and took a step back.

"Sure." She turned. "That's a great idea. I've got some fresh kombucha I can get out."

"Not the pavilion, right?" I asked.

"No." She laughed. "We can go to the circle. It's not being used right now."

"The circle?" I asked.

"A grassy space. It's shaded," Aaron said, picking up his dropped potato and spade. Putting them in his basket, he took his apron off and set it all with the others. He dusted himself off and tugged on the sweaty bandana around his neck, watching the silent Rhodes. "We use it at night, to commune around the bonfire."

"That sounds like a good idea," I said, following Charity.

"You said you're Mal?" Aaron asked, walking with us.

"Yep." I gave him a polite smile. "Nice to meet you."

"That's an interesting name."

"I like her name," Rhodes bit in, bristling. "It's unusual but strong, like her."

"Thanks," I said. It was one of the nicest things anyone had said about me.

Charity led us through the field to an open area behind the buildings. Just as described, there was a large circle with hay bales and cut sections of tree trunks scattered around. Trees surrounded the circle, far enough back from the bonfire, but close enough to the seating area to cast shade regardless of the time of day. There was less shade this close to noon, but some could still be found on the east side of the circle.

Aaron stood near one end of a tree log, hands stuffed in his loose oatmeal-colored pants. His eyes looked large as he watched Rhodes approach.

"I can help Charity get drinks." I touched Rhodes on the shoulder. "Okay?"

"Thanks," he said, dipping his head towards me.

Charity and I split off from the men. I followed her to a building attached to the pavilion. Walking in, it revealed a simple kitchen. It looked like they probably served dinner in the pavilion when it wasn't being used for meditation or yoga. I frowned, thinking of eating where they were practicing naked yoga.

"Thanks for the extra hands." She stretched to get mason jars from a shelf.

"What can I do?"

"Just put some ice in those." She pointed to a large, deep chest freezer.

On one side, I found racks of metal ice-cube trays. I picked it up and pulled the lever to release the ice, shaking them into the glasses.

"Just make sure to refill that before you put it back," she warned, getting a bottle of blush-colored liquid from the commercial-sized refrigerator. "We all help out here."

"Not a problem." I took them to the sink and turned on the tap, tipping them to fill the whole mold. I didn't mind doing my part, especially if it was going to make things easier for Rhodes.

"Mal?" Charity started.

I raised my eyebrows.

"Have you ever considered changing your name?"

"My name?"

"Well, it's just that *mal* means bad." She wrinkled her nose. "That's bad vibes, babe."

"Oh." I huffed. "That's not really my first name."

"Babe." She rolled her eyes. "Charity isn't my first name, either. But it's the one I choose to go by."

Washing the empty bottle in the sink, she set it with the other drying dishes and picked up two glasses, gesturing towards the door. I picked up the remaining two.

"My last name's Malone," I went on. "I was in the police academy. It's not uncommon to call others by surnames in the military or civil services. It just stuck."

She gave me a look.

"I also don't like my first name."

She stayed silent, walking backward through the door, holding it for me before letting it swing shut.

"Bad vibes, huh? I've always kinda liked it."

She shuttered. "Bad juju."

I turned away, so she couldn't see me fight the smile appearing on my face. "I'll take it under consideration."

As we crossed the lawn, I could see Rhodes still standing, his hands in fists at his side. Aaron sat on the tree log, shoulders slumped. Glancing at Charity, I picked up my pace back to the circle.

"You can't be serious," Rhodes shouted.

"Son—"

"Don't call me that," he cut in. "You haven't earned it."

"Marlon," he corrected. "I can't come."

"You *won't* come."

"I live here, don't you see?" He held his hands up, gesturing to the fields and buildings scattered around. "It's not that simple."

"I live in Chicago, but I left to come and see you."

"And I'm grateful," he said with a sad smile. "I've missed you."

"You can leave. You just choose not to."

I could see his jaw tick from where I stood, paused next to Charity, about ten feet away.

"I suppose you're right," Aaron admitted. "But they need me here. And I need them."

Rhodes spun away from his dad, running a hand over his similarly bald head and pacing a few steps. His shoulders bunched under his T-shirt. "Gran needs you. But once again, you don't do anything for me, for this family." His hands went to his chest. "My family. You had to go off and find another."

A buzzing sound interrupted the argument.

I looked around to see a drone moving between the buildings.

"What the hell?" Rhodes asked, finding it in the sky.

The drone spun towards us, dropping down in front of me.

"Mal." I heard a tinny voice that sounded familiar.

"Sam?" I asked, squinting into the drone.

"Is this yours?" Charity asked, shoulders raised, chin tucked. "We don't allow electronics here, especially with any sort of Wi-Fi or wireless signal. It's really bad for your health, messes with your chakras."

A man and a woman came out of a nearby building, heading towards us. From the look on their faces, they didn't seem happy.

"Uh," I said, backing up. "I'll be right back."

I headed off in the direction of the surrounding woods. I wasn't sure if I was surprised or not that the drone followed. Looking back at Rhodes, I figured he could handle the situation for a few more minutes.

"Mal!" I heard the drone say again. This time, I was certain it was Sam's voice.

"Just hang on a minute," I threw over my shoulder, walking between the trees to find a spot out of their view. I didn't want Rhodes dealing with any issues about the drone's proximity. Finally getting to an area I hoped was far enough, I spun to the drone, my arms waving in the air. "What the hell, Sam?"

"Hey, Mal. Everything okay?" I heard his voice go up.

"Uh, yeah. They were until you got here."

"Looked like Rhodes wasn't having a good conversation. Hey, was that his dad?"

"Yes, it's not going very well."

"But at least we found him!"

"You found him, Sam," I said, giving him his due credit. "But what are you doing here? Is there a problem?"

"No, I thought, well, Suzy and I both thought you were in trouble. You weren't answering your phone. And I tracked it to your car, left on the side of the road a ways away."

"We had to leave our phones in the car." I sighed. "It's only been an hour, maybe two."

"Well, I was trying to get ahold of you, and we were worried!"

"And how in the world did you get a drone from Chicago to Tennessee?"

"I didn't." The drone dropped to settle at my feet. "I hacked into a drone with a GoPro I found nearby and redirected it. I need to conserve this one's energy so I can return it before I strip my signal."

"Of course, you did." I sat on my heels so I could hear the tiny speaker better. "What do you need?"

"Well." His voice ticked up in excitement. "We got a ping on a sale."

"A sale?"

"A jewelry sale. An online auction went up with the piece of jewelry you had listed. Freddie Mercury was listed as the seller. What an idiot."

"Can you trace it back to Freddy Lamb?"

"Of course! That means we have him, right?"

"Maybe." I paused to think it through. "He could say Rosemary asked him to sell it. We need proof he's doing it behind her back."

"Oh."

"It's still really good news, Sam." I wasn't trying to burst his bubble. It was still a step in the right direction. "We now have proof he's selling it; we just need him to say it's not him. And I'd like to document the money transfer, too. Right now, it's just for sale. He hasn't actually accepted anything for it yet." I frowned. "But I'd hate for her to lose her jewelry."

"That's not a problem. I'll just buy the piece online, and we'll sell it back to her later. I'll record the sale and the transfer to Freddy's account."

"Thanks, Sam." I smiled at the drone. "You really are a sweet guy."

"Eh, don't mention it," he mumbled. I could practically hear him blush over the phone. I was so glad Suzy had someone like him in her life.

"Oh, and have Suzy call Rosemary to keep her informed. It's her decision if she wants to call it in to the cops in the meantime. I doubt she will, but still."

From the corner of my eye, I could see Rhodes still arguing with his dad, arms crossed over his chest. He turned and stomped away, back towards the trail we had taken to get here.

"I should probably get back." I stood, watching the scene.

"Oh, wait! I had another idea too. Well, Suzy and I were talking. I think it's a good one, but I wanted to run it by you first."

"Sam, I trust you. Whatever you think is right, go ahead," I said, heading out to follow as the drone lifted up.

"Really?"

"Really." I ducked around a branch towards the clearing, giving him a quick wave. "I'll call you later."

"Oh boy."

"Everything okay?" I asked, jogging up to Rhodes. He had made it all the way to the entrance before I caught up with him.

"He refuses to leave," he ground out, eyes focused ahead.

"I'm sorry, Rhodes."

"He says he can't handle the real world again, especially a big city like Chicago." He stomped, trampling over the weeds on the trail back to the road. He shook his head. "He said he'd think about it, but he's not coming back. It's what he always says. I can't believe I even thought…"

"Maybe he will." I winced, unsure what else to say. "It's been a long time."

He looked back at me. "No. God, I'm so embarrassed that's my dad. Sean should have been my dad."

"Sean is, in all the ways that matter." I hadn't known him long, but this wasn't like the Rhodes I knew. He was always in control of everything and having fun doing it. I could tell he was hurting, and there was nothing I could do about it.

"I remember another time at a commune when he pulled this crap. Couldn't leave it to come back to Chicago. It was for a little-league game. Made it to the All-Stars." The words poured from him like a cork had been pulled loose. "Probably didn't seem like a big deal to him. Sean had brought me for a long weekend, and he said the same thing back then. He couldn't handle it, wasn't strong enough to handle life without my mom. Needed to be in places like that, where they meditate when they're angry and not deal with problems. Just do some pot, and all your troubles will disappear."

I hadn't seen any pot, but I wasn't going to argue with him. I just let him rant as I followed the path back. It seemed much shorter than our walk out, I thought, as we saw the road in front of us. We stepped back over the chain and made our way to the Jeep.

"We can try again later, or tomorrow," I said hesitantly. We had to try again.

"No." He got into the Jeep and slammed the door.

When I got in, he had his head in his hands and was silent.

"Do you want some lunch?"

"Not really hungry right now."

"Let's just go back to the motel for a bit. I have some calls to make," I lied. He needed some alone time. "I'll grab some lunch and follow up on work, then check in on you, okay?"

"Sure," he mumbled, then looked over at me. "I'm sorry, Mal."

"Don't worry about it."

Chapter 15

Standing outside his door, I knocked again, hoping he was in a better mood than before. I had given him the day alone to decide what he wanted to do next.

The door slowly creaked open, revealing Rhodes, his eyes downcast.

"Hey," he said, tucking his hands into his back pockets.

"Hey. How're you doing?"

"Fine." He shrugged. "Look, I'm sorry I dragged you all this way for this. I should have known it would be a waste of time."

"Nah. Not a waste of time." I winked, trying to put the earlier events behind us. "I'm getting a paycheck."

He hmphed in reply. "It's his own loss anyway."

"Agreed. Miss Ellie is a mighty fine woman."

"The best."

"I was thinking we could grab a beer and maybe some dinner." I leaned casually against the corner of the doorframe. "I found a little pub a few blocks away that didn't look too scary."

"That sounds good." He nodded. "Let me grab my room key, and I'll be ready to go."

I waited for him to lock up, kicking some stray white rocks off the concrete pad in front of our motel doors. We walked silently down the street and around the corner to find the place just picking up with patrons looking to unwind after work.

We slid into a booth since the seats at the bar were already filling up.

"What can I get ya?" asked the waitress who made her way over.

"Do you have Guinness?" Rhodes asked, looking over the menu.

"Yep." She nodded.

"Make that two, please," I added, watching her take her time, maneuvering around the growing crowd back to the bar. "So, did you decide what you want to do? If you want, we can go back in the morning, or we can head home early tomorrow and get in by dinnertime."

He glanced down at his hands, clasped in front of him. "Look, Mal. I really appreciate all your help with this, but I don't think we should waste our time any further. I'd rather just get back home. If we can make it home tomorrow, I can make it to my next shift day, Friday."

I nodded. "That works for me."

"I mean, I'd like to think I could talk him into coming, but he's just not the kinda guy to come through for you." He screwed up his face. "I just don't understand how any son of my Gran's could end up like that. She was a force of nature back when I was a kid."

"I can see that. She'd have to be to put up with you guys." I smiled.

The waitress came by with our drinks and took our order. I took a long pull on the bottled beer, which was cool, but nice in this heat. I leaned back in the booth to relax. It had been a long day for me as well.

"It's just as well, you know? Probably better for Gran to remember him as her little boy, and not some doped-up weirdo, coming in and calling himself something crazy like Leaf." He shook his head, his lips in a thin line.

The guy wasn't like most people, but he hadn't seemed doped up to me. I thought he was nice, if a little sad around Rhodes, but I just let him continue to vent. At least he didn't seem as sad as he was earlier. Maybe that was an improvement? I wasn't really sure.

A half hour later, we had finished our burgers and were onto our second beer. Well, it was my second, his third, and his mood hadn't improved. I was trying to be understanding, but patience had never been my strong suit.

"We got a break in the jewelry case." I threw out, trying to change the subject. "That's why Sam sent the drone to find us."

"That's good." He nodded, taking another drink. "He's pretty good at all those techy things. I bet that really helps out in your line of work."

"It can."

"He has a business too, right? Making apps and stuff?"

"Yeah, and security systems now too."

"Wow, how does he have time to help you?"

"I think he just enjoys it." I shrugged. "He's got a great team at work. He can pretty much do what he wants."

"Must be nice." He swirled the beer in his bottle. "Not everyone gets to do that."

"He earned it."

"Not everyone earns being able to do what they want. Some people just rely on others to take care of them."

"It'll be good to get home and get back to my work. I need a new plan on the Dessi case." It probably wasn't the time to bring it up, but I needed to change the subject, and I was tired of just listening quietly. "My last plan just fell apart."

"You're still on that?" he said, his forehead creasing.

"You knew that."

"I knew you were trying to gather evidence. I didn't know you were pursuing him."

"It's kinda the same thing. I'm not half-assing this thing."

He threw back the rest of his beer.

"That's just great. You're going to end up getting kidnapped *again* or worse. Mal, you're no match for this guy!" He put his hands flat on the table between us, leaning in. "He's got hired killers working for him. You think you, all by yourself, can take him in? When the Chicago police department can't?"

"You're right. The CPD can't bring him in." I sat up straight. I couldn't believe I was having this conversation again. He had zero faith in me. "They can't do what I can. Their hands are tied by red tape."

"You're not above the law."

"No, I'm not. But I have a little more leeway than they do. I know what I'm doing."

"The hell, you do." He huffed, looking around the room for the waitress. "You need to back off where it's safe."

"Cause that's what *you* do." I stood. I was done being nice. He'd had all the leeway he was going to get. "You stay on the sidelines where it's safe, right? You don't get right into the fire to save others. Hell, you send your men into that fire. But that's safe, right?"

"I would never send my men in if I thought they couldn't handle it." He stood up next to the booth, meeting me. "Those guys are my family. I know what they're capable of and what they're not."

"But it's not always safe."

"No, they know what they signed up for. It's a damn sight safer than chasing a known mobster."

"I know what I'm doing too." I leaned in, my face drawn.

"Do you? Because from where I'm standing, you're just one woman, putting herself into God knows what danger, practically asking for trouble." He slammed his hand down on the table, officially drawing the rest of the room's attention. "Christ, Mal, you've got to come to your senses. I know you're trying here, but you're going to end up in a body bag!"

"You've got that wrong, and I'll tell you why," I spit out, throwing some money on the table. "I'm not just one woman. I have a family too. Remember those people who showed up at the fire station, looking for me? They're my family, and they have my back. Together, we're going to take Fabian Dessi down."

Ignoring the stares, I spun on my heel and walked out, slamming through the door on my way. He could make his own way back to the damn motel. He wasn't in any condition where he couldn't retrace his steps. And I wasn't going to sit here and continue being told I wasn't good enough.

Even if he didn't believe in me, I did. I didn't have the choice not to.

Meanwhile, at a stately manor surrounded by only slightly over-embellished gardens,

"Just be yourself," Suzy's voice came through Wyatt's speakers.

"I'm good at that." His mouth spread wide, even though she couldn't see him.

"I know. I just don't want you to get flustered when Freddy shows up, and I think he will. We want him to."

"I know, Suze. I deal with difficult people all the time. Remember, I deal with Sam." He chuckled.

"Ha, ha."

"I've got this."

"Okay. Thanks, Wyatt."

"Not a problem," he said, signing off.

He locked his Range Rover out of habit, not that he needed to in this community, this far from the road. Staring up at the large building, he whistled appreciatively.

"Who are you?" came a voice behind him.

He turned to see a young brunette, hair pulled up in a messy bun, oversized overalls hanging on a curvy frame. Her garden-gloved hands were on her hips, and her feet were spread wide.

"I'm Wyatt Parker, with Sentinel Security," he said, stretching his hand out in greeting.

She just looked at it, eyes narrowed. "Do you have an appointment?"

"Ms. Lamb knows I'm coming. Yes." He tried to still his grin.

"Then why are you just standing there, looking at the place?"

"I was sizing it up for security equipment."

"Oh." Her mouth pursed. "Well, Rosemary should be with you while you look at her property."

"Agreed." He turned to knock on the door. Damn, she was cute.

A man wearing a dress shirt and slacks opened the door. Probably the housekeeper, Nathan.

"Hello?"

"Hi, I'm Wyatt Parker, with Sentinel Security," he repeated, his hand out.

"She's expecting you," he answered, shaking his hand.

"Thank you." Wyatt slid a glance back to the young woman, eyebrow raised to note the difference in greeting. She shook her head, rolling her eyes.

"Please come in," the housekeeper said, stepping back. "She's in the parlor. I'll take you back."

He followed him through the entryway to a room to the left. Unfortunately, the gardener didn't come with them.

"Ms. Lamb," he said, seeing the elderly woman sitting in a curved high-backed chair.

"Oh, you can call me Rosemary." She rose to greet him.

"Wyatt Parker," he smiled, shaking her hand. "Please call me Wyatt."

He sat gingerly on the brocade couch, worried he'd get it dirty, and reviewed the bid he had prepared for the security coverage of her estate and the options she'd prefer.

"Did you bring references?"

"Of course." Selecting a sheet of paper from the folder he carried, he handed it over. He barely knew the woman but was proud of her for asking, even with Mal's recommendation. Too many people just took security companies for granted. It was obvious this lady wasn't senile. "Feel free to call any of the names on this list. I'll give you some time to follow up on them."

"No need," she shook her head. "I know some of the names here. If they're willing to provide their names and numbers for references, I'm comfortable having you secure my house."

"Great, then we can both sign the contract. It'll let you know how soon we can get everything installed."

"What's going on here!" an angry voice boomed from the doorway.

Wyatt stood out reflexively to meet the outraged man in a white linen suit. Presumably, this was Freddy. He wondered how the stately woman seated in the chair could have raised a dandy like him.

"I'm installing security coverage," she said, signing the paperwork. "Thank you, Wyatt."

"Like hell, you are!" He raced forward and snatched the papers from his mom.

Wyatt stepped forward, head down, barely able to contain the growl threatening to emerge from his throat. "You will be polite to your mother."

Freddy blinked, dropping the papers to the ground. Wyatt slowly bent to pick them up, his eyes never leaving Freddy's. He handed them back to Rosemary.

"Mother!" he said, turning. "Do you even know who this man is?"

"Of course, I do. He's accredited and has great references. I'm not an idiot."

Looking between them, he rocked back on his feet, his hands waving about. "But why do you think you need a security system? We have locks on the doors. This is a very safe neighborhood."

"We do, but it's been a long time coming. Most of our neighbors have security."

"And I cover quite a few of them." Wyatt leaned in.

"I'm just not sure it's a smart use of your money," he said, ignoring Wyatt. "Maybe we should talk about what's got you so worked up that you've gone off to hire someone to turn our house into Fort Knox! What are you so afraid of?"

"First of all, it's my house," Rosemary said gently. "And my money. I think it'll make me feel safer. I just heard about a shooting in the news, not long ago."

"That wasn't in this neighborhood."

"Even so."

He shot a look at Wyatt. "I need access to everything in case she forgets, as she often does."

"We can reset passwords any time we need to."

"And I need access to the codes," he pressed.

"Of course, as long as Rosemary agrees to it, I'll have you listed on the account as a backup."

"And Nathan, my housekeeper," she added.

Wyatt nodded. "I'm sure it will make you feel better, knowing your mother is safe."

Freddy's upper lip scrunched up, his hands tightening into fists. "When is it going to be installed?"

"Probably next week," Wyatt said, biting back a smirk.

"Fine." He stormed out of the room. "I'll show you out."

Wyatt took his time getting up and putting his papers back together.

"Just because the equipment isn't installed doesn't mean we're not going to be at work. I'm going to keep an eye on your house, starting today," he said, his voice low.

"That would be very kind of you."

"Just part of the service, ma'am." He winked, then glancing back to the doorway, he added, "Are you okay here?"

"Oh, yes." She batted him away. "He's a cad, but he's not going to hurt me."

"You sure?"

"Yes, but thank you, sweet boy." She smiled up at him, patting him on the arm.

"Are you coming?" Freddy hollered impatiently from the door.

He chuckled, sauntering out. It was the first time anyone had called him a sweet boy.

A timid knock sounded at my door.

I paused flipping through TV stations. It had taken me quite a while to cool down after the scene at the bar. Not ready to go back to the motel for the night, I had walked for blocks, but it wasn't the same as walking the streets of the city. Here, it was quiet and relaxed, grasshoppers buzzing and fireflies lighting the scene. It wasn't nearly as easy to let my mind roam, getting lost in the honking cars, shouting, and laughter.

The worst part was I couldn't seem to find a coffee shop. So, to the motel, it was, with its crappy coffee to sustain me. Still, it was better than nothing.

I took a deep breath before getting up to answer the door. There was no question as to who it was. I could ignore it, but I had to talk to him at some point. I was his ride back home tomorrow, after all.

"Yes?" I opened the door, looking expectantly at him.

Rhodes was leaning against the doorframe. Or rather, it was holding him up.

"Sorry," he slurred out. "I know I keep saying that, but I really mean it this time. I've really messed it all up."

I pursed my lips. "You were an ass."

"Yes. Ass." He pointed to himself with a thumb. "Major ass. Wait, captain. Captain Ass." He chuckled at himself, then whispered out of the side of his mouth, "I'm a captain."

I sighed, stepping out to the porch and pulling the door shut behind me. I wasn't going to let him in and have the conversation turn where it had before. I was done arguing with him.

"We can't keep doing this, Rhodes." I tucked my hands under my arms. "We have very different opinions on what I should be doing. And I respect myself too much to let you question that."

"You're right." His eyes dropped as he swayed. "I've been self-subsorbed, self-subsorbed, dang it. Self-*ab*sorbed. I don't like the thought of you getting hurt. Sssss-scares me."

I liked to think it was because he was being a little overprotective and that it wasn't that he thought I wasn't cut out for being a PI, but I really wasn't sure. And I had given him more than a few chances. More than I had given most people.

"It's what I do."

"I know. It's what I do too," he said quietly. "It's not a safe job."

"No, but it's who you are."

He nodded, but it made him stumble. I reached out to steady him, holding him upright. He looked down at me, eyes wistful, listing back and forth.

"We can talk about this tomorrow," I said, leaning back to look at him. He was only a little taller than me, but a lot heavier up top. I wasn't sure I could catch him if he went all the way down. "Let's get you inside."

"You're so beautiful," he said, inches away from me. His eyes softened, and he reached up a hand to touch my jaw. "I'm so sorry I let this stuff with my dad get in my head. These past two days, we could have been having a fun road trip."

I had thought the same thing. That maybe the time away would be good for us, to figure out where we were going, but it didn't seem like it was meant to be. Too many things kept getting in our way.

He leaned in, and I could smell his woodsy scent, like pine and leather. My hand, still on his muscled shoulder, gripped harder. He stopped an inch away, his eyes flashing up to mine, but I didn't move. I probably should have, but I didn't.

His lips met mine, warm and soft. But it wasn't like our first kiss, tentative and open. This kiss was unbridled with raging heat and pent-up frustration. He stumbled forward, pressing me against the door. Luckily, it was enough for me to come to my senses.

"Rhodes, we can't." I pushed his chest away. He was drunk, and we still had loads of things to work through.

"Why not?" He took two steps back, his chest heaving to catch his breath. He put out a hand to steady himself on the motel siding.

"You're drunk."

"I just wanted to feel something," he slurred under his breath.

Jutting my chin out, I widened my stance. I could forgive him for his distance and moodiness while dealing with his dad. Family could make you crazy like that, but to try to use me as a distraction? No.

Turning, I twisted my doorknob hard, slamming the door behind me.

Chapter 16

Opening my motel room door the next morning, I was surprised to see Rhodes sitting on the curb in front of my Jeep, elbows on his knees, duffel bag between his feet. He immediately lifted his head.

Jumping to his feet, he took a couple of hesitant steps toward me, eyes cast down. "I'm so very sorry, Mal."

I raised a hand, my mouth drawn.

He shuffled his feet.

"How long have you been sitting out here?"

"About two hours." His shoulders drooped. "I didn't want you to leave without me."

I raised an eyebrow. He really thought I'd just leave him? I might have been pissed, but I wasn't an ass. Like *he* had been.

"Not that I don't deserve that, but I hope you don't," he continued, lifting his gaze to meet mine and setting his jaw. "I didn't mean it the way it came out. I wasn't trying to use you."

I looked away, still hurt by his words the night before.

"I can't say it was a total lie." He grimaced, his face sour. "I wasn't thinking about anybody but myself, but I promise you, I don't think about you that way. I hold you in very high regard, or else I wouldn't have come to you in the first place. I just never should have let it get that far last night."

My heart twisted. I knew this wasn't like him. I had never seen him like he had been over the last few days, but I didn't like the way I was feeling around him lately, either. It wasn't healthy for either of us to continue down this road.

"I wasn't going to leave without you," I said, unlocking the Jeep.

"Thanks, Mal."

I just nodded and threw my backpack in the back seat. "I'm going to go check out."

"I'll come with you." He quickly got his bag and stowed it as well, rushing to keep up with me. "I can take care of the bill."

"You would have anyway."

"Yes, but this will save you the extra step of billing me for it."

I shrugged and headed to the office.

The ride home was long and uneventful, mostly because we barely spoke. He had tried to talk more in the beginning, but I just didn't see the point. He wasn't going to be the person I thought he was. It was just easier this way. So, after a few gentle attempts, he just stopped.

Rhodes had sat in the passenger seat, staring out the window, and I drove, radio off, getting lost in the landscape. We had stopped for food on the way back, but even then, we were both adrift in the sea of our own funk.

Sitting over an espresso in my favorite coffee spot, I let the waves of disappointment splash over me.

"That bad, huh?" Mo finally asked, hip leaning against the counter separating us. He had been giving me the side-eye since I plunked down in my seat.

I shrugged. I was getting good at it. Maybe I'd turn it into part of my exercise routine. Or maybe not. I got enough of it in my daily life.

"Another one, please." I lifted my tiny cup.

"You know this isn't a bar, right?" he said drolly, taking my cup to refill it.

I shrugged again; I was really meeting my new quota for the day.

"But you're a barista, right? Doesn't that mean this is a bar?"

"Your logic is flawed."

"I think you just don't have a good reason why a barista's counter isn't called a bar. It's a coffee bar." Hey, that sounded pretty good. But that could have been the caffeine talking.

"True."

"And you always listen to people's problems."

"True."

"And people tip you."

He raised an eyebrow.

"I tip you!" I said, sitting up straight.

It was his turn to shrug. Maybe I needed to be tipping him better.

"I don't really feel like arguing with you."

I smiled at him. It was kind of like winning.

"Except you're not really talking about your problems."

"I'm the strong, silent type."

"Really?"

"Hey!" I pouted. "I just dropped Rhodes off."

"Trip didn't go well?"

I shrugged, but he pursed his lips. I guess the shrugging wasn't going to cut it. And I really wanted that espresso he was pulling. "He's not himself."

"The thing with his dad? Sounds rough."

It wasn't my fault Rhodes had met me here. I hadn't shared it with Mo, but he had heard about the job right from the source.

"Yeah. I get that, but then he got drunk and was a complete ass."

Mo's nostrils flared. "What'd he do?" His voice held no emotion.

I waved him off. "Nothing happened. *I* wasn't drunk. And I had enough sense for the both of us."

"And he didn't press things?"

I shook my head.

"So, his dad's not coming?"

"I honestly don't know," I said, eyeing the espresso. "I did what I could."

Satisfied that I was okay, Maurice slid it over. I descended on it like a starving man at a buffet.

"Wait, slow down," I said, trying to understand what the Sam-bot was saying. "Wyatt's in on the case now?"

"I know, brilliant, right?" Sam's voice pitched higher. "Sentinel is there to make Rosemary feel safer, and it's given her a little confidence already. She stood up in front of Freddy! But the big advantage is to make it easier to see if Freddy or anyone else is getting on the property. We can easily track everything."

It was a solid idea. I guess I had to quit thinking so small. I was used to tailing people and getting background on them, but adding technology to my business was really proving to be an important move.

"Good job, Sam."

"Really?" His face filled more of the screen than normal. "You really mean that?"

"I really do," I reassured him. "But let's back up. What did Rosemary say about the jewelry sale?"

"Suzy told her about that. She was relieved we're buying it but said the same thing you did. He could just set her up and say she was forgetting she'd asked him to sell it. But still, the sale will be documented, and I can prove the money went to him."

"It's still good evidence."

"I'm hoping this will push Freddy to action."

"He can't argue about her safety, either."

"Exactly! And we can wrap the case!"

"It's a good move, Sam."

"Suzy and I came up with the details together, though," he said, biting his lip. "I didn't do it alone."

"Sam." I leaned over the corner of my desk towards the Sam-bot on the floor. "None of us do it alone."

I had tried for a very long time, had scrimped and saved and been stubborn to say that I did it all by myself. My success was due to no one but me. And I had barely been making it. I had learned the hard way that things worked out better this way. I was much happier, too.

"So, what's next?" he asked.

"I'm back to following Dessi around, forming a plan," I said blandly. I had already filled him in on my blown cover at Red. "We should sit down, the four of us."

"You, me, Suze, and Wyatt?"

"Yep. Pull the big guns out. Shut it down once and for all."

"Gotcha." He squinted his eyes. "I'll get my Z-6 rotary blaster cannon. Or, I know! The Star Forge! Dessi won't know what hit 'em."

"Star Wars reference again?"

He grinned at me, one-sided, like a little kid. "Maybe."

I rolled my eyes.

"What I really need is to get into that office." I tapped my pencil on the desk.

"Well, it's pretty guarded." Sam frowned. "But if you can, I can get you a bug with a long battery life."

"Won't that be pretty obvious? This is the mob, we're talking about."

"You won't get away with sticking a bug in a power source, but one with long battery life, that sits on standby when there's no sound to record? It might work."

Letting that sink in, I tried to think of a way to get back there. My cover was blown, but they didn't know I knew that. I could safely get away with milking that for a while. Mostly safely anyway.

"I might have an idea," I continued. "Let's meet up tomorrow night at your house. Can you see if Wyatt's free?"

"Sure thing! Are you bringing pizza again?"

"I can do that," I promised, turning back to my computer.

"Oh, before I go," Sam said, holding a finger up. "I have that information you wanted. That other thing."

"Really?" I said, surprised at the quick timing. "Thanks, Sam."

"It's what I do," he said, the Sam-bot rolling back to the lobby.

A few minutes later, a rubber band landed on my desk. I looked up to see Suzy's head popping into my doorway.

"So, how'd it really go?"

I let out a long sigh. I wasn't going to be able to get away with giving her the CliffsNotes like I had with Mo. Still, it was probably good for me to get it off my chest.

While going over the details of the past few days, it hit me that it wasn't the drunk part that had gotten to me; it was the realization that we weren't going to be able to make it work.

When had I gotten attached to the idea of pursuing something with Rhodes? Surprisingly enough, I had gotten invested in the relationship. And that made me feel a little sad since it had never even gotten past the early dating stage.

"Things will work out," Suzy said.

"I don't think they will." I shook my head. "But that's okay."

She nodded sadly, moving away from my door. "I'm going to take a short break, okay? Check on Marty."

"Sounds good. Let me know if you need anything."

Ten minutes later, I was still adding notes to my files when a delightful smell drifted in. I lifted my nose, following the scent.

"Maybe this will help," Suzy said, waltzing in with a mocha latte with my name on it. Literally. It was good to have friends.

On my way home that evening, stuffed pork chops from Mariano's deli in the car seat next to me, I spied a yellow convertible peeling out of a convenience-store lot.

The light in front of me clicked red, and I flicked a glance around to see cars packed at the intersection. I couldn't take the chance and ignore the light. My hand slammed the steering wheel. If only I could have caught the plates.

Unable to follow, I pulled into the lot, seeing the store owner, an Indian lady, struggling with a broom. Blood dripped from her hands as she swept broken glass from the tiled floor.

I made a quick call to the cops on my way to the door. Maybe they had some cars in the area.

"Are you okay?" I said, rushing up to her.

She drew back for a moment. She probably thought I was the girls, coming back for round two.

"Yes, I'll be fine."

I took the broom from her hands. "Let me do that. How bad are you cut?"

"Not bad." She lifted a shaking hand. "Just cut it on the glass."

"You sit down. I'll pick this up." I nodded to the floor. "Do you have a trash can?"

"Behind the counter." She pointed, walking around to sit in the chair.

I pulled napkins from the dispenser next to a small coffee-and-deli section and gently blotted at the fresh blood on her hand, keeping an eye out for shards of glass still in the cut. It seemed like only three small cuts. Luckily, none of them looked very deep. I didn't think she needed stitches.

"Have they been here before?" I asked, carrying her trash can back out to the floor. Picking up the broken liquor bottles, I threw them in, trying not to slip on the wet floor.

"Yes," she spat out. "It is the second time."

"When was the first?"

"Three or four weeks past."

"Did you call the cops?"

"Yes, but they had already gone."

"You have surveillance."

"But I have no idea who they are. The police could do nothing."

Just then, we both heard the sirens announcing the boys in blue.

"Do you need to call someone?" I asked. "A husband or a friend, maybe?"

"I texted him as soon as they left." She took a shuddering breath, slouching deeper into her chair. "He should be here soon."

"What happened here?" an officer said, making his way into the store, his eyes taking in the scene.

Letting the clerk rest a moment, I spoke up, "Three teenage girls, ages sixteen to eighteen, who've also been causing problems in a nearby burg, came in here to harass her and cause destruction. I believe there's a record of this being the second time they've hit this particular store."

He nodded, saying something to his partner, who was keeping an eye on the parking lot. The partner split off to make a round of the rest of the store, ensuring there was no one left on the premises.

"Did they make this mess?" he asked, nodding towards the tea spill.

"Yes," the clerk said.

"I just picked up the broken glass so no one cut themselves," I said. "She's got surveillance."

"Saanvi!"

We all turned to see an Indian man race into the store, concern etched on his face. The last vestiges Saanvi had held of her self-control crumbled at the sight of him, and tears streamed down her face.

Embracing her, he spoke softly into her hair.

"Do you need me here?" I asked the police officer.

He shook his head. "You'll need to write down your name and number, though, in case we have any questions."

Instead, I pulled one of my cards from the wallet in my back pocket and handed it over.

He scanned the card and looked back at me. "You were in the academy with Detective Rodriguez, right?"

"And Jen Swanson," I said, not wanting my name to be attached to that cheating slimeball, regardless of what she had said about him.

Nodding, he slid my card into his pocket. "We'll be in touch."

Chapter 17

No sooner had I backed out of the lot, my phone rang. It was Sam.

"This had better be good news," I said, hitting the hands-free button on the steering wheel.

"You need to get home now," Sam said urgently.

"Why? What happened?"

"There's someone in your place. An intruder."

"What?" I said, whipping back into traffic and following closely behind the car in front me, wishing it would go faster, but it was practically bumper-to-bumper at this time of the evening. My fist pounded on the steering wheel.

"The cops should be there any minute."

"What are you talking about?" I said, confused. "How do you know there's an intruder?"

"Well," he paused.

"Fill me in, Sam!"

"You had a bug in your apartment. I found it during a routine scan via Xavier, my drone."

My mind raced back to my place. I checked it for signs of forced entry on a regular basis. When would someone have made it in the house without me knowing it?

"When I killed the signal, I had Xavier drop a thermal reader on your roof," he continued. "Since I know when you're home, I could check if anyone came in to replace it or wait to ambush you."

"You did?" I blinked, trying to make sense of it while I banked a left-hand turn off the traffic-infested road. "I had no idea. Why didn't you tell me?"

"I didn't want to scare you," he said quietly.

Hooking a right, I was finally back into my neighborhood, just a few blocks from my place. Police cars lined the street in front of my apartment building. Pulling over to an empty spot across the street, I parked and tucked my phone into my back pocket.

The door of my building opened, and a couple of cops brought out a man in a hoodie, hood pulled low over his eyes. Something looked familiar about the guy. Grabbing my expandable baton, I took off at a dead run across the street to get there before he was loaded into the waiting cruiser, hoping to get a glimpse of him.

"Hey!" I shouted. "That's my place."

The cops hesitated, looking between themselves and me.

One man broke from the group to walk towards me. Detective Dillhole Rodrigez.

"Mal," he said, heading my way.

Could this day get any worse? All I wanted to do was go home and eat my dinner.

"Who's the guy?" I asked, still straining to see. I could only catch a partial view of his face, but I still couldn't place him.

"Driver's license says Eddie Leeman. Do you know him?"

I shook my head. "Who called this in?"

"I thought one of your guys did." He frowned. *Sam, of course.*

"Just checking that no one else was involved."

"What's going on, Mal?" He moved closer. "Are you in trouble? Abduction and now a burglary? Seems a little much for a coincidence."

I bristled. "Dessi's guys came after me because of Suzy's case. It's not like I went looking for that."

"And this guy?" He jabbed a thumb towards the apprehended culprit, tucking the other into his waistband. The five-o'clock shadow on his face was more pronounced than usual, highlighting his Mexican heritage. "Is this a result of digging into someone's background? Taking photos someone doesn't want taken?"

"My work puts me in interesting arenas." My eyes narrowed. "But that doesn't mean I'm asking for trouble, if that's what you're implying. I don't cause people to break the law."

"I wasn't saying that. I just worry that you're putting yourself in unsafe situations."

I had definitely heard enough of that sentiment lately. "It's so sweet of you to worry about me. Do you check in on all the private investigators in town? Even the male ones? I'm sure everyone appreciates your concern."

"Mal, come on." He spread his hands. "We used to be friends."

"'Used to' is the operative word. You probably think I put myself in the situation to get cheated on." I shouldered past him to get to the team loading the perp into the squad car. I only barely noticed the embarrassed look that crossed his face. Maybe it was hurt. I couldn't tell and didn't care at the moment.

Leaning in, I squinted through the back window of the cruiser. A young man, twenty-something, focused on an unseen point in front of him, patently ignoring me. There it was, the ping in the back of my memory. I could almost remember where I had seen him, but it fled before I could grab the tail end of it.

"This apartment yours?" An officer I didn't know approached me, pointing to the top-right unit.

"Yes, I'm Molly Malone," I said, grimacing at the use of my formal name.

George, a cop who worked for Rodriguez, joined us. "We found evidence of forced entry but had to really look for it. The guy's skilled. Any idea why he would be in your apartment?"

"I'm a private investigator," I said to the other officer, pulling out my card and handing it over for the second time tonight. "It's always possible it's related to a case, but I don't have any idea why he broke in."

"Okay, we'll just need to take your statement," he said, looking over my card.

My stomach growled for the stuffed pork chops in my passenger seat. It was going to be a long night.

An hour or so later, they finally left, taking their police cars and whirling lights with them.

I dragged myself up the stairs, pork chops in hand. They still had a slight coolness to them. Hopefully, they were still okay to cook.

The door across the hall opened, and Noelle peeked out. She took one look at me standing there and promptly slammed her door. I guessed having cops crawling all over your apartment building hadn't filled her with a sense of well-being.

Rolling my eyes, I let myself into my apartment, locking it behind me as usual. I tossed my keys on my kitchen bar, next to the little succulent, and froze, pieces clicking into place.

The ivy. When I was coming back upstairs from tossing the dead ivy in the dumpster, I passed Eddie Leeman in the stairway. I had run into Noelle that day too. Somehow, seeing the two in succession, plus the new little plant, had unearthed the memory.

I fingered Rodriguez's card where I had laid it on top of the pork chops in the grocery bag. It had seemed appropriate, swine on swine. My snort was replaced by a scowl. I'd have to call the swine now.

I took just enough time to slide the stuffed swine into my oven, not waiting for it to preheat, then pressed a couple of buttons on my phone.

"Is everything okay?" Sam's voice came over the line. The non-stuffed swine would have to wait.

"You called the cops before you called me." I stated the obvious.

"Uh."

"Why?"

"Mal, you'd have charged over there," he said in a rush.

"It's my place. *Of course*, I'd have charged over here."

"With no backup."

"Well." It was my turn to pause. He was right. I probably wouldn't have thought to call for backup. Memories of being grabbed in the parking lot at Mariano's flooded my mind, and I gripped the counter. Maybe I was being a little hell-bent on racing into things, trying to prove I could handle myself. My voice lowered. "Thanks, Sam."

"What are friends for?" he said softly.

Shaking off the warm bubbly feeling invading my chest, I said, "I've got a name for you. Eddie Leeman."

"The intruder?"

"Yep. I saw him coming down from my apartment steps about a week ago."

"That lines up with when the scan picked up the bug. Do the cops know?"

"About the bug?"

"That and that you've seen him before. Otherwise, it could look like a random B&E."

I smiled. Sam was getting pretty good at this. "No, I just remembered. I wanted to call you first."

"Who's the detective?"

"Rodriguez."

"That's what I figured." He laughed into the phone.

"Hey, Miss Ellie." I smiled at the older woman, who was sitting at her table, eating breakfast. Foggy eyes landed on me walking through the door, struggling to place me. "I'm Mal."

Recognition finally clicked into place. "Marlon's friend."

"That's right," I said, then raised my head towards Sean, who sat a glass of orange juice in front of her. "Hey."

"Hi," he said, walking up to me. "Everything okay?"

"Yeah, I just wanted to stop by and fill you in on Tennessee. I wasn't sure what Rhodes, er, Marlon updated you on."

It was early Saturday morning, and after last night, all I really wanted to do was grab an overly caffeinated latte. But I wanted to wrap up this case first. It just seemed better to do it in person, and I felt like I owed Sean an update as well, even though Rhodes had hired me.

"He called Thursday night when he got home but didn't talk long. Sounded like it didn't go very well, though."

"I'm really sorry we couldn't talk him into coming back with us." I wasn't sure what to say to him. I didn't want to give him any false hopes.

Sean was silent for a moment. "It's not that surprising. I appreciate you trying, though. It means a lot."

"I didn't do much."

"You tried. That's more than some people." He put a hand on my shoulder. "I'm glad Marlon's got you for a friend. I'm sure it wasn't easy for him to see his dad again after all this time."

I cringed inside, wondering if I should have been a little more understanding. Or more prepared for his actions. Maybe I could have done something different.

"Anyway, I just wanted to check in on Miss Ellie." I broke the uncomfortable closeness of the conversation, wandering over to his mother. "How are they treating you, Miss Ellie?"

Two blue-gray eyes met mine over her glass of juice. "Oh, everyone is just wonderful."

"That's great to hear." I smiled. "It looks like they've got you set up pretty good here."

"Oh, yes! My boys brought some of my things. I really like it. It's not as big as my house, but big houses are so much work to clean."

"You don't have to clean this place," Sean piped up.

"I don't?" She looked surprised.

"Nope." He shook his head. "Remember? They're going to come in and clean the place for you."

She nodded, watching him. "And they cook for me too."

"That's right. Someone will come to get you for meals if Marlon or I aren't here to take you."

"They make a mean meatloaf," she said, turning to me, eyes sparkling. "It's not as good as mine, mind you, but it's solid. Right amount of seasoning."

"She's right." Sean looked at me. "Hers is the best."

"Yours is pretty good too," she said to him. "But it's a bit heavy."

"I put bacon in it."

"Bacon." Her mouth turned down. "It doesn't go into a proper meatloaf."

"The guys like it." His shoulders tipped up. "I make it at the fire station."

"I bet they do." I laughed.

It looked like Miss Ellie was going to be okay here, with or without Aaron, but I still hoped he'd eventually visit, if only for his own sake. And for Rhodes'.

"Well, I should be going," I said.

After making my goodbyes, I headed out, wishing I could have done more for them. But I had done all I could.

You win some, you lose some.

Stepping out into the hot sun, I raised a hand to shade my eyes. A male figure was walking towards me. I recognized his wide V-shaped frame. Rhodes. My feet stalled. *And here I thought today was going to go better.*

"Hey," the shaded figure said, pausing.

"Hi." I moved over on the sidewalk in front of the building, to get a better look at him. "I stopped by to say a quick hi to Miss Ellie. She seems to be doing well."

"I think she's going to be happy here," he agreed, eyes still casting down every few words.

"I also wanted to talk to Sean. I felt bad we weren't able to bring Aaron back. He doesn't seem too upset about it."

"No." His mouth pressed into a thin line.

He looked up at me. Everything that lay unsaid floated between us in a thick fog.

I dipped my head, moving a foot out of the metaphorical smog, indicating my departure. I had said everything I had to say.

"I know it doesn't mean much to say it again, but I'm so sorry, Mal," he let out with a breath. His hand ran over his head. "What I did, well, I know it's practically unforgivable, to treat you like that, like nothing more than a mental diversion…"

The word hung between us in the gloom, agitating the heavy air. Constricting heat built inside me, bubbling up my throat at the reminder.

"I don't think of you like that," he went on.

"Then, how do you think of me?" I asked, nostrils flaring. I raised my chin. "I was a friend to you. I let you brood and muddle your way through everything that was going on."

"You were." He took the punishment I was meting out, relaxing slightly now that I was biting into him.

"I took the case with your dad. I know it was a paying case, but I also knew it would complicate things for us. But I have to know one thing." I paused. "Did you bring me this, ask for my help, just to have someone to go through it with? Some kind of amusement to keep you company?"

"What?" He looked up at me, startled. "I came to you because I wanted your help. I needed your help."

"But you constantly question why I'm involved with anything difficult."

"Not difficult," he stopped me, his face dead serious. "Dangerous. I just think the cops are better equipped—"

"I went through the same training *they* did—"

"You quit!" he said, his voice rising. "You didn't *finish* the training."

And there it was, a conversation so closely resembling the ones I'd had with my dad and Alex Rodriguez.

"I've done plenty of additional training since then," I ground out, not that he deserved the explanation. I could feel my face flush with anger. "I've trained with civilian teams and a couple of hand-to-hand combat groups. You have no idea how equipped I am."

"That's not it," he said, his hands spread wide, palms up in front of him. "I've seen what can happen when people get in over their heads. I've seen lots of women think they can handle a situation, and it goes bad. Really bad. I don't even want to talk about how bad. And fast."

"Your job is dangerous. There are women firefighters."

"There are. And women cops."

"Then it's just my job? You obviously don't hold what I do in any high regard. You hardly think I'm capable of it," I spit out. "I don't know if it's because I'm a woman or if it's just because it's me."

"Mal, I don't think—"

"It doesn't matter what you think," I cut him off. "Not anymore."

I wheeled around to leave, then came to an abrupt halt. "I'm going after Dessi tomorrow night. We have a plan, Sam and I, and it's going to go down tomorrow. And we'll get the evidence we need to put Dessi behind bars."

His jaw ticked as he rocked towards me and stopped but kept silent.

"That's what I thought," I said, striding away. He didn't try to stop me.

Chapter 18

Back at my apartment, the sound of my slamming cabinet door punctuated my mood. I set a plate down and loaded it with fried eggs, bacon, and potatoes O'Brien. It was a larger breakfast than I normally had, but I needed the comfort food.

Swiping my phone off the counter, I dialed Rodriguez. I had put off calling him last night, needing a break in the madness, but since my mood was already soured, it couldn't get worse.

"Hello?" I could hear feminine giggles in the background.

Yuck.

"It's Mal." My mouth twisted in disgust.

"Mal?" his voice came through, stunned. "Is everything okay?"

The giggling stopped short, and I could hear him fumble as he moved around, getting up or moving away for privacy.

"Right as rain," I said drily. "It's not random; it's premeditated."

"What, the B&E?"

"Yes, Eddie Leeman. I saw him in my apartment a week or so ago. Apparently, he planted a bug in my apartment."

"And you're just telling me now?"

"I just remembered his face, well, his hoodie and figure, coming down my stairs."

"What about the bug?"

"I only found out about it last night," I snapped. "Sam found the frequency and shut it off."

"And he didn't tell you?"

"He didn't. We talked about it. It's not your concern. Your concern is finding out what you can about Eddie Leeman," I snarled into the phone, still primed and loaded from my run-in with Rhodes. Heat spread across my forehead and down my back. "Or maybe you can go back to whatever's keeping you from your job. I just hope she's not married, not that it would stop you if she was. I'll fill you in on what *Sam* finds out about Eddie Leeman. Maybe."

Clicking "end" on my phone, I wheeled it across my countertop, where it slid to the backsplash with a light bang. I leaned over the counter, hands splayed flat, trying to control the shaking in my arms. I really needed to get it together. Relationships always had a way of screwing things up.

"Shit!" I exclaimed, realizing I had forgotten to stop by the coffee shop for my latte with extra espresso.

That evening, in a sterilized, but homey assisted-living room,

"What's wrong with you? You got a burr up your butt?" Sean asked his nephew.

"Nothing," he replied in a clipped tone from his grandmother's couch, where he sat sulking, hours later, his chin propped up by his hands. Neither had plans for the day, so they had decided to stick around and make sure she was settling in.

"Boys, don't start," Miss Ellie chided them. "Am I going to have to separate you two?"

He huffed but gave his gran a side smile. It wasn't anger at her, and maybe he needed to be more careful who he took his emotions out on. He'd made several mistakes lately.

Sean opened his mouth, but a knock on her door interrupted whatever smart-aleck comeback he had ready for his mom. They shared a look, unsure who it could be. He seriously doubted it would be Mal, coming back to talk it out. He had messed that one up royally. Dug his own grave and stepped in. And he'd accept the consequences, even if it would haunt him for the rest of his life. He deserved it.

Curious, he got up from his seat to answer the door. Pulling it wide, he stood face-to-face with his father.

"Hey, Brian." I waved at the man sitting in the Sentinel Security van parked at the Mennon stronghold. It had taken most of the afternoon and a long run to work off the bacon and eggs, but my bad mood had finally dissipated.

"Did you bring one of those for me?" he asked, eyeing the stack of pizzas I was carrying with interest. I thought I even saw a little drool forming. "I missed the Mantovani night last week."

"Of course." I slid off the top one and handed it to him through his open window. "Is Wyatt already here?"

"Yup, he got here a few minutes ago," he said, already tearing into the box and biting into a steaming slice. He pointed to the Range Rover parked next to him.

I nodded, heading up the stairs to knock on the thick metal door recently painted a dark teal to stand out against the masonry of the building. Suzy must be redecorating.

"Right on time," Wyatt said, opening the door. His eyes sparkled at the sight of the pizza boxes stacked high.

"As always," I said, stepping in. He took the boxes from me, making a beeline for the table. I couldn't blame him; there was something about that pizza. I might have gone a bit overboard on the order, but I knew how much his guys liked it. They'd eat the leftovers. That is if Wyatt left any. "Smart move with the home alarm system for Rosemary, by the way."

"It was those two," he said, pointing at Sam and Suzy. He was already digging into the pizza, filling plates for everyone.

"Two slices will do for me." Suzy held up her hand.

"Have you tried this pizza?" he asked, eyes wide.

"Yes," she said, laughing. "Two will do."

"Your loss." He sat down in front of his plate, piled high with four gooey slices.

"I'm just glad Rosemary feels like she has the upper hand," she went on.

"Somewhat," he said, frowning. "She's still being bulldozed by that good-for-nothing suit. I just wanted to stuff my fist in his face."

"I admire your self-control," I huffed. "It took all of mine to do the same. She doesn't deserve that."

"Definitely not. She's a sweetie."

I raised my eyebrow at that, wondering what had caused such a strong allegiance from Wyatt.

"So, are you ready for this?" Sam said, wagging his eyebrows up and down.

"What? The plan?" I sat at the table as Suzy set down a pitcher of margaritas. It was becoming a tradition. One I could really get behind.

"No, getting evidence to nail Dessi to the wall!" He sat straight up, his eyes on fire.

Suzy gazed at Sam with an open warmth.

"Oh, I'm ready for that, alright." So, it wasn't exactly a fully thought-out plan. I reflected on my conversation with Rhodes. But it was nearly there. Or rather, the beginnings of one.

"Tomorrow night, right?" Wyatt asked around mouthfuls of cheese.

I nodded. "It's Independence Day tomorrow—not that it's strictly necessary—but the place will be packed, and it'll be easier for me to plant the bug."

"Even on a Sunday night? They don't close early or anything, do they?" Suzy asked.

"Nope, they'll be open. I checked their Facebook page."

"You did?" Sam looked at me, eyes wide in surprise.

"I know how to use Google."

"With your Android phone." He guffawed.

"I looked it up on my laptop."

"Figures."

I rolled my eyes. "Anyway, you have the bug?"

"Yes, it's on the counter." He pointed to the kitchen. "It's charging."

"How much battery will we have?"

"Three hundred hours of active time. More in standby mode."

"That's quite a lot," Suzy commented.

"Not in an active bar, it's not," Wyatt weighed in.

"True." Sam nodded. "It's programmed to only pick up voices, but with all the ambient noise, it'll need to activate to identify the sound, then fall back to standby. And it's going to pick up a lot of side conversations. I'm guessing it'll be active at least half the day."

"They open at eleven for lunch and are open past midnight," I thought out loud. "That's maybe forty days."

"Maybe less."

We all looked around at each other, the food forgotten. After tomorrow night, my cover would most definitely be blown. No more poking about under their watchful eye. They'd know I knew exactly where I was. I wouldn't get another chance at Red. There might be other places, other warehouses to find, but this was the holy grail, where they met to discuss business. If we were going to figure out how and where Dessi was getting his hands dirty, we needed to make this work.

"Realistically, we've got a month," I said soberly. "We need to follow every lead we overhear."

"You just need to get it in that room," Sam said.

"I will."

"What can I do?" Wyatt asked.

"I need you to help with distraction."

"Wouldn't it be better with two distractions?" Sam asked, his puppy-dog eyes full of hope.

"Honestly, yes. I'm afraid Dessi has more than one person on his direct payroll, but." I looked between him and Suzy. No way would I risk what they had. "I need you on the outside surveillance and ready with a car. I'm going to need a quick exit."

"I'll disappear as soon as you take off," Wyatt said.

"And me?" Suzy asked.

"You're staying at home," Sam and I said at the same time.

"I need you listening in," I hurried to flesh her role out. "You can call in more of Wyatt's guys for backup if things go wrong. Or the cops if they go worse."

"I can do that." She smiled knowingly, watching the relief flood Sam's face as he realized she wasn't going to argue.

Taking a long sip of my margarita, I chewed on an ice chip. This could actually work. This *had* to work. We wouldn't get another chance like this.

"Speaking of payroll," Sam piped up. "Guess who else is on Dessi's payroll."

We all turned to look at him.

"Eddie Leeman."

At Wyatt's frown, I filled in, "The guy who broke into my apartment yesterday."

"I found bank-account transactions from Red Holdings, Red's parent company," he went on to explain. "What's interesting is that there are debit card transactions at the Dunkin' Donuts near your apartment for the past few weeks. He's been keeping tabs on you."

How had he been around that long, and I only saw him once?

It looked like we weren't the only ones upping our game.

Meanwhile, in a cute little doily covered seating area,

"What are you doing here?" Rhodes said, frowning.

Aaron hesitated at the door, glancing back down the hallway where the nurse was walking away. Taking a big gulp, he looked directly at him, hazel eyes matching his own, and said, "Sorry it took me so long to get here."

Rhodes chewed on it for a moment, then dipped his head, opening the door all the way. "Gran, you have a visitor."

"Who—Oh, Aaron!" his grandma said, straightening in her chair. "Come in, come in. We were just going to play cards."

And just like that, like he hadn't been gone for twenty-plus years, she got up and waved him in. Of course, that could be because she didn't realize it had been twenty-plus years. Sometimes, she did mistake Rhodes for his father.

The man in question locked eyes with him for a moment as he stepped in, and he knew they would have more talking to do before the night was over.

Great.

Deciding to make the most of it for his gran's sake, he mixed up a new batch of tea and got out some chips and salsa for the table. What he could really go for would be a beer, but after the previous few days, he figured he'd better lay off it for a while. It looked like it would be a long night.

"Whose turn to shuffle?" Sean asked, then turned to his estranged brother. "You do remember how to play Euchre, don't you?"

"I'm good if you all are." His dad's gaze flicked to his mother, silently asking if she could follow the game.

"Mom's gonna kick your ass." His eyes narrowed. She may be slipping, but cards were bred into her Midwestern soul. "She could beat you in her sleep."

"Sean!" his gran sounded. "Language."

"Sorry, Mom," he grumbled.

As soon as my phone hit the counter next to my plant with my keys, it lit up with the orange face of an orangutan. Letting out an unladylike snort, I swiped it up and hit the green button. It had been a long evening, full of pizza, margarita, and an unlikely game of charades. All I wanted was a long bath and a bed.

"I've got some interesting news," Rodriguez blurted out.

"Me too," I drawled out, plopping down on my couch. "You first."

"Well, you'll never guess who bailed Leeman out." He left it hanging.

"In person?" I exclaimed, standing back up. "Dessi signed him out in person? That ties him to whatever Leeman was doing, at least indirectly."

"Dessi?" he said, confused.

"It wasn't Dessi?"

"No, Mal. Not everything goes back to Dessi." I snorted again.

"It was Noelle Blair," he said, his enthusiasm squashed.

"My neighbor Noelle?"

"The one and the same," he confirmed. "And get this. She was crying that she sent Leeman over to see if you were home to borrow an iPhone charger, having an Android herself. She said he was really worried about getting a call from his boss and must have just *misunderstood* how close you two were and let himself in to get it."

"She doesn't even talk to me." I balked. "Also, I never leave the door unlocked."

That was unless I was taking out the trash. But never again; I was going to lock that thing obsessively, not that locked doors would keep the really bad guys out, but apparently, my place was being surveilled anyway. Was that even a word?

"According to Noelle, it was all a misunderstanding."

"My ass. We're not friends. She avoids me like the plague. Besides, if she was my friend, she'd know I don't have an iPhone, either."

"That's what I thought."

"What's that supposed to mean?"

"Nothing." He cleared his throat. "I just meant I've never heard you talk about her."

"You don't know my friends."

"I mean from before."

"Whatever." I brushed it off. I didn't have time for this. "There's something more here. I'd like to come in and talk to her at the station."

"I'm having her come back in and give a statement. You can be part of the questioning if you'd like," he offered.

"Fine." It was an olive branch, and I took it. "And there *is* a Dessi connection."

I filled him in on what Sam had found, but not that he was looking at his bank records; I left out the how.

Getting out my notebook, I sketched out notes on Noelle, my bath forgotten.

Chapter 19

Meanwhile, over a testosterone-filled four-person table,

"Ho!" Sean cried, throwing down his winning cards with a little too much force. "That takes the cake!"

Rhodes' eyes cut to his dad's across the table. It was the winning hand after three rounds, naming Sean and Gran as the victors. He might have had mixed feelings about partnering with his dad, but not about his gran's ability to still wipe the table with them.

"I may be a little rusty," his dad said.

"A little rusty!" his uncle huffed. "Have you *seen* cards in the last decade?"

A light shrug was his only answer as he gathered the cards together and shuffled, indicating practice. Maybe he wasn't as rusty as he carried on to be.

"Boys, I think I'm getting tired," his gran yawned.

"I'll pick up," Sean said, standing to help her up. "Ma, you can get ready for bed."

She nodded, heading to the restroom.

"They still have coffee in the kitchen," Sean continued without looking up. Apparently, he thought his brother and nephew could use a few minutes together.

"Do they have tea?" Aaron asked.

Rhodes let out a guttural sound between a snort and a growl. "Tea."

"They have tea bags next to the coffee cups. And a hot water tap on the coffee pot," Sean said, eyeballing his nephew to behave.

Grunting, he stalked out of the room, not waiting for his dad to follow.

Sure enough, the kitchen was empty and a pot of coffee sat on a burner, probably burnt by now. He poured a cup.

"I'm really glad you came to get me," Aaron said, taking his time to unwrap an herbal tea bag. "It's been good seeing you all."

Rhodes huffed, took a sip, and cringed at the brew. How long had it been sitting there?

"I'm sorry it took me so long to get here," he went on, filling the quiet.

"What took you so long?"

"Well, by the time I finished meditating on it, Mal had already left. I had to get a ride into town later that day from a visitor, and luckily, Amity let me borrow her car. I left that night."

"Mal left when I left." He made a face.

"No, I mean after she came back."

"She came back?"

"Yeah, a few hours later." Aaron walked over to sit at one of the tables outside the kitchen, taking a sip of his steeping tea. "She gave me a real talking-to, that friend of yours."

"She did?" his voice trailed off. The sinking feeling in his stomach dropped another few inches. Screwed up was too soft a word for what he had done. Even with his attitude, she had gone back. And after all of that, how did he repay her?

"I guess I just needed to see how selfish I was being. I'm really sorry, son."

"That's not actually what I meant." He shook his head, trying to clear his confusion with Mal and focus on the issues on the table between them. If Aaron wanted to talk, he'd talk. Apparently, he needed to. "What took you twenty-plus years? I was just a kid."

"Ah, that one's a little harder." His dad ran his hand over his head in a gesture he was so deeply familiar with. "It's not as easy for me. To be in this world."

"The real world, you mean."

"You can call it that, yes." He nodded, accepting the correction. "I wasn't like Dad or Sean, or you. I wasn't meant for service like they were. I wasn't as strong as you are."

"You mean the fire service."

"Any kind of public service like that, I guess. Fire, police, military. I'm not the confrontational type." He sighed. "Believe it or not, this conversation, as necessary as it is, is taxing."

"I'm so very sorry to tax you." His voice poured out with a thick syrup of sarcasm.

"I don't mean it like that. I'm glad I'm here. I'm not good at this." He shook his head sadly. "I just mean I crave harmony and peace. You know what it's like in a community of like-minded people. We all work together for a common goal."

He did; he gave a tight nod.

"When I found your mother, it was like I found the match to my soul. We traveled and celebrated life in a way I had never experienced before in my limited years." Memories tumbled through his eyes like galaxies of stars. "After Lily died"—his head dropped—"I couldn't go back to the way I had been living. It was a lie. It was too hard."

Rhodes stared into the sludge in his cup. He could almost understand. Things had been easy for him with women in the past, but that was because they needed something from him. He stepped in and took care of things, and they were more than happy to let him. Mal didn't need him like they had. She was so much stronger.

It scared him. Like he didn't have anything to offer her.

What he really needed to do was get his head out of his ass and get over her profession. Maybe at her side, she'd let him help her a little. And maybe he could learn to just enjoy her company and be there for her. The idea sounded freeing.

If it wasn't too late.

He wouldn't give him a second chance. It would have to be something major, to show her he accepted what she did, danger and all.

"I know it's not that easy to make things right between us," his father went on, staring into his own mug. "I missed so many, many years. I'm deeply sorry for that. But if you're willing, I'd like to come see you occasionally."

"Even in Chicago?" he asked, one corner of his mouth tipping up slightly.

"Even in Chicago." His dad's eyes focused directly on his.

"I can probably swing a trip down South occasionally, too." A shoulder jerked up. "Probably good to get a break from the smoggy city."

"I'd love that." His eyes softened and began to glisten. "And feel free to bring that friend of yours. She really is a keeper."

If he only knew how true that statement was.

Making a face, he downed the rest of the sludge and nodded his head. He had some thinking to do.

The place was already packed, if the cars in the lot were any indication. I approximated my arrival to equal the time it would take me to get here from the riverfront's firework show, adding some time for the slow drudgery of post-show traffic. Hopefully, people were already leaning into their celebratory drinks.

The furniture-store window looked as dull as ever. I checked my appearance in the rearview mirror: lip gloss on, hair plumped up even curlier and bigger than normal, low-cut blouse, boots laced tight. The bug was stashed in my bag, ready to go.

It had been a stress-filled day, going over the final details with Sam. He must have called a dozen times. The bug had charged until the very last moment. It was as full as absolutely possible, as I had relayed to my technologically advanced friend.

After pushing through the unmarked door at the rear of the beige store, I walked up to the heavy wooden door and waited for the tiny trap to open and ask for the passcode. Hopefully, they wouldn't know anything was different about tonight. I needed to keep up my undercover persona of Marina, blown though it was.

"Capone," I said when the door finally opened, and walked into the heavy crowd. People were decked out in red, white, and blue. Streamers hung from the ceiling, contrasting slightly with the twenties theme, but the bartenders wore color striped bands on their upper arms and around their foreheads instead of their normal black. Little flags were stuck into the decor in various places. It was louder and rowdier than I'd ever seen it.

Perfect.

Shoving between people, I made my way to the bar.

"Gin and tonic!" I hollered at James, whose eyes picked me up in the crowd quickly. How had I not noticed that before? Was I so vain I thought he was really that taken with Marina?

"Good to see you!" he said loudly over the noise.

I laughed as though I'd already had a few to drink, diving into my glass with enthusiasm when he handed it over. He might have known who I was, but he didn't know *I* knew he knew.

Swaying with the music, I let myself go loose and relaxed, playing up the drunk act. I didn't know how many of Red's employees knew about me, and didn't want to lose any advantage.

Dancing around the room, I carefully slid my near-full drink next to another on a table and backed away, eventually moving back to the bar for round two. My gestures becoming sloppier and bouncier. James laughed at my exuberance over my second drink. Whether he knew it was put on or not, I didn't care. I was Marina right now, and she was having a mighty fine time.

By the time I had ordered my third drink, I caught sight of Wyatt at the other end of the bar, flirting heavily with a blonde in a tight red dress. He laughed loudly at something she had to say and slung his arm over her shoulders, his weight making her stumble.

Perfect, it wouldn't be long now.

"Hi," a voice behind me said, making me stop dead. The blood drained from my face.

I knew that voice.

Turning, stomach in my throat, I saw Rhodes standing behind me.

"What are you doing here?" I looked around to see if anyone had noticed. "This isn't a good time."

"I know, actually," he said, his eyes going wide. "I've been driving around, looking for your car. I remember what you said. That you were going to be here tonight."

"How'd you get past the door?" I frowned; no way Sam or Suzy had told him. Not without telling me. It was the worst possible night to be dealing with an unplanned visit.

"I fumbled through it." He cringed. "I found something online on their Facebook page and tried all the gangster names until I got the right one. They were being helpful tonight."

Pulling him to a side table, I leaned in, one hand on his chest to keep up the act. I smiled coyly. "I'm sorry, but I'm undercover here. I can't mess this up."

"I know. That's why I'm here, to show you I support you." He put a hand up to cover mine, his eyes serious. "I want to help. In any way I can."

I blew out a sigh, looking around. Wyatt was getting louder, but it wasn't time yet. I had two, maybe three minutes. Absently, I realized Suzy was listening in on everyone's wires.

Forcing my face to stay in character, I swayed towards him. "Look, Rhodes, the best thing you can do is get out of here. I can't handle an interruption."

"Okay." His eyes cast down, then flicked back up in determination. "I'll leave, but you have to know that the only reason I questioned you at all is because I'm falling for you."

"You are?" I said, blinking. I knew we had chemistry, but I didn't realize his feelings had gotten that strong.

"And I can't stand the thought of losing you, which I know I've probably done already." His hand tightened around mine. "I hate the thought of you being hurt. And I've never been with someone who didn't need me, who wasn't a little broken. I'm always the guy who comes in and fixes things, takes control. You don't need that, and I honestly didn't know what to do with that."

I didn't feel all that unbroken at this moment. Emotions ran through me, pain from past relationships, reminders of missteps with Rhodes. Tears pricked at my eyes.

"A distraction," I said. "Isn't that what you tried to use me for?"

His head hung for a moment, shoulders following suit. "You're right. I have no excuse for that. I don't know how I let myself get that far gone. I was so twisted up about my dad."

I had baited him a little at the bar, though. It had been bad timing to bring up Dessi. Still, I wouldn't excuse his bad behavior.

"Whatever happens"—he stared into my eyes, as serious as I'd ever seen him—"please don't think you're incapable. You're one of the most capable women I've ever met. And Suzy is like family; I get protecting family. Your job is who you are. I don't like it, but I get it. I'll probably *never* like you being in danger, but I'll respect you and your choices. I can't imagine someone trying to talk me out of my job. So, I'll do what I can to get over it. And be there for you. If you'll let me."

It was so tempting.

"Do you think we've missed our chance?" My voice was barely a whisper. I didn't like the fragile nature of it, but there I was, being open, the room around me gone.

"God, I hope not." His eyebrows furrowed. "You'd be the one I'd regret for the rest of my life. The one that got away."

A loud shout behind me made me jerk out of my interlude.

This was it. It was time. I shook my head from the fog.

"The ball's in your court, but I want you to know I accept you. I believe in you. And I want to work it out, whatever it takes," he said, all in a rush. "I'm all in."

I couldn't wait; we'd never get a chance like this. If he left now, he wouldn't get in my way.

Backing away slowly, my eyes wide, I stumbled on purpose, then whispered, "I just want you to leave."

Chapter 20

Turning away, I slipped my hand into my purse, palming the bug. I would have to ignore the memory of the hurt reflecting in his eyes. This was my sting, damn it. He shouldn't have interfered.

I swallowed my emotions, my head down as I slipped through the crowd. Leaning on bodies as I passed. I looked like just another drunk heading to the restroom.

Let's do this.

"Who do you think you are?" Wyatt roared across the bar.

From my vantage point, I could see him take two unsteady steps back, grabbing people and knocking over a couple of chairs. He looked like a Viking bear gone angry with his dark-blond hair and blue eyes. The crowd scattered from him, forming a wall around the bar, and I slipped around behind them, going the other direction.

When I came even with the hallway to the restrooms and backrooms, liquid hit me in the face. Blinking, I didn't have to fake my stunned expression.

"Sorry," a woman said, looking down the hallway.

Angling my head, I saw the Asian-American woman hurrying from the backroom. Shit, Dessi had more people on his payroll than I had thought, but planting guests? It was so smart. I had to give him credit, even though it thoroughly messed up my plan.

The woman gave me an apologetic look and took her empty glass back to the bar.

"Can I help you?" The woman I knew of as Cynthia sneered at me. She wasn't very good at her cover. Maybe she didn't care.

"Sh-sorry," I slurred, tipping into her. Clutching at the lapels on her suit jacket, long and low-hipped over a skirt to fit into the twenties theme. She pitched back and snarled in return. "I's just—restroom." I pointed, my eyes glazed.

"Sure." She tugged firmly on her jacket, smoothing out any perceived creases. A hand reached up to check the feathered band around her forehead. "Go on, then."

I sagged, slumping towards the restroom door, banging on it to swing it open. It wasn't the direction I wanted to go, but I couldn't get past her.

"Don't touch me!" Wyatt's timber rang through the room, bouncing off the chandelier to resonate.

Out of the corner of my eye, I saw Cynthia's attention snap to Wyatt. A throng of people poured through the hallway between us to see what was happening. Dipping, I crouched and ran alongside them, angling around the corner to the back. I could see the doorway in front of me, only a few feet away.

On the other side of the bar, James' eyes caught mine and he lunged to break through the wall of people. But I was already through the door.

I found myself in a dim hallway. Surveying the hall, I saw a storage room to the left, and the sizzling sounds of fryers and metal banging on metal identified the kitchen farther down. But to the right were offices.

The one farther away had a single door, painted black with a shiny gold knob. That had to be Dessi's office. But to my direct right was more of a large office, two doors in and out, four windows in between, all with blinds drawn, but the doors stood open. I had only a moment to make a decision.

"Hey!" The loud crack of the door behind me hitting the hallway announced James' arrival. I flicked the thin plastic film covering the adhesive on the bottom of the bug. I only had to make it into that room.

Lurching forward, I dove in, searching the dark room for the best place to plant it. Under the table, Sam had said. And not in a plant; they'd be watered on schedule.

James was right behind me, grabbing my shoulder to wheel me back. I flailed sideways, grabbing a chair leg with my foot, to go over it and separate us. Scrambling over it, he landed on top of me. Reaching for the chair to my right, I fumbled with it, struggling to pull it closer, as if to throw it at him. In a sudden thrust, he swatted my arm away, locking my hands to my sides.

I went limp, not wanting to get any injuries by fighting back. He hadn't tried hitting me, so I didn't think his intention was to get violent, even outside of the customers' view.

"There's not even anyone in here," I sobbed, as though that had been the goal all along. "Where is everyone?"

Pulling me up, he sat me down hard on a chair.

"Stay there," he ordered, looking around. He planted his fists on his hips, pacing as he decided what to do. "We should take you to the boss."

My heart rate kicked up a notch.

"There she is!" Cynthia shouted, stomping into the room. "You let her get in the back?"

She stared James down, effectively dressing him down even from her lower vantage point.

He gulped loudly. "I'll go get the boss."

"Don't bother." She sneered, grabbing my arm roughly and jerking me upright. "I'll take her to him."

I stumbled, not even faking it. *See? This was why I wore boots.* I would have twisted an ankle by now, for sure.

Pushing me in front of her, she twisted my arm tightly behind me. Her fingers felt like slim steel bars biting into my forearm and shoulder. Out in the hallway, I cast a panicked look towards the black door when the barroom door crashed open again and people started spilling into the hall.

"Motherfucker!" Wyatt threw a punch, and a burly guy with a beard sailed past us, women around him rushing to help. He didn't even look my way as he pounded down the hallway after him, single-focused as though in a drunken rage.

Breaking from Cynthia's thin vice grips for fingers, I bolted into the crowd, ducking under an arm and shouldering my way through the throng of people. I had to get out of here.

"Stop her!" I heard her shout behind me.

Dancing from side to side, I bounded through the barroom, careening around tables towards the door. The bouncer stood in front of me, eyes narrowed, blocking my only way out. I cast a quick look behind me. So not an option. This was it.

I readied myself. He wasn't going to just let me through. But just as I came up to him, ready to knee him in the groin, a large shoulder came out from my left, blocking my vision. A huge fist knocked the bouncer to the ground. He was out cold.

I barely had enough time to follow the arm with my eyes as I sailed through the door. I would know that well-muscled forearm anywhere.

Rhodes.

His eyes held mine for a brief moment. Mine were bright with excitement but laced with panic. His held a little confusion and sadness. I didn't know what that meant, but it didn't look like good old-fashioned acceptance of my lifestyle. I didn't have time to think about it further.

I dashed into the furniture store, the Muzak at odds with the pounding of my heart, and rammed the door to my freedom.

The waiting car at the curb filled me with triumph. The door opened right on time, and I slid in as it rolled onto the street. The tires fishtailed and spun on the gravel, spitting out behind us. I had to catch the door to pull it shut.

"Oh boy!" Sam exclaimed, peeling out onto the road. "Suzy was giving me a play-by-play of what she could understand. That was incredible!"

My chest heaved as I sunk into the leather seat of his Tesla. I reached a shaky hand up to pull down the seat belt and click it in place.

"Crap!" I yelled, looking at the ceiling. Frustration tumbled this way and that inside of my chest. It hadn't gone as planned.

And why did Rhodes have to show up?

"Did you get it?" His eyes flicked to me, then back to the road, hands tight on the steering wheel.

"I couldn't reach the table, but yeah, I got it."

"Where?" His eyes glanced back to mine, edged in worry.

"Under a chair." I took another steadying breath.

"Do you think they're going to find it?" Suzy asked, fidgeting with the place mat in front of her at her dining room table.

"Who knows?" I shrugged. "There's no way they have a camera recording what's going on in that room."

"The chair isn't ideal," Sam piped up. "The audio may not be as strong from speakers clear across the room. But it should do. Unless they swap out chairs with another room."

"Let's hope not," Wyatt said from across the table, smiling like the devil, bloody lip and all. "There's only so much this pretty face can take."

"What about the frequency?" I asked Sam, ignoring his self-appreciation.

"Still off. I'll leave it off for forty-eight hours. They'll have done whatever sweep they'll do by then. I'll switch it on, on Tuesday night. See what's going on."

"I just hope they don't find it when they're cleaning." Suzy's lips pulled down in worry.

"They'll probably give the place a cursory glance," I told her. "But I acted surprised that the place was vacant. They believe I thought I was catching something in the act. I don't think they believe I was successful. Thanks for saving my ass back there." One corner of my mouth tipped up in acknowledgment to Wyatt.

"It's what I do." He shrugged confidently. "I saw that guy come in there after you and knew I needed to bring the party to you."

"It was what I needed to get out."

"What would you have done if she wasn't able to get away?" Sam asked, eyes as round as saucers.

"I'd have gone back-to-back with her if I had to. I wasn't leaving her there by herself."

I gave him a thankful smile. It was good to have friends.

"There's just one thing I can't figure out." Wyatt frowned.

"What's that?"

"Not that I'm doubting your abilities, but I saw the bouncer before I slipped out the back. He was huge. You didn't do that to him. He was passed out on the floor when I left. What the hell happened?"

"Rhodes." I sighed, looking at my hands in my lap.

"Yes, Rhodes." Suzy watched me, a dreamy look on her face. She had listened to the whole exchange on my wire.

"Why was he there?" Wyatt asked.

"Isn't that a good question?" I said drily.

The room all looked at me, waiting for my reply.

"I might have mentioned I was going in tonight when I ran into him yesterday at the retirement home."

"You told him our plan?" Sam asked, his nose wrinkling up.

"No! Of course not. He was driving by, looking for me." I huffed. "He wanted to help. To show his support."

"That's so sweet." Suzy's eyes got all glisteny.

"Kinda bad timing to jump into a job without any idea what was going on." Wyatt tilted his head. "But he did take out the bouncer, so there's that."

There was that.

I had a good chance of handling it without him, but maybe not without a few more scrapes and bruises than I currently had.

"So, he's making a show that he accepts your job," Suzy said excitedly. "He's showing you he's okay with what you do and trying to support you."

"Maybe he was." I frowned. "But I was undercover. I don't know that he got what he wanted."

It was doubtful he'd come back around now. I'd backed out right as he was pouring his heart out to me. I wouldn't blame him if he didn't feel the same now that he'd seen right into the fire of it all.

And I didn't want to push it. If he was okay with it, he knew where to find me. If not, well, I'd learn to live with it, even though I could still hear his words playing in my head.

He accepted me, but more than that, he *believed* in me. It was the words I'd always hoped to hear someone say to me.

"If it's meant to be, it'll be," Suzy said, casting a fond look at Sam, curly hair still wild from his thrilling car chase.

"What's our next move?" Wyatt broke into the conversation, steering it back on track. "You said the bug will be working in forty-eight hours? What happens then?"

"Then, we wait and listen," Sam said soberly.

"And we'll follow up on every single lead we possibly can." I nodded.

"And we put this bastard behind bars."

Chapter 21

Meanwhile, in a stark black-and-white living room with black leather couches,

"Hello? Jonathan?" came a frantic voice over his speakerphone.

"Hello, Frederick," Jonathan replied. "What can I do for you?"

"I'm—I can't," he stammered. "They've got the place surrounded!"

"What do you mean? They who?" He tried to be patient with the spoiled man-brat.

"My house! Er, my mom's house. I mean, the stupid, good-for-nothing security guys," he whined over the phone.

"Where are you now?" he asked, hearing road noise through the phone. "Let's talk it out."

"I sold that piece of jewelry."

"I thought we were waiting until she reported it missing!" he hissed.

"I needed the money!"

"You should have come to me! You must not be spending your money wisely."

"Well, I didn't! I can make some decisions on my own," he crowed. "Apparently, Mom's worried enough to get security, so I need to get in there to get another piece to hock before they install the system. I only have a couple more days."

Jonathan sighed loudly, rubbing his temple. He would never succeed if he insisted on being so stupid. Oh well, it mattered little. He had access to the Lamb fortune either way, through Rosemary or Freddy. Although Freddy would prove to be a longer investment. If Freddy succeeded, he could hold power of attorney over Rosemary. *That* would be the ideal investment. The thought made his mouth turn up in a deceitful smirk.

"Anyway, I need another piece," he continued, summing it up. "I need to push her over the edge, think she's losing things. She'll call the police, and they'll think she's crazy."

"But you've sold the other piece, Frederick."

"I, uh, oh, I hadn't thought of that. Well, I'll have this *new* piece to replant in the house, showing she's just forgetful. Or, I know!" he said excitedly. "I'll say she had me take it to the jeweler to get it cleaned! She just forgot, as always! The crazy old bat."

"Whatever you think's best."

"But I can't get in. That's what I'm trying to say!" he wailed. "And unless you can give me more money, I'll need to hock it too!"

"I'm already footing the bill for the lawyer and the doctor to proclaim her until you get your money," he said through pinched teeth. "Maybe you should just take two pieces!"

"Hey, that's a good idea! Except, that doesn't help me tonight. I still can't get in."

"Who is following you again, Frederick?" He pinched the bridge of his nose.

"Those security guys! Like I said!"

"You hadn't sai—Oh, never mind." He exhaled.

"You don't understand. These guys are like ninjas! But in a van. I drove down the street and tried going in the other way, and I found their van sitting there, just waiting for me. So, so, I drove down to the gas station, all the way outside of the subdivision, you know, down by Parchini's, and waited fifteen minutes before I tried again," he rushed to explain. "The same *exact* thing happened! I don't know what to do!"

"You must have gotten them at a bad time. Try again later tonight, much later. If they're still hanging around, try again tomorrow, maybe earlier, maybe later. And, Frederick? Try different cars."

"Hey, now! That's a good idea! I'll do that. Thanks, Jonathan," Freddy said. "And don't you worry. When this all goes down, you're getting set for life."

Oh, he'd better be, he thought.

Banging on my front door jolted me from my sleep in the early hours of the morning. Groggily, I stumbled to my door, wrapped in my robe. Peering through the peephole, I saw a blue uniform. Cops. *What in the world?*

"Hello?" I rubbed an eye. "What's so important that it couldn't wait until normal people wake up?"

The cops in front of me glanced back and forth between each other. Unfortunately, I didn't know either of them.

"Molly Malone?" the female cop asked.

"Yes," I sighed. I'd never get used to that name.

"Were you at a nightclub called Red last night?" the male cop asked.

Seriously? Dessi was going to play like this? Of all the underhanded...

My lips pursed tightly. "Yes, I was there. Along with quite a few other people after the fourth of July celebrations. What seems to be the problem?"

"We'd like you to come down to the station for a statement," the female said. Brooks, according to her uniform.

"What is the charge?"

"Disorderly conduct," the male cop, Frenzen, said. "The bar owner is also claiming destruction of property and assault on their bouncer."

"That's just fantastic." I sagged against the door. "I wasn't even drunk! You can test me, see!"

"It's too late to run a test." Brooks shook her head. "It'd be out of your system by now."

"Not if I were as drunk as you're stating," I argued.

"Everyone reacts differently." Frenzen stepped forward. "Just come on down and give your statement. Are you going to come peacefully?"

"It was part of an investigation. I was undercover last night," I hurried to explain. "I can show you my ID."

I left the door open and rushed to my wallet to pull out my card. The cops put their hands on their weapons, concerned at my hurried actions, and shared another look as they entered my apartment, closely tracking my movements.

"Look, I'll come with you to the station and explain it all," I went on, switching tactics. "I have no intention of causing any trouble."

"Good answer," Brooks said, stepping beside me to take my arm. "Molly Malone, you're under arrest."

Frenzen recited my Miranda rights.

Great. I hadn't even had coffee.

"Can I just change clothes first?" I tried to step back, finding Frenzen behind me.

They hesitated a moment. "Sure, but make it fast." She nodded, checking my bedroom down the hallway to clear it.

An hour later, I sat in front of Brooks, Frenzen, and Rodriguez. It was exactly where I didn't want to be, on the other end of an interrogation by Detective Dillhole with no caffeine in my system, whatsoever. My version of hell, as it were.

"I have certain investigative rights," I stated again.

"You do," Rodriguez said, his voice calm and agreeable. It made me sick. "But that doesn't allow for drunken and disorderly conduct."

"For the last time, I wasn't drunk," I got loud, then checked myself.

"Then how do you explain the accounts of knocking over barstools and running into guests?" Frenzen questioned. "According to the owner, that's how you were behaving. And explain the bouncer who was found passed out on the floor."

"First of all." I leaned forward in my chair, placing my hands on the table in front of me. "The owner wasn't even in the barroom. I didn't lay a hand on the bouncer. Did you see him? He's twice my size! If the owner saw anything at all, it was from a surveillance tape."

The two shared a look again. There it was.

"Is there a surveillance tape?" I pushed. "Because that could clear all of this up. I most certainly didn't assault the bouncer, and you're going to have to come up with a video if you think otherwise."

"Mal." Rodriguez's eyes look pained. "There's also a bartender who's claiming assault."

"I didn't hit him either! I was only trying to get away—to get out of there once another fight started. That's probably what they think I was involved in. I may have tripped in the crowd, but I certainly didn't hit anyone. Check the tape."

"Whether or not they have a video, this doesn't look good for your business," he went on as if we were friends. "Charged with disorderly conduct? That's a $10k fine and possibly incarceration. Mal, this is serious."

"That's not including the bar owner's charges. Destruction of property and assault is $1500 and thirty days in jail, on top of the disorderly conduct," Frenzen jumped in.

"They'd have to prove I was drunk," I ground out. "And I know I wasn't."

"The bartender said you ordered three gin and tonics and were already drunk when you arrived," Brooks said, reading from the file in front of her. "Why would he lie? Bartenders are typically good judges of people. They see a lot of drunk people every day."

"It was part of my cover," I repeated. "Rodriguez, Dessi owns that place. And the bartender is in on it."

"Is he now?" Frenzen asked, tilting his head. "In on *what* exactly?"

A low growl formed in my throat. Maybe I needed a lawyer. Unfortunately, I couldn't quite afford one. "I've gone over everything three times already. I've told you everything I can."

"You can't just go after Dessi like that," Rodriguez said. "I know you want to see him charged, and I understand that. I want to see any criminal locked up. But you can't just go in and bait him, start a fight with him in his place of business, hoping he's going to slip up."

"I've told you everything I can," I repeated, standing firm. "What's my bail?"

"It's really best to cooperate," the detective said.

"I've cooperated!" I threw my hands in the air.

"As I said," Rodriguez repeated, a cajoling note in his voice. "Red's pressing charges, so it'll have to go to court."

"Great."

"But they're letting you post bail."

"Because I'm not a threat."

"But you have to make your court date."

"I'll be there," I said, eyes narrowed.

"Hello?" I said, answering my phone. It was three hours later, and I was finally walking out of the precinct. I was in desperate need of caffeine. Things were getting serious.

"Mal, are you alright?" It was Jen.

"I couldn't be better." Sarcasm dripped from my voice. "Talked to your buddy Rodriguez, huh?" It wasn't fair, but right now, I wasn't feeling very fair. "I think you're right. He's such a nice guy. I really should just forgive him."

Silence filled the line, and I knew I had hurt Jen's feelings. At the moment, I didn't really care. I had gone into that place to get Dessi, the bad guy, and here the cops were questioning me. *I* was the one arrested. Not that criminal lowlife.

"He was just doing his job," she whispered. "Besides, he was there for you."

"Was he? I somehow missed his awesome support."

"He joined the investigation so he could help you."

"You know what would really be helpful? A little less help."

"Mal, be fair. He was making sure they were playing it by the books."

"Is that what he told you?" I asked, walking across the street. I had refused the ride back to my apartment in favor of walking. It was a long walk, but my mood could use it. "He questioned my actions and threatened me with the consequences."

"That's his job," she argued gently.

"They don't even have a video, do they?" I asked, doubting Dessi would release any surveillance of his club, that is if he had it, in case he was ever questioned on any other illicit activity. He would want to claim ignorance.

"You know I can't tell you that."

I snorted. "So, what exactly *did* he do for me?" I asked.

"He got you a fast court date. They're going to hear your case sometime late next week," she said helpfully. "That won't give them a lot of time to come up with evidence."

"There isn't any," I said, my teeth grating. "Or do you think I'm guilty too?"

She was quiet for a moment, then finally said, "I think you'd do a lot to see Dessi behind bars."

"Damn straight," I said and hung up the phone. It wasn't worth the argument, and I was done explaining myself. I didn't care what she thought. At least, right then.

"You look like shit," Mo said, frowning at me as he went about setting up for the day. The place had just opened.

"Thanks," I mumbled, taking a sip of my double espresso. "You say the sweetest things."

"You want to talk about it?" I heard him tap the espresso puck from its cup.

"Not particularly." I didn't raise my eyes to look at him as I spoke. I was too busy worrying about my business. What would that mean for a private investigator to have an arrest record? And if I was charged, would I be able to afford the fines, let alone the time in jail? A PI with a felony record, that didn't sound promising at all. I'd be stuck doing infidelity cases for the rest of my career.

"Mal," he said seriously.

Lifting my eyes, I looked at him. He was giving me the once-over.

"This isn't related to the fireman, is it?" he asked.

Rhodes. And there I had nearly forgotten about that issue. I felt like I was hanging on by threads.

"If you're in over your head, you can talk to me." His eyebrows drew together tight, concern on his face.

"I'm just having a really bad day." I sighed, feeling bad I had worried him. "My case just got a little outta hand. I've got it all under control."

Mo watched me, eyes narrowed like he didn't quite believe me. "You'd let me know if you need a hand?"

"Sure," I lied to appease him. I didn't want to get him involved in my legal troubles. I mean, what could he do?

Paying my tab, I shuffled across the street to the office. It was just about time for Suzy to come in, and I knew she'd be excited to rehash the night before. Luckily, two double espressos had gotten rid of my bodily exhaustion, even though my mental status was as weary as ever, weighed down not only by the arrest, but by the ruined chance with Rhodes and my recent fight with Jen.

Chapter 22

"Morning, Elliot Ness!" Suzy sang to me as I opened the door amidst the sounds of Corinne Bailey Rae. At least she had something mellow playing today.

I raised my sunglasses and squinted in, trying to give her a smile.

"What's wrong?" she said, noticing it was tighter than normal.

"Just woke up too early." I shrugged. "Late night."

"You should have slept in! A hero like you!"

"I'm no hero." I exhaled with a sigh, the bond documents weighing heavily in my pants pocket. Last night's victory seemed so far away. And I didn't want to weigh her down with my problem. It was just that, mine. My choice, my actions, and mine to figure out how to get out of. "I just want to get back to work until we can get that frequency on and listen in on Dessi."

"No problem, Mal," she said with an upbeat tone, but there was an undercurrent of concern.

I was settled in my seat for less than five minutes before the Sam-bot rolled in.

"Hey, Sam."

"Hey!" he said, waving. He looked relatively normal in a Firefly T-shirt and trench coat. "Wyatt got an interesting call this morning."

"What's that?"

"Brian was monitoring the area around the Lamb estate last night, and Freddy's car was seen driving around with his lights off."

"Really?" I settled back in my chair. So the little weasel was getting impatient. "What'd he do?"

"Well, those guys chased him off; that's what they did!" Sam chortled. "Apparently, they cut him off from every direction. I bet he was spitting mad!"

I bet he was just that. It was time to get Rosemary to make a decision on this thing.

"Did Wyatt call Rosemary yet?"

"Not yet. He figured you might want to fill her in since it's your case. Maybe use it to persuade her, he said."

"My thoughts exactly. I'll give her a call. Thanks, Sam." I hung up.

Still in the process of thinking through my plan, I dialed her number.

"Hello?" her gentle voice came through my receiver.

"Ms. Lamb, this is Detective Malone."

"Dear, I told you to call me Rosemary," she gently scolded.

"Rosemary." I smiled, unable to help myself. "Sentinel Security reported Freddy driving by your house last night, lights off. They believe he was trying to get in."

"Oh, my. That's not good news."

"No, ma'am. It's not. I wanted to warn you things might be starting to move. You should keep an eye on things at home. Be careful what you say. Think about what you do. You don't know how he's going to play this thing or what he's going to do."

"I think he's going to try to steal more jewelry, now that he pawned the first piece," she said gruffly. "But thanks."

"You're also going to think about what you want to do. The time has come," I leveled with her.

"You're right, dear," she replied sadly. "The boy's not going to learn unless I confront him. But I'd like to have proof in front of him, so he can't use it against me. I'm just not sure I'm ready for legal action just yet. It really depends on what he says."

"I thought you might say that. And I have an idea."

"Hello?" I answered my ringing phone. It was coming from a restricted number.

"Bugsy," came the oddly gravelly mellow tones of the one-and-only Domenico Poggiali. He was a suspected leader in organized crime in Chicago, from a somewhat opposing side to Dessi's Marchi. He also thought it was hilarious to call me Bugsy Malone.

"To what do I owe the pleasure?"

"Little bird says you're in trouble."

How did he know about that so quickly?

"Nah, not so much." I tried for a lighthearted approach.

"So, you're not on bail and getting served court papers as we speak?"

My gaze flicked to the lobby outside of my office. No one was here yet.

"Probably soon," I said reluctantly.

"Do you need help?" he offered temptingly, but we both knew it didn't come without a cost.

"I got it, Dom, but thanks." I sat back in my chair. "Your son's doing well."

"Yes, he is. Thanks." He chuckled. "He always tells me when you visit Pete's pizza shop."

"He's a talented kid. I can't wait to see where he goes. Him being your kid, I'm expecting great things."

"Me too." I could hear the smile in his voice.

"Dessi's been causing quite a scene around town. I'm sure you've heard about the shootings." Maybe I could find something out from him.

"Unfortunately, yes." He signed. "It's not the sort of business that should be done in public."

"It was in a warehouse."

"Yes, I meant the manner of business he was conducting and how it escalated. That warehouse is in an up-and-coming neighborhood. Innocents got shot. Marchi's guys knew what they were getting into. The locals, not so much. We may have questionable businesses, but there's no excuse for that. There are rules."

"The manner of business?" I said, hoping he'd say more.

"Are you hoping for intel?" He cut right to the chase. "I'd be happy to oblige. You know it doesn't come free, but I've made my interest well known. I'd be happy to have you on the team, even if it's just for the repayment of a debt."

"Respectfully, I'm going to have to pass." It's not like I could pick the method of repayment, and we both knew it'd never end there. I liked Dom, but he was still part of Chicago's underworld.

"As much as I'd like to see him off the streets, I don't snitch. Not unless I'm getting something out of it anyway. That's just business, you understand."

"I do." I looked up to see someone walk into the lobby outside. "Looks like that company arrived."

"Think on it," he said before hanging up.

"Mal?" Suzy said hesitantly. "Someone's here for you."

"Coming." I pushed up from my desk with a groan. This was going to be fun.

A police officer stood next to the desk, watching me approach. "Molly Malone?"

"That's me."

"Please sign here." He handed me a clipboard and a white envelope.

I scribbled my signature and handed it back to him.

"Have a nice day," he said, turning to walk back out the door.

And just like that, it really felt real. After staring at the envelope, I looked up to see Suzy watching me, eyes like saucers. Crap. I had forgotten she was there, too busy being caught up in feeling sorry for myself. Not that I regretted my actions of the night before.

"What's that, Mal?" she said quietly.

"Court date." I folded it in half and stuffed it in my back pocket, along with the other damning documents.

"For?"

"Dessi sued me."

Her eyes cast to the Sam-bot in the corner, then back to me. "We'll get you a good lawyer."

"Suze." I sat down across from her in one of the two chairs in the waiting area, the thick paperwork in my pocket making itself known. "You can't just bail me out anytime there's trouble. You came here to help me, and you do. Sam brought technology and research skills I never dreamed I'd have at my disposal. I had a working business before, but not like this. I'm so much more effective, and I'm actually making a little money. I'd never have been able to take on someone like Dessi a year ago."

"But we're not bailing you out," she said exasperatedly. "We help each other out! You saved me."

"You were well on your way out of that place when I found you."

"Who knows?" She raised her shoulders, her hands out wide. "Who knows who would have gotten to me first. Let us do this. Let us help you."

"No." I shook my head. "You've already done so much. I don't think I'll ever be able to repay you as it is. It's fine, really, Suze. I have a license to investigate. I really don't think it will be a problem. Worst-case scenario, they get me on a little destruction of property. That's all they can really prove if they get witnesses to lie for them. I'll pay a little fine and move on."

"But what about the record? Isn't that bad for your profession?"

"Maybe?" I gave her a little side smile, trying to sell it. Sam didn't need to spend money on this; it was a little issue. What was more important was Suzy and getting Dessi locked away. Besides, I was finally making a little headway financially. Any lawyer the Mennons hired would be expensive to the max. "Maybe it just shows I'm an in-it-to-win-it investigator. Maybe it'll give me a little edge."

I didn't like it, but I couldn't let them help. It was my fault anyway. I should have been more on it, shouldn't have slipped up as I had.

Suzy's mouth made a little moue, showing her displeasure, but she said nothing else.

I leaned forward to get up, but she stopped me. "What about Rhodes?"

"What do you mean?"

"What'd you decide to do about his declaration of love?"

"You didn't see the look in his eye when I ran out of that place. He was *not* impressed," I rolled my eyes. "Plus, he obviously felt like he had to come to my rescue."

"You needed the assistance."

"Yes, I did," I admitted, dipping my head. "It certainly helped. I'm not sure how I'd have gotten by that bouncer, but I'd have given it my all."

"You left it in his hands last time, and you know where that led you." She gave me a knowing look. "Nowhere. It just festered until he came to see you."

"But he did," I said helpfully.

"He did. But do you want to chance that again?"

I didn't like that she was right, but still, she didn't see his face. I really didn't think I had a chance in hell. It's one thing for him to make a decision to try to ignore an irritation, but living with it, day in and day out, sometimes wore on a person. And he had gotten an up-close and personal view of my life. At least, my life right now.

At least this time wasn't really my fault. He'd put himself in that situation, but the times before? I could have edged him into it far easier than I had. I was so sure I needed to prove myself by proclaiming it a little louder than necessary.

"Suzy," I said quietly, being more vulnerable than normal. "Do you think I pushed him away?"

"What do you mean?"

I shrugged, my mouth twisting up. I didn't like the feeling, but I needed to know. And I trusted Suzy to be honest with me. "I don't know. I mean, do you think I messed things up with him, pursuing Sully, throwing the Dessi job at him, letting him know I didn't need help, as a way of pushing him away?"

Looking down at my hands where they sat in my lap, I thought about all the problems that had sprung up between men and me.

"Do you think I did that with Alex too?" I went on, unable to stop now. "Jen thinks I'm too hard on him for a onetime mistake. But I don't think I should have been okay with him cheating on me! I just don't think I'll *ever* be okay with that." My voice raised, then quieted. "But do you think I pushed him away all that time, too? I thought we were happy once, but maybe I was throwing at him all the ways I didn't need him either."

Suzy sat there in silence for a minute, weighing my words. "Listen to me, Mal. What Detective Rodriguez did is inexcusable. He behaved badly and lost you as a result. He did *not* deserve you. Maybe he's changed, maybe he hasn't. That's for whoever chooses to look past his indiscretions to decide. As for Rhodes, I don't know. Maybe you pushed him a little, but he's still responsible for behaving the way he did, too. At least he got to the point where he talked to you about it. We all have fears, Mal. I do all the time, even with Sam. That's why I talk to him about it, and he talks to me. And why you should too. Talk to Rhodes, I mean."

"I guess I just don't want to be born to walk alone." My mind ruminated back to the road trip in the Jeep.

Suzy gave me a little frown, not getting the Whitesnake reference, but said, "Call him. You might be surprised."

"I'll think about it," I said, walking slowly back to my office, barely registering my surroundings, deep in contemplation.

I did have one other thing I could talk to him about, ease into the conversation and see how he reacted. I knew there was only one way to find out for sure where he stood, but the thought of calling him sent my stomach into a tumble. And the temptation to just dump myself into work like I normally did was so much more appealing than dealing with those emotions…or his rejection.

Or maybe I was more worried about the court case than I had thought.

Chapter 23

Later that day, after grabbing a few groceries from Mariano's, I headed home. I was considering another case but was worried it would take me away from pursuing any leads that came my way once the bug was activated. I just needed to make sure we had enough funds to get us through the next month. That was assuming I'd be around in another month, and not in jail.

Maybe I could call Rodriguez and ask him to push the court date out until then. If I did have to face some repercussions, it would be so much easier if it was after Dessi was arrested. I snorted, imagining Dessi and I both behind bars at the same time.

As I neared Humboldt Ave and the convenience store on the corner, a flash of yellow caught my eye. It was the convertible, and three girls were in the store, terrorizing Saanvi again.

Eyes narrowed, I gunned it through a yellow light and spun my Jeep into the lot. My fingers raced over my cell phone to dial Officer Mathews, the only officer other than Jen I kept on speed dial for cases like this.

"Drop it!" I shouted at the blonde in pigtails, punching through the door. She had Saanvi's broom high overhead and was shaking it towards the Indian woman, who was trying hard to maintain control. Her chin was set, eyes pinched, even though they winced with every broom thrust her way. "Drop it right now!"

Twirling on one foot to see me, her eyes shot daggers. "Who do you think you are?"

The brunette grinned maniacally, dropping a large bottle of Snapple. She made a little hop when it broke on impact, spraying her bare legs with tea and glass shards. Inwardly, I cheered at her bad choice; she obviously hadn't realized how close it was. A few tiny rivulets of blood ran down her legs into her high-heeled ankle-high boots.

"I'm Detective Malone." I widened my stance. "I'm detaining you three for vandalism of this property and others."

"You're not a cop," the brunette said, running a hand over one leg, wincing at the glass shards still stuck to her. "You don't have a badge."

"No, I'm not, but I can make a citizen's arrest, like any other citizen in this town."

Standing between them and the door, I tried to keep them contained. I didn't want to lose them again, although I did get their license plate number this time at least.

"It's not our fault, ma'am," another blonde said, twirling the ends of her hair, giving me big doe eyes. "This lady yelled at us and told us to leave. That's not the way you treat someone!"

"I'll tell you how you don't treat someone." I lowered my voice, descending on her. "You don't scare and torment shop owners. You don't beat them with a broom. You don't throw their magazines on the ground and kick them! Don't you tell me about how you're supposed to treat someone, you little hellion!"

In that instant, her innocent, little-girl expression dropped, and she growled, running towards me on knee-high boots. I'd never seen anyone run in heels like that. She didn't even slip in the spilled tea.

When she made it to me, I braced and sidestepped, shooting my arm out to sideline her. It caught her in her chest, taking her feet out from under her before she fell hard on her back. She gasped where she lay, trying to get air back into her lungs.

"You're going to regret that," the brunette said, circling me with Demonic Pigtails. Pigtails still held her broom aloft, ready to pummel me. The brunette bent down to get a chunk of the broken bottle large enough to grasp.

I had tried being nice, but apparently, there wasn't an innocent or scared bone in their bodies. And weirdly, they didn't look high, not that I was an expert. They looked way too clear-eyed. Deranged and demoniacal, but not chemically imbalanced.

My right hand snaked behind me to grab my expandable baton from its holster. I deployed it downward, parallel to my leg, bringing it up close to my chest to use as a shield. Miss Innocent had finally gotten control of her breathing and was struggling to get back up. I smirked when she slipped in the tea puddle. *Not so coordinated now.*

"Back up slowly and get down on your knees," I commanded, not really convinced it would do any good.

"Look at her, thinking she can take us down," Pigtails taunted, moving to my left.

"You're going to pay for that," Miss Innocent spat out, still heaving, but having circled around to my right. I spun to keep them both in my view.

The brunette crouched, holding the broken bottle in front of her, her face twisted in anger. More blood dripped down her leg, but her steps were sure-footed.

She lunged, swiping out with the glass. I brought the baton down in a sweep to block the attack, gaze flicking from side to side to keep an eye on the other two. Pigtails swung the broom, trying to build on the attack. I pivoted, whipping my wrist to bring the baton across her exposed left ribs, not as hard as I could, but enough to send a message. She obviously wasn't prepared to block and cried out in pain, jumping back a step.

What were these girls doing out here?

The brunette charged again, stabbing twice, then swiping out at my forearm, getting a minor slash but still drawing blood. Miss Innocent took that moment to jump on my back. I stumbled away, knowing she didn't have a weapon in her hands, running backward to slam her into the wall behind me. She slid off into a squat on the ground, gasping for breath once more.

The other two pounced on me, the glass in the brunette's hand too close for comfort. I lashed out with my baton, striking fast and hard on her forearm and Pigtail's shoulder. They backed off, holding their arms gingerly. A strong baton whip was like being hit with a tire iron.

"Let's try this again, girls," I said, taking a deep breath. I could hear Miss Innocent whimper behind me. "Line up and settle down. We'll see to those cuts on your legs."

A grunting noise was the only thing that warned me before I got hit from behind as Miss Innocent jumped back on me, arms and legs wrapping around me with such force that I was sure she was going to take me down. I stumbled, twisting to brace against the squirming weight. My baton was useless from this angle.

I was knocked forward by a thrust from behind me, but the demon-child backpack I was carrying slid in a heap to the floor. Whirling, I saw Saanvi, standing there like a guardian angel, her metal chair held high, ready for round two.

Immediately, we went back-to-back, watching the final two for their next moves.

"What's it going to be, girls?" I asked, but it didn't matter, because Mathews took that moment to walk in.

"What's going on here?" she said, taking in the scene, her gun drawn. Stevens, another cop I knew from the academy, came in, breaking off to clear the rest of the store.

Miss Innocent started to cry on the floor. "She-she attacked me!"

She pointed to Saanvi, who slowly lowered her chair, her eyes flickering down in fear.

"She threw a jar at me and cut me!" the brunette crowed, tears leaking from her eyes. "I was trying to protect myself but didn't know what to do." The broken bottle held loose in her hands fell in a clatter to the ground as her shoulders collapsed forward and her chest heaved.

I caught Pigtail's eyes narrow at me as she dropped her broom to the ground, backing up. "I saw the whole thing, officers. The Muslim lady attacked us, and the woman helped, screaming something about Allah."

Fear washed over Saanvi's face, draining any light from her eyes.

I had seen a lot in my relatively short career, but I'd never seen a bunch of spoiled teenage children try to set up someone to ruin their lives.

"You stupid girls know there's a camera, don't you?" I shook my head.

All three of them stopped, looking at each other, mouths hanging open.

"What?" Pigtails asked.

"Do you know who my daddy is?" Miss Innocent said, struggling to get up.

Mathews stopped her, slapping cuffs on her hands. She had obviously seen enough to step into the situation. "Can you get me the tape?" she asked Saanvi.

"Uh, of course," she said numbly, still visibly shaken.

Stevens came back in to help to secure the girls.

"We'll need you to come down for a statement once you collect the recording."

"Yes, Officer." She dipped her head in gratitude.

"You too," Mathews nodded to me.

I shrugged. I was spending more time there than I'd like.

The girls continued to argue, a cacophony of dispute that they were being mistreated and there would be hell to pay.

"You good, Malone?" Stevens asked me, eyeing the cut on my arm.

"It's shallow." I wrinkled my chin. "I'll live."

"Do you need to have it seen?"

"Nah." I bent to slam my baton into the tiled floor, collapsing it. "I'm good, but thanks."

He gave me a slight nod, securing Miss Innocent, who gave another whimper before unleashing another stream of insults. "Your boss will be hearing from my mother!"

"And tell Melissa hi for me." I winked to Stevens, watching them walk out.

I knew there was evil out there, but I hadn't seen it quite as firsthand as I did today. Thank goodness at least someone who was wronged was finding justice.

"We're here to make a statement for Officer Mathews," I announced when we walked into the precinct thirty minutes later. I had waited with Saanvi until her husband arrived and reassured them Mathews was a fair cop. Offering them a ride felt like the right thing to do. They both seemed nervous.

The officer on duty nodded, making a note on his notepad, then got up to let us in. "They've got a room ready to see you."

"I know where it is," I nodded, leading the way.

George came to the window and held the door open for me. "Is this twice in one day?"

"Appears so."

"I think you just miss us."

"You have no idea." I clapped him on the shoulder, guiding Saanvi and her husband to the back.

I gave my statement, making sure to tie all the evidence I had to the other encounter and Marty's newsstand vandalism as well. I told them Sam would be in touch with video evidence and repeated the license plate of the yellow convertible.

An hour later, when we were wrapped up. I broke off and headed down the hall. I had hoped to see if Jen was still on the clock, try to talk things out, but ran into Rodriguez instead. It was turning out to be a banner day.

"Mal," he said, jogging to me. "I was looking for you."

"You were?" I frowned. "Why? Do you have another violation to throw at me?"

He squirmed, which felt great, really, but then he spoke.

"George told me you were here." He looked behind him down the hallway. "I know you're out on bail and all, but we've got Noelle in questioning right now. I wondered if you wanted to join us."

Of all that I was expecting, this certainly was not it. He was virtually holding out an olive branch to me. And I wasn't going to bite off my nose to spite my face and refuse it.

"That would be—Thank you," I said, watching him closely.

"We'd leave your presence off the books, of course." He looked down and shuffled his feet.

I hmphed. "Of course." And rolled my eyes as I headed past him to the interrogation rooms.

It wasn't hard to find Noelle; her tear-streaked face looked up in surprise when Rodriguez and I walked in.

"What's she doing here?" she cried, trying to stand. Her feet got caught in the chair legs, and she plunked back down again. "She's who they're after! She's a *bad person*."

"Says who?" I said, hooking a chair with my foot and perching on the edge, leaning forward.

She looked back and forth between Rodriguez, George, and me before taking a deep breath and defiantly facing the lead detective in the room. "Eddie's keeping an eye on her for the cops. He's undercover. I'm not supposed to tell you, but since you're cops too, I guess it's okay. You need to arrest that woman!"

She pointed angrily to me, her story about Eddie needing to borrow my iPhone charger gone. She probably knew the idea that we were friends wouldn't hold up in my presence. The two men flanking me turned to look at me with a frown.

"What'd you do now, Mal?" George guffawed.

"Miss Blair." Rodriguez focused on Noelle. "I will assure you Eddie is not an undercover cop. I ran him through our databases. His file didn't require restricted access, nor did he come up as being a member of the force. But I have to level with you, Miss Blair. Eddie has quite a record."

"He said you would say that." She blew it off. "He didn't always make good choices, and he's very talented at computers. That's why your people recruited him. And he's trying really hard to make amends."

Rodriguez looked at me, his face hard with disappointment. I knew that face. He hated liars as much as I did, which is why I was so hurt by his betrayal.

"I'm sorry to say that's just not true," he said, pulling a file out. "Eddie Leeman is under the employ of a dangerous man."

Her eyes went narrow, wanting to argue, then finally welled with tears. I could see things clicking in place in her head, probably from seeds of doubt she had been carrying.

"I thought..." she stammered. "He was staying at my place to keep an eye on her comings and goings. He needed to get into her apartment."

"Why?"

"He needed to plant a bug."

There it was. Hard evidence that Leeman was behind the bug. I just needed the tie to Dessi.

"Did he mention the name of his boss?" I asked, ignoring the detective's warning look. I wasn't stupid enough to use Dessi's name and get it thrown out for leading the witness.

"No." She frowned, and my heart sunk.

"His boss works for the local mafia. We have reason to believe he's following Detective Malone here for them."

"Detective Malone?" Her voice pitched high. "But you're *crazy*! You come home at all hours of the night, banged up, looking wild. You can't be a cop!"

"I'm not a cop." I sat up straighter. "I'm a private investigator. I have an office downtown, across from Grounds."

"It seems Leeman set you up," Rodriguez said, sliding a notebook and pen in front of her. "I'd like you to write down everything you know."

"But we're in love," she trailed off, eyes unfocused.

Chapter 24

"We've got Eddie set up for questioning next door," Rodriguez said, head tilting to the door to our right. We had left Noelle in the room to make her official statement. "You want to join in one more?"

"Definitely," I said, not liking being monitored in my own home.

"You're going to have to try to stay quiet," he warned me. "I don't want to have to explain to the chief why you're in there."

He was always bending rules. At least this time, it benefited me.

I gave him a tight nod, agreeing to behave.

Eddie Leeman's eyes followed me when we walked in. It looked like it shook him up that I was there. *Good.* He hadn't expected me to have such close ties to the law enforcement in town.

"I think you know Detective Malone?" Rodriguez dropped his file on the table and indicated me casually, without even casting me a glance. George joined us, sitting at the end of the table. "We've got Noelle sitting next door, writing down her full and complete statement, detailing how you used her to keep an eye on the detective, trying to find the best way to break into her apartment."

Leeman's eyes shifted nervously towards the wall behind him, his hands cuffed to the table. Sweat beaded up on his forehead and his upper lip. He knew he'd been had.

"She said you two are pretty close," he said, perusing the case file. Then finally, he raised his head to meet Eddie's face. "It sounds like you got in over your head, Eddie. She even said you were only acting out because of your boss and were nervous about making him happy."

"Uh," he started, his eyes shifting back and forth between us, foot bobbing up and down with pent-up nerves. "My boss?"

Rodriguez nodded understandably, his pen poised over the file. "Just for conversation's sake, who is that exactly?"

Eddie's foot went still, and the blood drained from his face. "I was following her for myself."

Crap.

Man, it was hard to stay silent. I bit the inside of my lip to keep from exploding on him.

"You mentioned your boss, though," Rodriguez continued, looking vaguely interested. "Who is he?"

"Uh." His eyes, opened wide, shifted left to right. He swallowed. "I'm working freelance right now. I don't really have a boss."

"Let's go back to why you planted the bug in the detective's apartment," he redirected.

"I-I was trying to listen in on her."

"That makes sense, Eddie." He nodded. "Just help us understand why. Did someone ask you to?"

"No." He shook his head. "I wanted to get close to her. Because I'm really into her, I-I, uh, think she's really hot."

Rodriguez's nostrils flared, and I could see him attempting to keep his face under control. George did a worse job of it, having to cough to cover his half smirk.

"I see," he said, back under control. "Eddie, I have to say, man. It doesn't look good. You could be charged with stalking, a little B&E, and unlawful surveillance. If someone hired you to do these things, you'd still get a charge, naturally, but it wouldn't be nearly as harsh."

Leeman's foot resumed its nervous bobbing, and he bent over the table, his breathing labored. He looked stressed enough to pass out. "No. It was just me. No one else was involved."

The detective's nose scrunched almost imperceptibly. They had lost this one. He wasn't going to rat on Dessi.

"You know he won't come to save you when you go under, don't you?" He switched tactics, nodding at me, his eyes set. "Why don't you tell him what happened to Mr. Jones."

It was a last-ditch effort but also great timing. "We had an APB out on Jeremy's car," I said, referring to the guy Dessi had paid to take Suzy out. "We found the car fairly soon; Jeremy was much later." I gave Rodriguez and George a sad look, slowly shaking my head. "He was in a bad way when we finally found him *weeks* later."

"Beat up, bruised to shit," George finally spoke up, head down. "He could barely speak. But when he did..."

"When he did, he took all the blame onto himself." Rodriguez's eyes bored a hole into Eddie's. "Guess who's sitting pretty in his comfy office, without a care in the world? And guess who's in a maximum-security prison? I think you get the picture. I'll give you some time to think about it."

We all stood as one, exiting the room. It was like we had practiced or something. But then again, we had.

"Nice work back there," I said, head to one side. "Good timing."

"It's the job." He shrugged it off.

I nodded, then turned to leave.

"Mal." He stopped me.

I waited, turning back to look at him.

"Good luck in the coming weeks."

I pulled a face. "Thanks." I didn't need a reminder. I headed out.

Finally out of the hallway, I took a moment to freshen up in the restroom. The day hadn't gone anything like I expected it to, but then again, when had it? Maybe I needed to change my expectations.

After washing my hands, I grabbed a paper towel, dried them, and tossed it in the bin before leaving. Walking back down the hallway past the interrogation rooms to the offices, I considered stopping in and saying thanks to Rodriguez for letting me sit in on the investigations. Maybe Jen was right.

A giggle from his office made me stop in my tracks. It was the same sound I had heard when I called him Saturday morning. The back part of my brain that told me I should pay attention came alive.

There it was again. I frowned. Did I know that voice?

Finally, it clicked, but not liking the answer, I couldn't leave it without investigating. Closing those last few steps between where I stood and his doorway, I looked in to get all the proof I needed. Rodriguez stood at his desk, an intimate smile spread across his face. Jen stood in front of him, leaning into him, looking up at him like he was a god.

Unfortunately, I knew from prior experience that he was not, in fact, a god. Even though he did slightly resemble one at times.

The non-god in question's eyes flicked to me, seeing me standing there, and went on alert. He froze, stiffening. Jen turned, eyes wide when she registered my presence.

I blew out a snort, spun on my foot, and headed out, ignoring her calls to my back. So, that's why she had tried so hard to clear Det. Scumbag's name with me. And here I had thought she was trying to get us back together.

I had heard enough bullshit today to be able to listen to any more.

Back at my apartment, I poured two hefty fingers of Irish whiskey and sank down on my couch to take the edge off the day. The fingers of my left hand rubbed the back of my neck. *Why couldn't my life be more normal?* It felt like I was running into roadblocks wherever I went, not to mention the sting of betrayal that colored the edges.

How would I deal with the court case coming so soon? I had bluffed my way around Suzy, but deep down, I was pitifully worried about how it was going to turn out. Dessi had the best possible lawyers, and even if Sam and Suzy paid for someone to defend me, it would take someone special to have enough balls to go against Dessi's lawyers. People who opposed him often disappeared.

I took a long sip from my whiskey and settled back in further.

At least the day was over. It was getting late, and I hadn't even eaten yet, but I could handle that in a minute. Remembering I hadn't turned my phone back on after I went into the investigation room, I pulled it out and pressed the power key.

It took a few moments to power up before multiple notifications popped on the screen. I made a mental note to turn more of those off. I hated reminders that weren't phone calls, text messages, or important emails.

My phone dinged again and again, a voicemail icon finally appearing. I sighed; it was probably Jen. I wasn't in the mood to hear what she had to say just yet. I nearly ignored it altogether, until I saw whose name popped up under it, a name that made my heart pause.

Rhodes.

Tapping it, my feet swung to the ground. Hope welled up within me; maybe Suzy was right.

"This is Rhodes." His voice came through haltingly with a little caution. "I, uh, just wanted to call and say thanks." Another pause. I could hear sounds from the fire station in the background. "I wanted you to know your plan worked. My dad showed up. Friday night, actually. Gran acted like he'd never left. Ha! But we, uh. We had a nice visit. And that was all thanks to you, Mal. I just wanted you to know that. No matter what's happened between us. I'll always be grateful for that. So, thanks."

I stared at the phone, trying to process what he had said. I was glad Leaf, er, Aaron had decided to change his mind. The family needed him.

As much as I wanted to hear acceptance in his words after last night's events, I simply didn't. He certainly didn't resume his admiration and dedication as he had the night before. Hell, he hadn't even brought it up.

It sounded more like a goodbye to me.

Chapter 25

"I hope you know what you're doing, Mal," Wyatt said, his face showing up in split-screen with Sam's on my Sam-bot screen. "I didn't like letting Freddy into that sweet little old lady's house."

"Oh, I have a plan," I reassured him, rolling my chair back to my desk to grab my morning coffee. I had let myself sleep in a bit this morning after the night I had, hoping today would be better. Could it really get worse? *Check that. It can always get worse.* "Rosemary knows what's happening, and she's given her blessing to allowing him in. She also said we were free to view her bedroom video if we think he's gotten in."

"So, you have footage of Freddy driving to the house?" Sam asked. "You can tell he broke in?"

"He came back, as we had expected, but was driving a different vehicle. Like that would stop us from paying attention to him." He snorted. "Sam gave me a list of the many ridiculous vehicles he owns. We have footage of him parking down the street. Brian was parked across the street with his lights off. Freddy didn't even pay attention to the car. Idiot. The video shows him entering the house at 2:30 a.m."

"Perfect." I grinned. "And Sam? What did you get?"

"We captured him five minutes later. He must have taken his time, moving quietly inside the house.

He showed up in the sitting room cam, poking around for a few minutes, then crossing to Rosemary's door and entering."

"Creep." Wyatt's mouth wrinkled.

I agreed. His own mother was asleep in the same room he was sneaking into.

"The feed picked up in her room once he moved into view of the jewelry cabinet. He wasn't wearing shoes; he must have taken them off to quiet his steps. He stalled for a moment at the foot of her bed, probably to ensure his mom stayed asleep. Since it's only video, I can't hear if there was any noise from her shifting in the bed or anything. Once he made it to the cabinet, he slowly opened it and removed a few pieces. It looked like a couple of necklaces, a bracelet, and maybe a ring or small earrings? It was hard to tell in the feed. It was clear, had a high pixel content, but it was dark in the room. The model I used has some night-sight capabilities, but since she sleeps in near-total darkness, there's only so much I can do to help that."

The view on the Sam-bot on Sam's side switched over to the feed from Rosemary's room. It was a little faded, but I was surprised to see how much detail it had picked up.

"And the video is time-stamped?" Wyatt asked.

"Yes. So... That's it, then, right?" Sam asked.

"It appears to be." I nodded, confirming the evidence. "It's better than I could have hoped for. Bundle this with the documentation of the jewelry sale on the other piece and our testimonies, and I can't imagine Freddy would have a leg to stand on in court to declare her incompetence. It's obvious he's trying to set her up."

"Good." Wyatt gave a swift, hard nod. "So, what's next? You had a plan?"

"Yes, I'll call Rosemary and fill her in on what happened last night. She probably hasn't noticed the loss of the jewelry yet, but she can confirm what was taken. Sam, if you can keep an eye on the auction site to see if he lists anything, that would be great."

"Way ahead of you." His eyes searched for something off the camera. "I resumed the automated searches once I saw the video."

"With the clear view of him pocketing it, we should be set. But if he lists it, it helps reinforce our case. Any additional evidence at this point is just gravy," I said. "Are you guys free tonight?"

"Tonight?" they answered in unison.

"Rosemary and I have a plan. She's ready to confront Freddy once we have the right evidence, which we do. I'll text the time after I talk to her."

"Are the cops coming too?" Wyatt asked, eyes narrowed.

"Not yet." I shook my head. "But I'm hoping she'll allow us to call them in once it all comes out."

"And you want me there?" Sam asked, eyes shiny with excitement.

"Hell, yeah." I tilted my head. "You're part of this team, and you have to explain all that technical jargon. We need you. And Wyatt, I could use the extra muscle if any of Rosemary's staff are involved."

"I doubt it, but I'll be there." He gave a short nod before his connection flicked off.

Sam's face filled the screen. "Tomorrow morning clears the forty-eight hours. Dessi's likely cleared the room as much as he's going to. I'm going to turn on the audio feed for the bug and cross my fingers."

"Thanks." I wasn't sure what I'd do without him.

"It's a live feed, so I'll record them and send them to you to review too. It only turns on when it recognizes voices, but it might still be a bit to wade through."

"That's okay. Believe me, I'm ready for this. I'm going to follow up on every possible lead. If they're meeting in Lincoln Park one day and Park Ridge the next, it doesn't matter. I'll be there, watching."

"I have a parabolic mic and a sound amplifier you can use," he said helpfully. "You can pick up audio from your car unless they're in a building, then you'll need to get closer."

"That's great, Sam. I'll need it."

"Mal?" he asked, his face serious. "I really appreciate everything you've done for Suze and me. I was so afraid when I came to you. And you've stuck with us this whole time."

"You really don't get it," I said, lowering my head. "You two have done more for me in the past few months than anyone ever has. You're both helping with my business, but you've also become family to me."

"We *are* family," he emphasized.

"Exactly." I gave him a half smile. "We've got each other's backs."

"That's why we want to help out with a lawyer."

Ah, so that's why he decided to get all touchy-feely this morning.

"I really appreciate it. I do," I said, ignoring his rebuttals. "But it's not going to be a big deal. I've honestly got this. My investigative license allows for all sorts of these things. Dessi's just grasping at straws."

He studied my expression like he wasn't sure he believed me. "But his lawyers are good, Mal."

"I know, but I'm really not worried. He's just trying to shake me. I'm good, honest."

"Okay." He pursed his lips. "But please keep it in mind."

"Will do, Sam. Thanks."

Looking up from the now-blank screen of the Sam-bot, I saw Suzy standing in the doorway.

"Did you put him up to that?" I asked lightheartedly, leaning back casually in my chair.

"Had to try again. Can't fault a girl for it."

"Never." I smiled. "But I'm all good here, thanks."

She nodded, stepping into the room.

"Did you think any more on calling Rhodes?" She sat down in the chair across from me, leaning forward, her soft brown eyes looking concerned.

"I didn't have to." My mouth twisted. "He called me."

Her eyebrows raised hopefully.

"Don't get excited just yet." I raised a hand, continuing, "I had my phone off while I was at the precinct, giving my statement against the girls."

She nodded, her and Sam having been briefed when I came in that morning. "And?"

"I missed his call, but he left a voicemail." I paused, shaking my head. "Leaf showed up at Miss Ellie's Friday night. He was just thanking me for that."

"Did he bring up his visit at Red?"

"Not a word."

"He did say the ball was in your court," she said helpfully. "He was so sure that night. I heard everything he said. Maybe he's just waiting for your answer."

"Things changed back there. He didn't ask me to return his call. That voicemail was goodbye, Suz."

"If that's what you want to do." She stood and walked back to the door. "But if it were me, I wouldn't let pride stand between Sam and me. Never have."

I watched her back as she walked away, wishing it was that easy. A little voice in the back of my head said *maybe it is,* but the black hole of fear surrounding it squashed it.

Fiddling with my pencil, I tried to push my brain onto the next thing on my to-do stack. It was easier than the content presently filling it. Finally finding my way through the muck, I picked up my phone and called Rosemary.

"Ms. Lamb speaking."

"Hi! It's Mal," I said. "It's official. We've got what you wanted."

"You do?" she asked, voice soft. "I guess it's time, then."

"He visited last night. You should be missing a few more pieces of jewelry."

"A few?" She sounded surprised. "The boy's getting greedy."

I hated hearing the pain in her voice. I couldn't imagine what it felt like to have your own child going against your back.

"Can you verify and catalog what's missing?"

"Of course. And I'm protected should it go bad?"

"Entirely," I assured her. "We have videotapes, sales documentation, everything to confront him safely. It's time. Just tell me when you want us there."

We settled on a time that night. I'd ask Wyatt's guys to drop us off earlier so Freddy wouldn't suspect anything.

My ringing phone broke me from final tweaks on the night's plan.

"Hello?" I answered it.

"Mal? This is Officer Mathews. I wanted to thank you for last night's statement. It looks like the end of the story for those girls. I'm so glad you called me. I've been looking for them for quite a while now."

"Your number is one of the few I keep on my phone." I shrugged, not that she could see. "So, were they arrested?"

"They will be, and the evidence you gave us is enough to make the charges stick. They'll be released on bail, most likely."

"Even with the vandalism they caused? Surely, they're still a threat to the shop owners."

"Even so, but rest assured the parents are good and embarrassed. I don't think we'll have trouble with them supporting us going forward."

"Oh, yeah?"

"They put the fear of God in them." She laughed.

"I'm glad someone finally did." I shuttered, remembering their fearless faces.

"And a few of the cops around here might be giving them a much-needed lesson in respect. We're holding them the full forty-eight hours before we officially charge them, just to delay paperwork on bail."

"How're they holding up?"

"No makeup, no internet? No one caring about anything they say?" she chuckled. "You can guess."

"Fantastic." I leaned back in my chair, putting an arm behind my head. "But they really caused some damage. I hope they're going to be held accountable for that. Their parents obviously haven't been very hands-on."

"Oh, they're going to be. They all assured me they would have supervision on them at all times, even if they have to hire someone."

"A babysitter. I guess it's better than nothing."

"Suppose so. With the money these families have, I don't think I stand a chance in hell of withholding bail, so I was happy with the compromise. And make no mistake, they're going to be charged. I've already talked to the DA; we're going to attempt to charge them as adults. It might not hold up—they're barely seventeen—but it'll at least pack a punch in what happens to them."

"Thanks. Did you tell Saanvi yet?"

"I already called her and another shop owner across town. Marty is next. You know him, right?"

"Yes, he's just down the street from the office. He will be glad to hear they're off the street and that his stand should be safe."

"At least from the girls. Can't guarantee something else won't develop, but we're doing what we can."

"We appreciate it," I said, hanging up.

Marty was watering plants on his display when I stopped by later that afternoon. He stopped when he saw me, a wide smile spreading across his face. I guess Mathews had already gotten ahold of him.

He bypassed the coffee I was holding out towards him, ignoring it to pull me into a big hug. Laughing, I struggled not to spill it or the one I had brought for myself.

"Thanks, Mal!" he said earnestly when he pulled away, his hands clasped together in front of him. "You don't know what this means to me."

"I didn't do much, Marty," I said. "I don't mind keeping an eye on this neighborhood. We all work together to keep each other safe."

"Well, I am deeply appreciative. I didn't know what to do about them. You were the only person I could think of to come to."

"I'm happy you did. If you hadn't, I wouldn't have recognized them at the convenience store."

"I can't do much," he said, looking over at his small newsstand. "But I'd like to offer you free newspapers whenever you need one."

"Really?" I said, eyebrows up. "That's actually going to save me a lot of money. You know I have to keep up to speed with all the local news."

Turning to grab the top paper off a stack nearby, he held it out to me, his chest puffed up with pride at being able to offer something in return.

"Thanks." I held it up, turning to leave. "Have a nice day."

"You too." He nodded lightly. His hands stuffed in his back pockets, rocking back on his heels. He cast a look to the sky. It was a nice, clear afternoon with surprisingly few clouds. He seemed at peace on his bustling little corner of Roscoe Village while the cars whizzed by.

I needed that. It was something I had gotten right today. I hoped it boded well for the evening's plans.

Chapter 26

"Mo-om!" Freddy hollered, stomping through the house to the living room. "Nathan had to let me in. What's the meaning of this?"

Skidding to a halt when he saw me standing next to Rosemary's chair, fury zipped through him, igniting his eyes.

"Hello, Frederick." Rosemary stood. "Thank you for agreeing to come over this evening."

He pursed his lips, his chin jutting out. "And what's *she* doing here? I thought we talked about this. I was going to handle any press conversations."

"I'm not with the press, Freddy." I stepped forward, standing side by side with Rosemary. "I was helping your mom with a personal matter."

"I think you need to get out of this house." He grunted. "I need to talk to my mother in private. You can wait outside."

"She will *not*," Rosemary said, chin raising. "She's going to stay."

"I have something to show you." I walked over to the side table. Opening a box that was sitting on it, I pulled out the diamond necklace inside, moving so he could see it."

"What the hell do you think you're doing with that?" His face twisted as he stalked towards me. He shook so hard in his anger, the drape in his linen pants rippled. He snatched it from me. "Give that to me; that's mine!"

"It's not, actually," Rosemary spoke up, causing him to spin around in shock. "It's mine. And I paid her to find it."

"It's not yours. It's partially *mine!*" His nose pointed upward, perfectly layered hair shifting backward with the jolt. "Dad paid for it."

"And he gave it to me, not you. He also left all his money to me in his will. Interestingly enough, I paid two times for that particular necklace. You unwisely listed it for far less than its actual worth."

"I have no idea what you're talking about," he started to backtrack.

"That's okay. My team has all the evidence showing you put it up for sale and documented the money transfer into your account. That should be enough to jog your memory." I gave him my back, walking across the room. "You have more than just that, though, don't you, guys?"

Sam and Wyatt entered the room when I addressed them, causing a string of profanities to spew from Freddy's mouth. I was glad Sam had foregone a costume tonight. The evening's affair might have felt a little differently had he worn his Jedi robes. Although his T-shirt still clearly bore a photo of baby Yoda.

"I'd ask you not to talk like that in front of your mother," Wyatt growled. "But sadly, you lack any manners or common sense."

"You all need to leave right now!" Freddy commanded, attempting to gain control of the situation.

"I think you're done giving orders," I said, mouth in a thin line.

"I don't know what you're implying." He looked around the room, then shifted away from Wyatt's angry glare. "I'm sure this can all be explained."

"I have you on camera, entering Ms. Lamb's estate last night at 2:30 a.m. It shows you going to her private bedroom and taking several pieces of jewelry while she herself was in the room, asleep," Sam filled in, flicking on the TV at one end of the room. Videos and photographs flicked over the screen. "I have photographs of her jewelry cabinet before and after the robbery, plus proof of the robbery. Proof of breaking and entering her house. We have witnesses who saw you driving around her house the night before but were chased off by the security team she had hired to protect herself. A security team you vehemently objected to her contracting. And finally, we have the piece of jewelry you stole previously, sold online, and collected money from its sale. The financial information is all documented as well. There is *nothing* to explain. The facts speak for themselves."

The visual of Freddy's hunched-over form creeping through his mother's room was the most difficult to watch, and I heard him gulp out loud when it came onto the screen, clear and unable to deny.

"It's a deep fake," his voice shook.

"It's not," Sam said calmly. "And I have the original recording, with its untouched digital fingerprint."

A hush fell over the room as Freddy weighed his odds. It was apparent his goose was proverbially cooked. Panic replaced his fury as he began backtracking with a seriousness that belied his situation.

"It was all Jonathan's idea," he expelled all at once. "He talked me into it, saying we needed to do it for your own health and welfare."

"Do you honestly think I'm senile?" Rosemary spoke up.

"Uh, no?" he said quietly. "I, uh, Jonathan—"

"Jonathan what?" I asked.

"Jonathan said part of that money was rightfully mine. I was just taking it back." Splotchy red and white patches appeared on his cheeks. "He-he said Dad meant for me to have a comfortable lifestyle and that she should be sharing more of it with me."

"He did, did he?" his mother asked quietly. "Do you honestly think your lifestyle isn't comfortable enough? I've given you all you ever wanted, probably too much. I've bailed you out at every turn. Not now. Freddy, son, I love you, but you're going to have to answer for your choices.

Freddy collapsed on the sofa, head cradled in his hands, crying.

"But, Mother!" he wailed, lifting his head. "I'm your son! You can't just turn me over to the cops. How can you treat me like this? I made a mistake. I know I make lots of mistakes, but I just have a harder time than most. It's not been easy on me, losing Dad. I no longer have a male role model."

"Oh, I could turn you over to the cops, pretty easily, in fact, and I probably should. But I'm not going to. You're still my son, and this was your house, growing up, so I'm not going to, but you're cut off, Freddy. Completely."

"What am I going to do for money?" he whined.

"I think you're going to have to get a job."

"But I don't have any skills. I've never been prepared for anything like this."

"What about that expensive degree your father and I paid for?"

"Marketing?" he huffed, his nose running. "I was never going to be in marketing. I just picked whatever seemed the easiest."

"After changing your major three times."

He shrugged, wiping his nose on his linen jacket sleeve.

"All of this is on record so you don't get my power of attorney. If you do well over the next few years and learn a lesson, you'll still be in my will and get your portion of your dad's money. But you won't get mine; it's going to charity or wherever else I decide to put it."

He looked up, his red-rimmed eyes hopeful.

"You're not getting free rein of this house. You're not even going to have a key. Sentinel Security's already changed the locks and set up the security cameras. It was done today. You'll have to knock, just like everyone else."

I had to admit I was a little disappointed in her for not calling the cops on him, but then again, I'd never had a kid. At least she was making him pay, in her own way. I just hoped she held to her decisions.

"He's here," Wyatt said suddenly, looking out the window. "I'll let him in and get the others."

"Who's here?" Freddy said, looking frightened. "I thought you weren't calling the cops."

"Are you ready?" I asked Rosemary, ignoring the spoiled adult brat.

"As ready as I'll ever be."

A few minutes later, Wyatt led a surprised Jonathan, Nathan, Hillary, Rachel, and Tommy into the room. Rosemary had asked the rest of the crew over earlier, leaving them to wait in the backroom for a house meeting where she had wanted to talk to Freddy alone first.

"What's going on here, Rosemary?" Jonathan asked, studying everyone's body language.

The rest of the group cast fearful glances back and forth between themselves. We had already worked out that Jonathan was involved, but we wanted to make sure the rest of them were innocent. I didn't want to leave her with them if they had been plotting against her as well.

The images of Freddy were still playing on the screen, exhibiting his deceit.

"I think you know what's going on," I answered for her.

"Surely, you don't think I had anything to do with this." He gestured to the screen, his mouth turned down in disgust.

"She's got us, Jonathan," Freddy said, his head back in his hands where he sat on the couch.

"I don't know what you're referring to," he said in a haughty tone.

"They know everything. It's too late." He crumbled into a sodden mess.

"As you can surely make out, I'm no reporter," I filled Jonathan in. "You see, I got to thinking. Why did you call Paul to verify my story instead of Freddy?"

"Frederick seemed so worried about his mom; I offered to help out," he said evenly. "I often help my clients with trivial matters. It's just part of the service I offer that makes me so different from my competitors. And what makes them stay devoted clients."

"So, I had Sam look into you," I went on, ignoring how well he stroked his own ego. "You're not so innocent."

"Why, what ever do you mean?"

"Sam, you want to relay your findings?"

"I'd be happy to." He beamed. "All of your clients are older people. You've wormed your way into several of their wills. Those you haven't, you've charged well over the normal fees to manage their wealth." He made air quotes over the word *managed*.

"It's not my fault if my clients choose to leave me in their will." He shrugged. "There's no law against it. Who am I to refuse?"

"I'm sure you had more to do with that than you're leading us to believe." My eyes tightened at the corners. "They probably thought you were executing their will with that benevolence."

"I'm still not hearing any hard facts here." He sighed. "Rosemary, I'm sorry you feel I was connected to your son's unfortunate acts, but I'll be in my office next week, should you want to discuss it further. We can take whatever legal actions you'd like on your funds long term. I hope you have a lovely weekend."

He turned to leave.

"Is that why you secured a lawyer against Ms. Lamb?" Sam spoke up, causing Jonathan to halt in his tracks. "And a doctor who specializes in determining competency in the elderly? Who has a record of declaring them incompetent?"

"How did you find that out?" He turned back to us, sneering, his true colors finally emerging.

"I should probably tell you, Sam there is a whiz with computers." I gave him a sideways grin. "You'd never guess what he was able to find."

"I told you they have us, Jonathan," Freddy said, his head hanging low.

"Shut up, you stupid imbecile," Jonathan shouted. "If you would have just been less greedy, no one would have known about the jewelry. We'd have gotten the payload."

"Charles always believed in you." Rosemary shook her head at Jonathan.

"He was just as stupid as his son," he spat out.

"I wouldn't say you're all that smart either." I shook my head. "You're going down for your own dishonesty."

"You'll never be able to prove that." He smiled. "However he got that information, it was gathered illegally."

"I'm so sorry, Ms. Lamb," Nathan said suddenly from where he was listening, hovering with his coworkers. "I too have betrayed you."

"What did you do, Nathan?" she asked.

"I called Freddy whenever you had a visitor and reported it to him." He looked forlornly at the floor. "I shouldn't have done it, but he made me believe it was in your best interest. He was worried about you and claimed he needed to know if people were here to bother you. You have a large estate, financially, and are subject to a lot of people trying to get ahold of it. I thought, coming from your son, it was okay."

"That's okay." She cast him a kind expression. "I knew you wouldn't betray me."

His eyes filled with guilt. "That's not entirely true." He took in a large breath and let it out before he continued, "There's more. He told us that if we didn't listen to him, we'd be fired as soon as he gained control of your money. I'm so sorry, ma'am. I was—we were—all frightened. But I promise you, I never gave him any more details. I only told him when someone came over."

"That's how he knew when I was visiting Rosemary," I reflected.

"Me too." Wyatt frowned. "He nearly chased me off the property."

"I hated doing it. I thought it was a good thing that she was getting security," he said enthusiastically. "I hated the thought of her here, alone. I wanted her safer, too. After that, I really questioned what Freddy meant about getting control of her money. It didn't sound like he had her best interests at heart, even though that's what he kept saying."

"Were all of you approached by Freddy?" Rosemary asked the rest of the crew.

They all looked down, distraught.

"I was the only one who notified Freddy, though," Nathan spoke up.

"Is that true?"

They all looked at each other, then nodded.

"But you were tempted," she clarified.

They all nodded again.

"That's only because he threatened our jobs," Hillary finally spoke up, giving Freddy an evil look, dark enough that he melted into the couch. "I didn't do as he asked, but he said we'd lose our jobs if we didn't support him. I admit I considered it, albeit briefly. I'll accept my consequences."

She cast an embarrassed look in Wyatt's direction before looking back at the floor.

"That's understandable. And easy to fix. I'll grant you all a severance package should anything happen to me. I should have done it anyway."

"Are you serious?" Hillary said, her eyes shining. "You're not going to fire us for what we said here?"

"Of course not, child." She shook her head.

"It looks like that's it," I said. "It was only Freddy and Jonathan. Your crew supported you the whole time."

"Of course," Freddy said sourly. "Her perfect crew wouldn't do anything like that."

"I think I'm done here," Jonathan spoke back up, turning to go.

"Not quite." I raised a finger to get his attention. "Sam said that was the final piece of evidence, but it's not really. It's this conversation. It's all on camera." I pointed to a small camera on the table. Mr. Gladstar, your confession has been recorded."

"You can't record me without my consent," he exploded, enraged.

Wyatt stepped forward, between him and Rosemary. "We can if we're in a private residence."

"Can we please call the cops on him?" I asked regarding Jonathan.

"Oh, yes, definitely," Rosemary said with a decisive nod.

Smirking, I dialed Officer Mathews. It would be twice in one week, but she would appreciate the apprehension record.

Maybe it was a good day, after all.

The next morning, we all sat, anxiously waiting for Sam to turn on the audio from the bug I had hastily stashed under a chair in Red's back conference room.

Suzy and I sat in my office, focused on the Sam-bot on the floor, watching Wyatt's face from where he sat in his SUV and Sam's face as he worked to activate the feed.

I think we were all holding our breaths as the signal came on, fuzzy and quiet at first.

"I just have to adjust the frequency." His eyes narrowed as he worked to configure it.

The static cleared up, then resumed as he typed on his computer until it finally cleared and we could hear low voices.

"I think that's it." He leaned towards his computer's speaker. "Hang on."

I could hear some sounds, but they were faint.

"That may just be hallway voices," he said. "It'll likely be louder when they're in the actual conference room."

"That's Dessi," I said, straining to hear. "And I can hear other people."

"Back at the warehouse," the words rang out clear as day.

The side of Sam's cheek raised slightly in a grimace. "That may be the bug's location. I'm wondering if the speaker got jammed when it was placed."

"Jammed?" I asked.

"If you mashed it hard, it might have warped the side of the microphone. I expected some distortion due to its placement at the table, but not this acute."

"Well, I was fighting off someone trying to stop me at the time," I said defensively.

"It's not your fault," Sam said offhandedly. "It's the bug. It's delicate at that size, but we needed it to get any level of precision in the audio file."

We all listened dejectedly at partial conversations, bummed it wasn't better. We had put all our eggs in this basket.

"I'm sorry, Mal." Sam's forehead scrunched in frustration.

"It's okay, Sam. It's still better than we had before." I fought the feeling of failure. "We'll still get leads. Tonight, it looks like we're going to be sitting at the warehouse. See what happens."

"We?" he said, forehead smoothing out.

Suzy caught my eye and smiled, thankful.

"We." I nodded.

"Need me there?" Wyatt asked.

I shook my head. "We'll call if we get into any trouble."

It wasn't what I had been hoping for, but it was something. We might just have to wait a little while longer. I just hoped that after my court date, I'd still be around to follow up on the leads too.

Chapter 27

Sitting in the hall outside the courtroom, I fiddled with my hair, trying to calm down the curls in order to look more presentable. Now that the day was here, I was wondering why I had so strongly rejected help from the Mennons. I had felt in way over my head, but I hadn't wanted to bring them down with me, whatever happened.

Dessi's lawyer sat across the hallway from me, face set solemnly, refusing to look at me. His suit looked like it cost more than I had in my business bank account. Brushing lint off the black slacks I had picked up at Zara, I sat up a little straighter.

The click of the door beside me ratcheted up my heart rate, knowing that my fate would soon be decided.

"The State versus Molly Malone," the bailiff called out from the door, holding it open.

Awkwardly, I rose, gathering the notes I had brought with me from preliminary research in my defense.

Mr. Fancy Pants rose elegantly, lifting his briefcase, and followed, his mouth pursed lightly. It looked like he already knew what was going to happen. My heart dropped to my stomach, where it felt like it melted in an acid bath called despair.

It looked like Dessi wasn't going to show, so sure his lawyer would handle the situation to his benefit. I watched the door, despondent at my insistence in doing this alone. Again.

Just before the bailiff closed the door, though, Maurice walked in, decked out in a suit and tie, file folder in hand.

What was he doing here?

Nodding to the judge, he took the empty seat next to me and leaned in. "Morning, Mal."

I could smell the scent of coffee grounds drifting off him, and I wondered if his entire house smelled like the heavenly bean.

"What are you doing here, Mo?" I asked under my breath.

"What does it look like?" He straightened his tie. "I'm saving your ass."

"But do you even know what you're doing?"

"Do you think I was always a coffee-store owner?" He raised an eyebrow. "Honestly, Mal."

"But how did you know to come?" I asked, amazed. "Did Suzy ask you?"

"Arrests are public record."

My mouth hung open dumbly for a moment while the judge called the room to order.

Maurice stood up, taking command of the case from my perspective, setting the stage with Dessi's lawyer, Mr. Kingston, each dressing the other down. I sat nervously, astounded by the side of my friend I'd never seen before. My mind replayed every conversation I ever had with him. No wonder he was always asking good questions when I ran through cases with him.

They called James in for his statement. Mr. Kingston asked questions that laid out my actions the night of July fourth.

It was Maurice's turn to question the witness.

"James." He looked at him. "Was the defendant here a regular at the speakeasy known as Red?"

"Yes."

"Had you had any previous issues with her?"

"No, sir." He looked nervously at Mr. Kingston.

"Hadn't you gotten along before the night in question?"

"How is that relevant?" Mr. Kingston broke in.

"I'm trying to understand the witness's relationship to the defendant."

"Overruled," the judge spoke up. "I'm curious."

"Yes, we got along." James swallowed.

"Didn't you see her heading to the backroom?"

"Yes, but—"

"Was there anyone in the room?" Maurice cut him off.

"N-No, but—"

"Did you see her break anything or cause any issues there?"

"She ran into someone." He glanced at Mr. Kingston.

"Did she hit them?"

"No."

"Did that person go to the hospital?"

"No."

"No further questions, Your Honor," he said. "Unless they have any real proof, any video evidence that she was drunk, broke anything, or hit anyone, I'm requesting this sham to be excused so we can all go home."

"Mr. Kingston?" the judge asked. "Any further evidence or witnesses to call?"

"No, sir," he answered, his nostrils flaring.

"I'm forced to call the case due to lack of evidence. The court finds the defendant not guilty." He slammed his gavel down and shook his head. "The court is adjourned."

The corner of Mo's lips curled up as he leaned into me. "He never had anything, Mal. Dessi was just trying to shake you."

I nodded numbly as we made our way out of the courtroom and walked down the hall.

"Dot your I's and cross your T's for a while," he advised, watching Mr. Kingston approach.

"Mr. Dessi intends to file a restraining order." He narrowed his eyes at Mal.

"On what charges?" Maurice asked, challenging the other lawyer.

"Harassment."

"Have fun with that," he scoffed, leading me away. To me, he said, "That won't stick either. But they'll probably have you on a list, barring you from entering Red. Don't try that one again."

"I won't."

"Without the restraining order, it'll all be dependent on who's at the front door, letting people in, but still, it's not a good idea to go back in there. I'm serious, Mal. They know who you are."

"I won't, Mo," I promised.

"I know I can't keep you from following him." His lips pressed firmly. "I care about Suzy too. I want to see him locked away as much as you do, but as long as he doesn't actually file that restraining order, you won't get charged for following him and being in his proximity. If he does, lay low at least until it goes to court. I'll represent you. It won't hold up."

"Thanks, Mo." I hugged him, comforted by his support. But I was still worried. "I just hope I can succeed. I'm doing what I can, but it feels like I'm taking one step forward, two steps back."

"You'll figure it out." He clapped me on the back. "You just need to figure out his biggest weakness. Then exploit it."

Hmm. That gave me something to think about. "I'll work on it."

"Now, onto more important manners." Pulling at his tie, he yanked it over his head and stuffed it in his pocket.

"What's that?" I hurried to keep up as he strode down the hallway to the metal detectors at the exit.

"What kind of coffee do you want to celebrate? I'm thinking maybe a lavender-rosemary latte. I made a simple syrup last night."

"Sounds wonderful." I smiled. I had opened my heart to my friends more in the past year, but I hadn't really learned to trust them. Maybe I needed to stick my neck out and ask for help sometimes, even when it wasn't comfortable. It was just so much easier to be the one helping and not the one asking. Less fear of rejection.

After a celebratory cup of coffee and a retelling of the events to Suzy and Sam, I sat at my desk. It was such a weight lifted off my shoulders. It was a relief to know I would be there to stay on the case and see it till the end.

Reflecting, I stared at my phone, the knowledge that I needed to open my heart more eating away at me.

Taking a steadying breath, I picked it up. It answered on the first ring.

"Mal," Jen's voice said.

"Hey."

"I'm really sorry. I can't imagine how that looked," she rushed to explain.

"I know how it looked. It looked like you're in a relationship of some sort with Rodriguez." I paused. "And while that means I'm questioning your sanity and think you should go to the nearest hospital to request an STD and maybe a sobriety test… I'm happy if you're happy."

Jen made a muted sound, then said, "Thanks, Mal."

"I wish you would have told me about it, though."

"I tried. I really did."

"The conversation on the way to Red," I said, remembering our argument in her car.

"Yeah, but it didn't go as planned. I'm sorry I got pissy about it; I just didn't know how to handle it, and I handled it badly."

"I get it. I do that too sometimes." My mind went back to when I pushed Rhodes on the subject of my job.

"So, you're not upset I'm dating him? He *is* your ex."

"Oh, have at him. I certainly don't want him." I laughed, rocking back in my chair. "But I would keep an eye on the situation. You know his history."

"I do, and I think it's different with us. That's not to say you two weren't a great couple. Hell, back then, we all thought you guys were the perfect couple. But…" She trailed off.

"Times have changed, and so have we." I relented. "We were both very passionate people and fought just as much as we got along."

"Exactly."

"Not really a forever match."

"Does this mean you'll forgive me?"

"Of course. What are friends for?"

"And you'll come over and hang out at Hungry Brain soon? Rodriguez and George told me about your court case. We could celebrate."

"With you two? Together?" I mulled that over. "I can do that, but don't expect me to let up on Rodriguez. I might double down a little harder now that he's got you to live up to. I'm never going to think he's worthy of you, Jen."

"Thanks, Mal." I could hear her smile over the phone. "And don't worry; I wouldn't expect anything less."

Another chunk of my heart fell back into place, making me feel better after mending things with Jen.

As soon as I hung up the phone, it rang again. It was Rodriguez. What were the odds?

"Hello?"

"Uh, hi, Mal," he said nonchalantly, as if nothing was wrong.

"Yes?" I said, not ready to give him a break just yet.

"I heard the good news. I'm glad Dessi didn't get away with it. I heard you had a good lawyer."

"Thanks. I did."

"And I wanted to fill you in on Leeman. Dessi lawyered him up too." He huffed. "I thought after our questioning the other night, we might have a chance with him, get him to talk, but an unannounced lawyer arrived for him."

"Let me guess. It was Mr. Kingston."

"You got it. Once he showed up, Leeman clammed right up, refused to say another word. The man was terrified. Took the fall, hook, line, and sinker."

"While Dessi walks free."

"Just like you said he would."

"And Noelle?"

"She's facing some light accomplice charges, but since it doesn't seem she was acting out of malice and she has no criminal history, my guess is she'll get a slap on the wrist and a little probation."

"That's good." I nodded. She just got in over her head. Too bad she didn't have any friends to bail her out. She had found the wrong kind of friends.

"Okay, well." The line went quiet as he paused. "About what you saw the other day."

"Yes?" I couldn't help but smile. I was enjoying this a little too much.

"I just wanted to say. You know now that Jen and I are together."

"I do."

"I think you should call her, Mal. She's really torn up about this. You two have been friends since the academy."

"I just got off the phone with her."

"You did? Well, shit." He blew out. "And you're letting me go on and on like an idiot."

"You *are* an idiot, Rodriguez."

A grunt of surprise came over the phone. "You're going to keep that up?"

"You bet," I said, smiling as I hung up.

An hour later, I was bent over, making final notes in Rosemary Lamb's case, glad things had wrapped up the way they had. I should have completed it earlier, but the stress of the looming trial had really taken its toll on me. Between that and following up on the two leads we had, which ended up being absolutely nothing as of yet, I hadn't taken a moment to let myself reflect on anything else.

Jonathan Gladstar would get his due rewards, and Freddy would too, even if they were a little less than he truly deserved. He was still miserable and learning his own lesson, which soothed my nerves at least a little. The best part was that her team, her own group of people she relied on, still had her back. I felt satisfied that she was safe in that big house all by herself.

A light tap on my door brought my head up.

"I'm sorry to bother you, Mal." Marty stuck his head in, pulling his ball cap off.

"You're no bother," I said, standing up. "Please come in."

"I brought you your paper." He held it aloft. "You didn't come by for it today."

"Thanks, Marty. You're a savior." I walked around my desk to take it. "I've been a bit busy today."

"I also wanted to come by and update you on the trio."

"The trio?"

"The girls," he clarified

"What's happened?"

"Well, they've been officially arrested, but are out on bail. Their parents bailed them out; Officer Mathews said to expect that." He grinned suddenly, his eyes sparkling. "Their parents brought them by, made them apologize to me."

"They did?" I was glad to hear that. Apparently, they were doing something right, even if it was a bit late. "How'd that go over?"

"Well, they're pretty scared right now, and really unhappy, especially that brown-haired one."

I snorted. "I bet."

"The parents, they're keeping them under house arrest, but not together, mind you. They're not allowed any freedom, any internet, or cell phones. They're really miserable." He beamed. "I think the parents are hoping they'll learn a bit of a lesson and not be as mouthy when they go in front of the judge."

"That would be a good move."

"Anyway, the only freedom they have is twice a week, they come by and sweep my street corner and pick up a bit. I've got them scraping off old gum and stuff, all the crappy jobs." He chortled in laughter, and I couldn't help but join him. "All monitored, of course."

"How long does that go on?"

"Until their court date, however long that is." He shrugged. "But I'm going to milk it while I've got it."

"I would too," I agreed. "Sounds like fair punishment to me. Are they learning anything?"

"I don't know yet," he said, looking down at the hat in his hands. "But I hope so."

Chapter 28

Locking up, I headed out to grab some dinner before going home and listening through another day's worth of audio. It was recording approximately six hours a day, mostly offhanded remarks coming down the hallway. The plan was to split it between Sam and me, but more often than not, we each listened to it all, worried the other would miss something. We hadn't recorded any decent length of conversation, indicating a meeting in the conference room, but I was still hopeful. We were a week and a couple of days down on our four-to-six weeks. Even if it wasn't fun, I'd continue to listen to the recording in the background of whatever else I was doing.

But I had another stop to make before all of that.

There was still one item outstanding on my to-do list, another uncomfortable conversation I needed to stick my neck out on. Vulnerability wasn't my strong suit, but I had dual purposes for the visit. So if it all went south, I could backtrack and still get out partially unscathed. It was something.

Standing in front of Rhodes' house, I raised my hand to knock. I knew he parked in the garage, so I couldn't tell if he was home or not. A dim light shone through his curtains, so there was a good chance. And I knew it wasn't his workday. *Crap, I was stalling, and I knew it.*

Letting my hand fall, I rapped it against the door, quickly and succinctly.

Nothing happened right away, and I worried I had knocked too quietly. Or maybe he wasn't home. The thought didn't fill me with the relief I had expected.

Before I could try again, the door opened, bringing with it the scent of grilled meat. Rhodes stood there, barefoot, in a cutoff T-shirt and worn jeans, wiping his hands on a towel. His eyebrows raised in surprise when he saw me.

"Mal," he said, throwing the towel over his shoulder. "I wasn't expecting to see you."

"I know." I cast my eyes down. That wasn't exactly a welcoming reply. "I'm sorry to bother you at home. I probably should have called."

"That's okay." He turned to cast a look behind him. I hoped to God he didn't have anyone there with him. "It's just that I have food on the grill."

"I'm sorry. Of course." I sidestepped. "I can come back. Or call you later."

"Do you want to come in?" he finally said, stepping aside. "We can talk out back."

I hesitated, not if he had another girl here. I didn't need that kind of embarrassment. But surely, he wouldn't have invited me in if he did. Taking a chance, I nodded. "Sure."

Following him through a house I hadn't been in since our date night months ago, I felt my trepidation increase from the mixture of memories that arose.

He walked out onto the wooden deck that I remembered him saying he and a few of the other firefighters had built after he bought the place. Hurrying to the grill, he opened it, letting out a billow of smoke.

"I hope it didn't burn." I winced.

"Nah, it's okay." He turned to toss a smile back at me, then quickly went back to flip burgers and turn brats. After adjusting the heat, he wiped his hands again and flicked the towel back to his right shoulder before turning his attention to me. "Now, what can I help you with?"

Oh boy, my turn. Here it goes.

"Well," I started, unable to find the right words. "I got your message. Sorry it took me so long to get back in touch. I'm so glad your dad came."

He gave a short nod. "I'm really grateful you went back and gave it another shot. I wasn't going to. It means a lot to me that you did that for Gran and me."

"I know." I shrugged. "I'm an impartial party. It makes it easier for me to have the conversation."

"I kind of screwed that up, didn't I?" He looked at me, meeting my eyes.

"You were emotional. You had your reasons."

He nodded.

"It sounds like you all mended some fences," I said, not ready to dive into the nitty-gritty.

"I wouldn't quite say that. We only had one good night. He had to return the car the next day. But I'm hopeful. It's going to take some time to get past all of those years. He said he'd come back to visit, and I said I would too."

"That's great to hear." I shuffled my feet, deciding where to go next. I drew a deep breath. It was now or never. "About the last time I saw you."

It was his turn to wince. "I'm sorry I hit you with that on your job. I know it wasn't the best timing. I really shouldn't have."

And that told me absolutely nothing. Sink or swim. Sink or swim.

I chose to swim.

"I'm sorry I had to rush off like that," I hurried on, unable to stop now that I'd decided. "And what you saw... I was undercover, you know." I raised one shoulder and a corner of my mouth. "I know it looked bad. And I wasn't sure how I was going to handle that bouncer at all. It would have been bad. I probably would have made it. Probably. Maybe. But thanks for your help. You didn't get in trouble for that, did you?" I said suddenly, realizing for the first time that he could have.

This wasn't going as I had hoped. I felt like an idiot.

"No." He shook his head, his eyes twinkling slightly, like he was busy contemplating me. "The big guy came out from the back after you left. He's one of yours, isn't he?" At my nod, he continued. "He caused a commotion and melted out the door in the middle of it. I tagged along."

"I'm glad to hear it. I can't believe I didn't think of that sooner." I let out a big exhale. "But I wanted to come by to check if I've...scared you off. If your offer was—is—still on the table."

He paused, still watching me intently.

I raced on, distinctly uncomfortable and unable to help it. "I know that was probably more than you signed up for, and I'm clearly too late in my arrival here. We've had so many setbacks, but—"

A grin split his face as he grabbed my arm, pulling me into him. Wrapping his arms around me, he brought his face down to mine, gently laying a kiss on my lips.

"Does that give you the answer to the question you can't seem to get out?"

Shocked, I blinked at him, still in front of my face. "You let me ramble on."

"I could have let it go on longer," he said, grinning. "I decided to take it easy on you."

Rolling my eyes, I collapsed in his arms. "You're an ass."

A low rumble of laughter reverberated from his wide chest. I enjoyed the feel of it against me.

"So, what's next?" I asked, leaning back to look at him.

"You're staying for dinner." He kissed my cheek, breaking away to turn the meat. "It's almost ready. Want to grab a plate?"

I watched him, shocked. Now that the stress of his dad had been resolved, easygoing Rhodes was back. I had missed this. Shaking my head, I headed inside, only barely catching a glance of him closing his eyes for a quiet breath of relief over the grill. It sent tendrils of warmth throughout my chest. He'd been as nervous as I was.

I found a plate and brought it out to him. He piled it high with meat and carried it towards the door.

"Hell, let's eat outside," he said, setting it on the picnic table instead and brushing past me. "Want a beer?"

A half an hour later, after our bellies were full and we were lingering over the last of our beer, I pulled out a slip of paper from my back pocket. "This might not be the right time."

"What's that?" He sat down his beer.

I handed the paper to him. "It's Lily's parents' names and phone numbers. Sam got her last name from your birth certificate and did his Jedi magic to find the family. They live in Joliet. Up to you if you want to contact them."

His eyes met mine, shining briefly with emotion, then he studied the names on the paper. "Thank you. I've always held family sacred, family I've been born into and family I chose. But for the most part, it's been easy for me, the fire department, the center. But I'm starting to realize that sometimes, sometimes we have to fight for it."

He took my hand and gave me a wink.

"Even if I have to learn to love death metal," he went on, his face completely serious. It took me a moment to remember the conversation in my Jeep. When I remembered, a bubble of laughter spilled out.

It had taken me a while, but I was starting to learn he was right.

"You made up?" Suzy clapped her hands, jumping up to wrap me in a hug when I filled her in on the night before.

"It would seem so." I shrugged, too happy to argue. "Who knows where it'll end up, but we're giving it a try."

"So, tell me everything," she brushed past my hesitancy.

"I stayed for dinner," I started.

"But did you stay for breakfast?" She wagged her eyebrows. She was picking up too many physical traits from Sam.

"No." I shook my head, still smiling. "It was just dinner. But there was a mighty heated kiss by the Jeep."

"Ah." Suzy sighed, collapsing back into her chair. "I just knew you two were going to make it."

"You did?"

"Of course. The heat coming off either of you when talking about the other is palpable."

"Is it?"

"Definitely. We're talking about super high on the Scoville scale," she said, her eyes sparkling.

"If you say so." I chuckled, making my way to my office.

"Wait, wait!" She held up her hands. "What's next?"

"Well, he wanted to know what I was doing tonight." I turned back to grin.

"Date night!" she squealed.

"Who knows where it'll end up." I winked at her before continuing my way to my office.

Sitting down at my desk, I wasn't sure where to start. I had listened to a few more hours of audio after I went home the night before, but there was nothing yet to go on. I opened my laptop, scanning my emails, worrying about Ms. Lamb and the other wealthy people who had put their faith in Jonathan. An idea popped into my mind.

"My favorite PI," Paul's voice answered on the first ring. "What can I do for you? Do you need another favor?"

"Not this time. I've got something for you, another story." I smirked, twisting in my chair. "Have you ever heard of Jonathan Gladstar?"

After filling him in on the financial advisor, I knew his story would make a splash across the news. We had plenty of evidence against him, but now no matter what happened to him legally, his career would be over. No one would trust someone with that bad of a reputation again, even if he got out of jail on good behavior.

Besides, it was always a good thing to have a bank of credits with the good reporter.

"Mal," Suzy called from the lobby.
"Yeah, Suze."
"You've got a call. It's Maurice."
Frowning, I picked up my phone. He never called me here. Maybe it was about the court case. "Hey, Mo."
"You've got a visitor here," he said, his voice tight. "Dessi came in half an hour ago, got a coffee and biscotti, and sat down. I was keeping an eye on him, ready to call law enforcement if I had to."
"Oh, crap."

"Finally, I went by and asked him if he needed anything." He huffed. "He looked up and said, 'Just let her know I'm here.'"

"I'll be right over," I said, hanging up the phone.

Walking out the door, I headed straight to the Sentinel van parked nearby. I wasn't going to be an idiot twice. Luckily, it was Brian.

"Hey." I leaned in the passenger window. "Dessi's across the street, asking for me. Mind giving me backup?"

"I can have another guy out here in a few minutes." He nodded. "I've got your back."

"Perfect."

I headed over. I knew Mo had cameras too, but it wouldn't hurt to have Brian ready in case things went bad. He was technically here to protect Suzy, but since it was from the guy currently across the street, I didn't think he'd mind breaking his station, especially with another guy on the way. I also knew he'd be calling Wyatt for orders as I entered Grounds.

Spotting Dessi in the back, I turned instead to the counter, taking my time to order a dry cappuccino. It would give me the few extra minutes I needed to play down my stress. Taking my time, I made my way over, weaving through the other tables.

"You rang?" I slowly slid into the chair opposite him.

A smug expression crossed his face. "Don't feel too foolish. Many people have tried and failed to catch me."

I kept my face blank to show no emotion. He thought I'd failed at my attempt at Red. *Cute.*

"You never really had any shot of making it." He scoffed. "Everyone in the place knew about you already. It must feel really awful that you didn't know that whole time."

He reached forward to pat my hand, but I ripped it away instead, letting my contempt show. It was good for him to think we hadn't succeeded in anything.

"But then you parried with your hidden-lawyer trick. Even I was unaware of Maurice's hidden talents." He waved a hand to the front of the store. "Nicely done, by the way."

My eyes narrowed, not liking his attention turning to Mo.

"Don't worry. I'm not going to hurt your little friend. Yet." He pursed his lips. "As long as he doesn't continue to get in my way. I just wanted to stop by and make sure you didn't feel too foolish. I mean, you made a fool of yourself, of course, but I do hope you don't stop this little tennis game we're playing. I'm having way too much fun."

I let my mouth fall open in shock.

"But don't try getting back into Red." He wagged his finger at me, clucking his tongue. "You won't be able to get in to hear any juicy details."

With that, he rose from the chair, dusted off his pants, and gave me a polite nod before leaving, obviously very pleased with himself.

Tilting my head, I leaned back in my chair, watching his dramatic exit as it hit me.

That was his weakness. Pride.

I crossed my hands across my stomach. I could work with that.

"What was that about?" Mo said, taking the seat Dessi left, sliding my cappuccino across the table.

I took a sip, savoring the heavily whipped foam. "He was just rubbing my nose in it. He thinks we failed."

"And you haven't?"

"Nope, I have a plan."

Epilogue

"Somehow, I pictured this as much more serious." Rhodes gave me a side grin as he stuffed another heavily salted French fry in his mouth, pausing to wipe his fingers on one of the many napkins set between us in my Jeep.

"This is *very* serious." I lowered my voice, setting my burger down in my take-out container and reaching for my lemonade. "We're on the lookout for bad guys."

After filling in the team on Dessi's visit, Sam told me he overheard a mention of the video-gaming wine bar in Oakbrook in the audio feed. We hadn't seen much, but here we were. Sam hadn't taken much convincing to swap his seat with Rhodes for the night after I told him it would be a date.

I was still a little frustrated with the condition of the audio, and the chair wasn't the best placement from the head of the table. It all depended on who was talking in the room. But we were learning the players, so that was something.

Time would tell.

"You sure you don't mind the change of plans tonight?" I scrunched my nose. "This probably wasn't what you had in mind when you asked me out."

"I'm with you, aren't I?" He leaned close to peer down at my seat. "Besides, these seats slide back if we decide to neck, right?"

I laughed out loud; maybe things would turn out okay, after all.

Jen Flanagan

From the Author:
Thank you so much for reading my book. I sincerely hope you enjoyed Mal and her friends.

If you do, the nicest thing you can do is leave me a good review on Amazon, Bookbub, Goodreads, or wherever you review books.

Connect with me online:
Website: **jenflanaganbooks.com**
Follow me on Amazon
Facebook: **@jenflanaganbooks**
Instagram: **@jenflanagan_author**
Bookbub: **@jen_flanagan**

Please visit my blog at **jenflanaganbooks.com** for upcoming books, comments, and minor musings.

What's Next?
Anxious to find out what happens next with Mal and her friends? Will the team be able to find a way to get Dessi off the streets for good?

Turn the page to read the first chapter of *Under Pressure.*

Under Pressure

Rhodes joins Mal and the team as they come up with an elaborate plan to put Dessi down once and for all in this heart-pounding installment of the Detective Malone series. Brace for intrigue, deception, and twists. The con is on!

Mal and her unlikely team have hit enough dead ends to last a lifetime and the building threat of criminal mastermind Dessi holds them in a state of danger. One single, illegally-planted bug in the conference room of underground criminals is the ace in the hole—that is, if they can actually catch something incriminating.

Each lead guides them down another path of disappointment. Not even a side-case at a local pet store can pull the team from their plummeting spirits. Time is running out and loyalties are challenged, forcing them to attack Dessi head-on if they're going to end this thing.

The two teams embark on a complicated game of cat and mouse, and even with all the coffee in the world, Mal doesn't know who will come out on top.

Chapter 1

"There's no security set up back here." Sam's eyes were on the door in front of us, his mouth turned down. "And no surveillance. What's wrong with them?"

"Isn't that a good thing?" I was kneeling, already at work, picking the lock. It clicked on my first try. Triumphantly, I swung it open and stood to collect my bag before heading in. After sitting for the past two hours, waiting for the drop off, my legs had gotten stiff.

"Well, yes, for us." He huffed, stomping in behind me in his all-black spy outfit. He stopped short when he realized he couldn't see. "But I could have disabled it."

"Of course you could." I hustled past him, my flashlight aimed in front of me. I made a beeline to the front of the store, on the hunt for the new deliveries.

"Wait!" he whispered loudly, switching on his headlamp. He froze as he scanned the building. Light bounced off the walls erratically. "Did you hear something?"

"No one's here. You thermal scanned the place." I held a hand in front of my face to block my eyes from the light. "Careful with that thing. Keep it aimed low. We don't need anyone calling the cops because they saw something suspicious."

"Sorry." He lowered his head, taking a hesitant step forward. "I guess you're right. Unless they have newer technology I missed."

I looked around the dry-cleaning shop, guiding my light slowly around. Beige walls surrounded us with a long rack on one side, a small office portioned off in the back, and a countertop in the front with chipped Formica. "I think we're good."

"If you say so." Relaxing, my unofficial business partner—consultant was the legal term—started poking through things.

"Hang on. Don't contaminate the evidence!" Presenting rubber gloves to him, I held up my already gloved hands. "Just because there's no one here, doesn't mean we should be leaving a trail. We need to find it, check it out, and get out."

He and his wife, Suzy, had stumbled into my life when she went missing and I was the private investigator he'd hired to find her. As fate would have it, we got her back, and I'd been stuck with them ever since. They were the friends I never knew I needed.

"We can check it out once we get out. I have a friend who can test whatever's on it."

"That's if it looks like evidence. No sense tipping our hand until we need to. If it comes up missing, it'll be a dead giveaway that someone's paying too much attention."

"But you heard it too. The audio came through, clearly stating they needed to drop something off. There was an accident."

"Something about an accident. And I'm not sure it was really clear."

"I'm almost positive he mentioned a little accident." He stuck his gloved hands into one of the bags of unprocessed clothes sitting behind the outdated counter. "Something like that."

A while back, we had planted a bug in the conference room of a local crime boss's Chicago speakeasy. The same one who happened to have ordered Suzy's kidnapping and death months ago. We'd been following up on any lead we could.

"It may be nothing." I walked over to where the cleaned clothes were hanging, a beam of light guiding my way. They were all pressed and wrapped in plastic. Storage tubs were stacked against the wall behind them.

"Yes, but we're losing battery life. We estimated four to six weeks, but the bar's been busy, and we've been recording a lot of audio."

Silence hung between us in the dark, both of us knowing time was closing in on us. Realistically, at this point, we only had a matter of days left. And with the plan we'd hashed to get it planted, it'd be back to square one if we didn't get any solid leads, anything to go on to get us closer to real evidence, enough to lock Fabian Dessi behind bars for good.

"Maybe they're disposing of a body here," he went on, spotting the plastic storage containers. Rushing over to them, he tripped over a bag of clothes hidden in the skirts of long hanging dresses. The bag ripped, sending dress shirts and sweaters flying.

"Hang on, Sam." I rushed to help, trying to locate all of the clothes and gather them back together. There was nothing to be done about the bag, but we were able to heap it together without being too obvious. I wrapped skirts around it, hoping whoever found it would run into it themselves and think they did it.

"The containers are a little small to store a body." Sam bent to open a lid. "Maybe they cut it in pieces."

Wrinkling my nose, I joined him, peering in. His headlamp lit up the interior of the box, landing on jugs of chemical solvents.

"Huh."

"The two guys in the sedan we watched only brought a bag."

"This could be where they clean up their crimes, though." He rushed to the next container. "I'll check the others."

"They said their boss wanted it cleaned right away, that it was his favorite shirt." I slowly made my way back through the shadowy storeroom and found the ledger on the counter. Each entry matched a number and a pick up date. "They said they'd be back tomorrow."

The last entry in the book had the number 533026 next to it, with tomorrow's pick up date. The description listed a men's blue button-up shirt. I didn't remember anyone coming in after them. Bending down, I started going through the bags at my feet, looking for a blue dress shirt matching that number.

"Find anything?" Sam shouted.

"Shhhh."

"Sorry."

"Not yet, but I think I have the number of the order." I started going through a second bag. Finding a black skirt marked 533024, I gripped my flashlight between my teeth so I could use both hands. I was close. Sifting between a cashmere sweater and a vest, I saw a flash of blue. As I pulled it out, I checked the tag. 533026. Lamp still firmly clasped between my teeth, I said quietly, "Found it."

Light bounced off the ceiling as Sam hopped across the tiled floor to join me.

When I shook out the shirt on top of the other clothes, the hair on the back of my neck rose and a chill danced down my back. Dark-red spread across the left side. My blood turned cold.

"See!" The would-be detective next to me clasped his hands in excitement, bouncing on the balls of his feet. "It's blood. We can get it DNA tested."

I leaned closer, inspecting the splatter pattern.

"It looks awfully thick. It might be something else." We had to be sure.

He swiped the shirt from my hands and sniffed it.

"Careful!" I semi-shouted, sending a panicked glance towards the front window. "If we ruin the evidence, it's useless."

Frowning at the shirt, I leaned in to give it a sniff. It smelled like oregano and basil. Probably marinara sauce. To be honest, it smelled pretty good.

"I still think it's blood." Sam's chin pulled up, defiant. "They said it was an accident."

Deflated, my body sagged. It was just another in a long line of failed leads. "Their boss, or somebody else, spilled the sauce on his shirt. Come on, let's get out of here before someone calls us in."

"We have to test it to be sure." Holding tight to the garment, his eyes remained trained on the spot.

"If it comes up missing, they'll know something's up. Dessi's already on our case after the night in his speakeasy. We need to lie low until we know something for sure." Gingerly, I eased the shirt from his hands.

"But-but this is it, Mal! This is someone's blood. I know it!" He stared right at me, blinding me with the light before ripping the shirt back to inspect it closer.

"Hang on," I started, but he was poking at the stain with his gloved finger. A bit of sauce rubbed off.

"See?" I tried to point out. "Blood isn't that thick."

Shoulders drooping, he suddenly tensed, sucking in air and clenched the shirt. "This has to be it."

I wasn't sure what he was planning, but it didn't look good. I reached out to take the shirt, but he pulled it out of my reach. Off-balance, I braced myself on the bag of clothes, but they were too soft. Unable to gain purchase on the slippery plastic, I slid, slumping onto the floor.

Sam's eyes were lasered in on the stain as he sniffed and inspected it closer and closer to his face.

"No," I said, drawing back, but it was too late.

Fueled by desperation, Sam stuck his tongue on it.

My mouth turned down in disgust, and I sat back on my heels.

"Huh." He frowned. "Maybe it is marinara."

Rolling my eyes, I started stuffing the spilled articles of clothing back into the bag. Then I held out my hand, waiting for him to give me the shirt so I could add it to the rest and slide everything back where we found it.

"Come on, let's go." I headed towards the door.

Following, he smacked his lips. "I'm gonna need to get that recipe. It's pretty good."

It was a quiet drive back to my office. Sam's unusually silent self carefully packed his fancy surveillance equipment into the bags he had left in the back seat. He always had the best stuff. It made sense, really, since he owned his own tech company, creating apps, security systems, and stuff.

"We'll get a good lead, Sam." I tucked my small bag in the back with my run-of-the-mill binoculars. I hated to see him lose his optimism. Normally, this discussion went the other way around.

He nodded, fingers stilling over a zipper. "I don't want this to be Suzy's life," he finally said. "No one should live in fear every day."

I hardly thought Suzy felt like that, but I got his point. He had been paying Sentinel Security to follow her around ever since he got her back. Wyatt Parker, who owned the security business, had since become a close friend of ours and an accomplice in seeing Dessi locked away.

"But what would Wyatt's guys do if they didn't have you adding to Wyatt's schedule." I flicked my eyes towards him to see his reaction. "And how would Wyatt afford that Land Rover without all the work? You've got to account for half of his business."

That got a smirk from my techie-geek friend. "I doubt it's half, but yeah, he might have to downsize some."

My phone chose that moment to ring.

"Speaking of the devil," I muttered, pressing the phone icon on my steering wheel.

"Any luck?" Wyatt's voice came over the Jeep's speakers.

"Not tonight," I jumped in. "Spilled sauce on a favorite shirt. Apparently, that takes two people to correct."

I heard a humph over the phone line.

"Next time," I said, wishing I still believed it.

"Hey, Columbo." I was just pulling away from where I had dropped Sam off at his car, near my office. Even through my phone's speaker, Rhodes' voice sent a warm wave down my back.

"Hey, yourself." I hummed pleasantly at his reference to the TV detective. Cute. Unconsciously, I fiddled with my auburn waves.

"Any luck?"

"Not this time," I repeated, unable to pull together any enthusiasm this time.

"Next time." He supplied the optimism for me.

"Thanks."

"Want to come over? I can put a pot of coffee on."

The man did say the sweetest things. He definitely knew how to brighten the evening. Coffee was, after all, one of the top three best pleasures in life.

"Actually, Jen asked me to stop by Hungry Brain if I had time. I haven't seen her in weeks." Not since she and I made up, after recently discovering one of my oldest friends had been secretly dating a cheating ex of mine. But it was her choice, and she knew the score. And since he seemed to be making her happy, I was willing to see where it went, for her sake. The bar was a local hangout for cops and a usual for us.

"Oh, sure. Of course," His voice was light, but I could hear a thread of disappointment in it.

"The crew's all there tonight," I said, meaning the team I had gone through the police academy with. It was where I had met Jen and the slimeball also known as Alex Rodriguez. They'd finished training; I hadn't. It wasn't entirely Alex's fault. Let's just say my temper had raged more than was healthy after his indiscretion. Thankfully, I discovered I actually did do better in the less-structured private-investigation sector.

"Then you should go. I've had you all to myself these past weeks. Enjoy yourself."

Everything was still new between us, having only recently officially started dating after spending the last few months dancing around each other. But things were starting to get serious. At least, I thought they were.

"You want to come?" I blurted out.

He paused a moment. "Are you sure?"

"No," I answered honestly. "But come anyway."

"Will your ex be there?"

"Probably."

"Okay." He laughed. "What could go wrong?"

It was one of the things I liked best about him. He had the best laugh.

Pushing through the crowd at Hungry's thirty minutes later, I pointed to the back patio with one hand and laced the fingers of my other with Rhodes', who followed behind me. He turned sideways to better navigate his broad shoulders through the small bar frequented by the local cops and firefighters.

It had been a while since I was attached to anyone like this, and the feeling was equal parts scary and exciting. The last time I had arrived here with someone, it was with my ex. The same one I expected to see tonight. Awkward.

"Hey!" Jen's eyes lit up when she caught sight of me on the patio. Her mirth quickly migrated south to create a full-on teeth grin to display her delight when she spied Rhodes. She hurried over to me. "Omigod! I'm so glad you brought him. How are you guys?"

"Good," I said, hugging her.

"Nice to see you," Rhodes said, surprised when she angled in for a hug. I had to remind myself that they'd met when I was admitted to the hospital after escaping from Dessi's thugs.

A few of the guys from the academy saw me and headed over.

"So, who's this?" Stevens caught sight of us in the casual space illuminated with twinkling lights strung from the wooden beams above.

I cast an apologetic glance towards Rhodes, tightening my hold on him. It might be the first time I felt protective over a guy. What did that mean?

"Marlon Rhodes," he spoke before I had a chance to introduce him.

"This is Stevens." I gestured to the guy giving my—was he my boyfriend?—the once-over. Two other officers had now flanked him. "And that's Walker and Bradshaw."

"Nice to meet you." He nodded, shaking their hands. "You all went through the academy together, right?"

"Yeah," Stevens said, rocking back on his feet. "Until Mal left us. Jen was left as the only token female in our class."

Jen laughed, lifting her cocktail to take a sip, but I stalled. It had never occurred to me before. I wondered if it had been hard on her. You'd never know with her perpetually sunny disposition, but still.

"What do you do, Marlon?" Walker lifted his chin, giving him the obligatory once-over.

"He's a fire captain in Bricktown," I said, giving his hand a squeeze.

"Couldn't cut it for police?" He sniggered.

"Well, you know how it is." Rhodes gave him a sideways grin. "I could handle the heat."
The guys let out a hearty chuckle, clapping him on the back. And just like that, he had been accepted.

"Mal." A voice behind me made me turn. I took a deep breath in an effort to keep my face straight.

"Rodriguez." I nodded to the detective in question and his partner, George Michalski.

"You made it." Jen rushed up to him and stretched to plant a kiss on his lips, then stilled, looking warily back at me.

I shook my head, waving her off. It was weird, but I was most definitely not jealous.

"Sorry it took me so long," he said quietly to her, his hand on her hip. "I had someone in questioning."

Rhodes leaned in. "You good, Malone?"

"Absolutely." I winked at him, turning back to the guys. "Okay. I still don't have a beer in my hands. Who's buying?"

"I gotcha, Mal." George raised his hand, motioning for the waitress.

Rhodes ordered a beer as well, his body at ease with a wide stance. To the casual observer, it looked like he was relaxed, but I knew him better. He was taking in every conversation and social cue in the group.

"So, Rhodes, is it?" Detective Dillhole addressed him. At his nod, he continued. "I hear you're a firefighter."

"That's correct," he answered, not bothering to correct him on his status with the crew.

"Oh, cut the crap, Alex." Stevens slapped him on the shoulder. "We already went through all that. He's okay."

I wasn't sure if he was being supportive of me, Rhodes, or if he had beef with Rodriguez. Accepting my beer, I toasted those around me, hoping my history wouldn't mess up anything in my future.

<u>Jen Flanagan Fiction Books</u>

Orca Cove Series:
Saltwater Cures
Uncharted Waters (coming 2024)

Books in the Detective Malone Series:
Bad Company
Here I Go Again
Under Pressure

<u>Willa Daniels Non-Fiction Books</u>

Stand-alone books:
The Art of Living Seasonally

The Natural Path Series:
An Introduction to Herbalism
An Introduction to Soap Making (coming 2024)
Home and Cleaning Solutions (coming 2024)
Body and Skincare Solutions (coming 2024)